D1632378

THE SUN'S NET

These stories, centred on the people of the Orkneys, mingle legend with actuality, the workaday with the sacramental, and range widely in time and in theme: from the strange romance between an English prisoner of war and the daughter of his Scottish captor at Bannockburn, through mutiny and piracy in the 18th century, to a timeless revenant from the field of battle who finds that life goes on and the seed is sown whichever way the tide of war may turn.

By the same Author

*

Poems

FISHERMEN WITH PLOUGHS
POEMS NEW AND SELECTED
LOAVES AND FISHES
THE YEAR OF THE WHALE
WINTERFOLD

Short Stories

A CALENDAR OF LOVE
A TIME TO KEEP
HAWKFALL

Play

A SPELL FOR GREEN CORN

Novels

GREENVOE
MAGNUS

Travel

AN ORKNEY TAPESTRY

THE
SUN'S NET

Stories by

GEORGE
MACKAY BROWN

1976

THE HOGARTH PRESS

LONDON

Published by
The Hogarth Press Ltd
42 William IV Street
London WC2

*

Clarke, Irwin & Co. Ltd
Toronto

All rights reserved. No part of this publication
may be reproduced, stored in a retrieval
system, or transmitted in any form, or by
any means, electronic, mechanical, photo-
copying, recording or otherwise, without the
prior permission of
The Hogarth Press Ltd.

2563
1

ISBN 0 7012 0419 2

© George Mackay Brown 1976

Printed in Great Britain by
Redwood Burn Limited
Trowbridge and Esher

FIFE EDUCATIONAL
RESOURCES CENTRE

CONTENTS

A WINTER TALE

DOCTOR

I was appointed doctor in the island of Njalsay in the late summer of 1973. I came too late for the regatta and the agricultural show, but I was in time for the Harvest Home, and saw how well islanders enjoy themselves on a festive occasion. That night I got to know all the healthy ones, old and young, that I was unlikely to meet in the course of my duties.

In fact the community was almost the most healthy one in my experience. There were a few chronic sick — arthritics, asthmatics, melancholics — but I had a great deal of time to myself as the great darkness of winter began to close in. I began to read again the novels of Hardy. I arranged in a new album my collection of Commonwealth stamps.

I look after myself in the doctor's house on the brae. Mrs Pegal comes twice a week to clean the place, and she looks after my laundry. But I cook my own food; the island steaks and fish and potatoes are delicious. Occasionally, on a Sunday, I am invited for supper at the manse or the schoolhouse.

So my first three months in Njalsay have passed, uneventfully on the whole. I had been told that the islanders were difficult folk to get acquainted with. I did not find it that way. They are shy, certainly, and they have an exaggerated respect for "professional people", which springs no doubt from the calvinistic attitude to education and the ethic of "getting on in the world". . . . . It is all a nonsense, of course. Once you break down that class wall you discover a kind humorous friendly folk. (There are exceptions, of course – a bad egg here and there.) I was soon friendly with the blacksmith-engineer Tom Selwick and the farmers who gather in his workshop in the evenings, to tell stories mainly and argue politics. I don't go there every night; but I much prefer my evenings with Tom Selwick to those at the manse and school-house.

I should say a word, in passing, (though I am no expert) on the social and economic set-up of the island. Njalsay is an affluent place, now in the late twentieth century, compared to the Njalsay of earlier times. No islanders go hungry or in rags; every farm and croft has its car and television; a banker comes from the town once a week to look after the island's money. But, in spite of that, Njalsay is a dying community. Every year the population dwindles. The young folk, for a generation and more, have been leaving the island to get work in the offices and shops of the town, and sometimes much further away. It could be argued that they were not needed, in any case; machines were doing more and more of the labour of men and animals. Crofts were absorbed into bigger neighbouring farms, and gradually the croft-houses fell into ruins. And in another part of the island the boundaries between two farms would be cancelled by the stroke of a lawyer's pen; and one of the farmers would retire to a big house in the town, which was twelve miles away by sea (but only seven minutes away by the planes of the new efficient inter-island air service). Then another farmer's wife and young ones would be happy to be finished forever with "the filth and dung and brutishness of the earth". Did they feel, perhaps, after a year or two of buying their food and clothes over shop counters, a certain lack; the dark earth-rhythms which had dominated their lives for generations still operant, but with nothing to glut themselves on, only the empty rituals of "getting and spending", and a more refined and empty mode of social intercourse?

'They go', said old Josh Cott from his sickbed to me one day. 'They go, they drift away, they clear out. They think they're "bettering themselves". They sell their animals. They get rid of the acres that the same family has worked for generations. I'm sorry for them, doctor. I tell you one thing, I'm not leaving Klonbreck. Never. And Dod, he's promised me he'll never leave Klonbreck or sell it. I'm very glad to think there might be Cotts in Klonbreck still in a hundred years' time'. . . .

Poor old Josh Cott — it's true enough he won't be leaving his croft and island, for he is dying slowly of sclerosis, and I doubt if he'll see another seed-time. But I wouldn't attach too much importance to the sacred promises of the likes of Dod Cott, his only son. Dod is all for tinkering with mechanical things — cars and wireless sets and watches — and Dod's wife fancies herself in the short skirts and knee-high boots that she buys (mail-order) from the south; once the old man is dead I can't see her lingering overlong among the earth-smells of Klonbreck.

But a dying man cherishes impossible hopes; it

would surely be wrong to take them from him. A last
seed throbs in the winter earth.

* * *

Death has come to the old man up at Klonbreck
sooner than I thought. Early on Sunday morning I
closed his eyes. He will lie in Njalsay earth, but I think
he may be the last of his race to do so.

His son covered his face with his hands. And Doreen
said, "Poor old dad", but it was only mouth-mime,
a passing mask of regret.

Josh Cott's death was the first to happen since I
came. It has been followed, in the course of a few
days, by two others – a small feast of death in Njalsay.
On Tuesday it was old Miss Tina Luthman, a spinster
who lived alone in a house near the pier that her
father had built at the turn of the century. This Tina
had always kept herself rather aloof; she considered
herself a cut above the other women of Njalsay.
Hadn't her father made his money as the island's
general merchant? Here again the foolish snobbery
showed itself – the family whose symbols are counters,
ledgers, letter-heads is superior to those whose heraldry
is plough and flail. . . . It was comical, in fact – Miss
Luthman was so poor she had to live with the utmost
meagreness, she had to count every penny. Yet she
wrapped herself in this web-thin garment of social
superiority. None but the minister's wife or the
teacher's wife drank afternoon tea with her. Once,
many years ago, at the time of a royal wedding, she
had knitted with her own hands a beautiful shawl and

sent it to the bride. In due course, back came a printed acknowledgment — thousands of them must have been sent out to every corner of the globe. Miss Tina framed hers; it hung above her mantelpiece; it was her proudest possession.

Poor Miss Tina — for the last five years she had been terribly crippled with arthritis. But, through all her sufferings, she clung to her gentility — that was the thing, it seemed, that kept her going for so long. But on Tuesday afternoon it was all over for her at last. When I came down the stair from her death-chamber her little gilt clock ticked away under the framed acknowledgement from royalty.

These deaths — old Josh Cott and Miss Tina Lethman — were in the course of nature. The third death shocked the whole island — it even made me blanch, who am accustomed to death's slow weatherings and sudden bolts. A young fisherman called Ragnar Holm killed himself on Friday evening. He was twentyfive, and he lived with his mother in a small house where the burn empties itself tumultuously into the sea. I had passed him once or twice on the island road, and had always gotten a wave and a smile; and one evening I even exchanged a few words with him in the smithy. That night the men's talk had all been about politics. Most of the island men are cautious progressives — liberalism is as far as they will go. They keep some kind of ancestral memory of the bad rule of the lairds, and so Toryism is out. They have nothing in common with the organised industrial workers in cities; the notion of strikes and industrial action is foreign to them, it is almost against nature —

will the ripe corn wait till some dispute between the
farmer and his reapers is settled? Will the sow refrain
from farrowing till she gets better husks?. . . . The
rhythms of farm and factory are different things. The
only socialists in Njalsay are Peter Kringle who has
been a deep-sea sailor, and Mr Prinn the schoolmaster.

But now, I gathered that night in the smithy,
Njalsay had a third socialist, Ragnar Holm. He hadn't
thought deeply about it, that much was obvious, and
he was poor at expressing himself. But I could see, all
the same, that he had a sincere concern for the poor
of the world. It was a socialism of the heart, rather
than Peter Kringle's rancorous kind, or the teacher's
New Statesman kind.

That night in the smithy — the only time I ever
spoke to him — Ragnar was so carried away by "the
evils of South African apartheid" that the other men
gradually fell silent around him. He became conscious
of all the eyes that were on him — he hadn't meant it
to be that way at all, it was just a small private
exchange of opinions between himself and me. He got
flustered and tonguetied; he lost the thread of his
argument; at last he burst out with, 'It's terrible,
wicked, evil!' — and blushed — and turned, and took
his inarticulate passion out into the night with him.

'That Ragnar', said the farmer of Osgarth, 'he
fairly gets carried away!'

The other men smiled and puffed at their pipes —
they were inclined to be against displays of enthusiasm
on any subject whatsoever.

'But still,' said Jake Nelson, 'he's a fine boy, Ragnar.'
'And I'll tell you another thing,' said Bill Rerwick,

who was a crofter-fisherman, 'there's not a better man than Ragnar at the haddock-fishing.'

'His father was a good man before him,' said Tom Selwick. 'Ragnar'll cool down when he's a year or two older'. . . .

On Friday evening, while I was toasting bread and poaching an egg for my supper, there came a loud knocking at the door. Whoever the caller was, he didn't wait for me to answer. The door was thrust open, and a vivid face appeared. Tom Selwick was so transformed with shock and excitement that it took me a second or two to recognize him.

'Come!' he said. 'For God's sake! It's Ragnar, something's happened to him down at the boatshed — something terrible!' He wouldn't wait for me to get the car out of the garage. He was off across the fields to the boatshed half-a-mile away, running and leaping. Round the door of the boatshed a few other islanders were gathered. Shocked white faces made way for me. A fisherman gave me the lantern he carried.

Ragnar Holm had hanged himself with a shred of net. There was nothing I could do, except cut him down and then break the news to the mother. But she already knew — perhaps some old woman had told her, perhaps she had heard the crash of the fishbox and the creaking of rafter-and-man-and-twine; and guessed. 'Yes', she said, 'Ragnar. I thought this might happen. I expected it. It's come to this. Yes, indeed. He's by with it, he's by with it'. . . . I had not expected such quietness and acceptance. I thought to myself, 'Life has made you ready for anything, old one'. But then she suddenly wailed and rose to her feet and flung herself across the bed. 'Ragnar, Ragnar,' she cried, 'why did you have to do it? There was a long good life before you! There was plenty of love for you, Ragnar, my boy!'. . . . I was glad that at this point three neighbouring women came in at the door. I left her to them. I was glad to get away from such desolation and pain. . . . Up at the house, the egg lay cold on sodden toast, and the teapot was cold. I poured myself a half tumbler of whisky.

Between the suicide and the funeral of the young fisherman, I have gotten one or two scraps of information, but nothing at all that could provide a likely clue as to why a young healthy hard-working lad should want to end his life. The heredity on both sides is sound — the father had died in the course of nature ten years before — nearly everyone on the mother's side specialised in longevity. He had intelligence, a natural courtesy and gentleness, a proper concern for the things that happen not only in his island but in the larger world outside. He went to dances and darts-matches and concerts; he was popular with the island girls, though it seemed at the time he had no steady "date". His boat provided little in the way of wealth — no small fishing-boat has ever done that, in the whole history of the island — but there was no real poverty, and no debt. It is an utterly baffling mystery. All we can be sure of is this — there are minds that have to endure terrors and anguishes and imaginings of which we tougher mortals know nothing, fortunately.

They buried Ragnar Holm today, on a dark midwinter afternoon.

There, when the other island men were in the churchyard, was that Peter Kringle — I saw him myself — down at the shore, minutely going over Ragnar's boat with eye and hand. No doubt he will make an offer for it; I hope not this side of Hogmanay, till the mother's pain has mended a little.

(In honesty I should mention here the much smaller pain that led me, against the drift, to seek solitude and darkness. That pain had a name given to it in the late nineteenth century by a famous ostracised writer. The "temple of love" has many courts — in one of which it was a crime, until lately, to display trophies. From the wounds of a small defeat in that contention I have sought the cure of silence.)

*   *   *

The days get shorter; darkness encroaches rapidly as we near the solstice. Last Saturday I got a note through my letter-box: Mrs Grantham would be pleased if I could come to dinner the following evening, Sunday, at 7.30 p.m. (Mrs Grantham is the lady of the manse.)

I do not like getting such invitations, on the whole. I am one of those pernickety bachelors who have their day carefully mapped — so many hours for reading and listening to music; such and such a time for my stamp collection; the recharging of my pipe every two hours or so. These evenings out ruin the careful pattern. Besides, I like to eat when I'm hungry, and then what I fancy. (I am thought to be a passable cook.)

I am also something of a coward − I am all for peace in the community, at almost any cost. I phoned to Mrs Grantham after the evening surgery to say that I would be delighted to have dinner with the minister and herself. (This was the first time I have been invited to anything other than a supper-time snack.)

It proved to be one of those distasteful evenings that one swears will never be repeated as far as oneself is concerned; but of course it happens again and again. The bruised mind renews itself every morning. Cheerfulness sends its fresh springs up through the stone.

I found there were other guests than myself. Prinn the school-master and his wife were there, and also a friend of the minister who had been a contemporary of his at the university, a Robert McCracken, lawyer, from Glasgow.

I must say the food was first-rate; I could congratulate Meg Grantham with genuine warmth. There was even a couple of bottles of good wine − a thing I hadn't expected in a manse − and brandy afterwards. The two-mile walk in the cold air, also, had made me hungry.

It was the talk that ruined the whole evening. How dreadful it is when you can't speak easily and naturally to your fellow-diners, and listen tolerantly to what he or she has to say. Here, on this night, cleverness was all. You had to keep a sharp ear open for subtle puns

— you had to rummage desperately through your mind for witty things to say. And laughter — though nothing really funny was said all night, as I remember — played like summer lightning across the dining table. A hypocrite again, I did my best to add my leaven of cheerfulness to the symposium.

Prinn was in his high and scathing mood. I have heard him in that vein before. He is the knowledgeable man in a community of fools and morons (present company excepted.) He sticks in his barbs right and left, indiscriminately — his tongue wounds people who seem to me to be better than him in every respect. Worst of all is when he catalogues his pupils as "louts" and "objects" and "yokels". . . . And Isobel Prinn sitting opposite with that thin smile on her face — her don of a husband, having to hide his talents in such barren soil. Prinn even spoke about "that fisherman who hanged himself because the "morbus orcadensis" had got into him". . . .

For a time, while Mrs Grantham and Mrs Prinn were in the kitchen doing the washing-up, the Glasgow solicitor held the stage. His speciality — at least this night — was stories with a vein of smut in them. I hated myself for smiling at the end of every well-turned piece of filth; McCracken certainly knew how to put them across. I don't mind the earthiness of Shakespeare, Chaucer, Burns — there's a cleanness at the heart of the bawdry — but this slick modern filth is rootless and functionless, it stinks in the mind, it leaves a stain. I wished for the two women to finish their dish-washing and come back. Meantime McCracken had finished another story. Prinn roared with mirth. I screwed my face into a smile. What shocked me more than a little was the reaction of Mr Grantham; his chuckles were as false as Prinn's and my own — falser, because he had to show that being a man of the cloth didn't at all mean that he was a glumpot. By no means; he could relish a clever story in any vein, he was the complete man of the world.

The two women came back out of the kitchen; McCracken's latest story remained half-told. 'Blast you women!' shouted Prinn. 'Couldn't you have waited another two minutes!'. . . .

And now, late at night, the minister came into his own. Whether one or other of us prompted him I don't remember, but he began to explain his attitude to scripture.

'Now James', said his wife, 'no shop, please!'

'Yes, Jimmy, you carry on', said McCracken. 'It'll do me good. It'll make up for all the sermons that I've missed in the last ten years.'

Mrs Prinn said she thought one religion was as good as another — they all had something, didn't they? Basically they were the same.

It was as if the minister was determined to show us all just exactly how broadminded and modern he was. The miracles — they were demolished in no long time — they were simply vivid ways of impressing primitive minds. The feeding of ten thousand people with five barley loaves and two small fishes — what educated man could accept that nowadays? It was obviously a way of getting people to share out what they had. The crowd on the hillside that day was made up of certain prudent folk who had taken parcels of food with them, and others who had simply rushed off to listen to the Galilean spell-binder without a thought of food or drink. The loaves and fishes in the boy's basket — once the disciples had distributed these to a hungry few, the others took the hint, and so the whole assembly had enough and to spare. . . .

'But the Virgin Birth?' said Prinn. 'And the Resurrection? Surely, as a minister, you are bound to believe them?'

Mr Grantham made no answer. His forefinger stroked his cigarette. He looked round the table, from face to face, smiling, and shook his head.

I found enough courage to say that if I was a minister and couldn't accept these things, then I would resign and look for another job. . . .

Mr Grantham said he was trying to be honest in the light of modern knowledge — other men of his profession thought as he did. 'We ministers are a part of the society we live in,' he went on. 'We take our colouring from it, and we contribute our own special skill. Society nowadays will have nothing to do with miracles. Miracles were very beautiful, some of them, and served their turn in their place and age. But we modern ministers, whether we like it or not, are living in an age of scepticism and pragmatism.'

'But would you say what you've just said,' I persisted, 'to your session clerk?'

Four faces frowned at me.

'That old idiot!' said Prinn. 'For God's sake. Dung and mud and money in the bank — that's Smith's religion, that's the only miracle old Obadiah knows anything about!'

FIFE EDUCATIONAL
RESOURCES CENTRE

The minister held up his hand. 'Charity,' he said, 'charity, Philip, now. . . .' He turned to me and said, 'No, I wouldn't say what I've said to that good old man, because he isn't ready to receive it. He never will be, this side of the grave – he's a fundamentalist, he was brought up in the old literal tradition. And I hope he never asks me – I would find it very difficult to begin to explain'. . . .

McCracken joined in the discussion then. He, it seemed, was knowledgeable on the subject of myth and religion; at any rate, he had done some reading here and there that had some bearing. He put forward the proposition, after a time, that probably no such person as Jesus of Nazareth had walked the earth; at least, not the figure as represented in the gospels, as god-hero. The fact was that everything Jesus is reported as saying and preaching had already been uttered by earlier prophets and holy men. The huge rhythms of existence – the opposites and complements such as winter and summer, birth and death, fertility and barrenness – all religion was an attempt to come to terms with these mighty forces that dominate the life of the tribe. The corn king dies and rises again and nourishes his people. Oh, there might indeed have been a small-time carpenter-turned-preacher on the shores of Galilee in the first century A.D. – it was the merest accident, a quirk of history (who could explain it?) that the attributes of the mythical priest-king, the seasonal god, had been attached to this enigmatic figure. . . .

I did expect our host to assert himself at this point, but he actually seemed to accept what McCracken had said as a fair enough basis for argument; managing to suggest at the same time, with a tolerant shake of the head, that really his friend was venturing into deeper waters than he could, as a layman, understand.

Soon after that the evening came to an end.

I said my goodbyes and took my leave first of all, declining an offer of a lift in the Prinns' car. The walk, I said, would help me to sleep. (McCracken I hoped I might never meet again — he was leaving for Glasgow in the morning, to be home for the festive season.)

It struck me, walking homewards through the first swirling snowflakes, how much kinder and sweeter the atmosphere of that house and that company might have been if only Mrs Grantham and Mrs Prinn had had children.

It struck me, then, that there hadn't been a single birth in Njalsay since I had come to the island; only, last week, that little feast of death. It seemed like a foreshadowing of the day when the only people in the island were the dead in the churchyard.

Beyond the farm of Osgarth there is a lonely stretch with no houses at all. For a quarter of a mile or so you walk in complete darkness on a moonless winter night — tonight there were no stars even, and the snow was falling thicker than ever. Just over the ridge the road turns left, and you look down on the cluster of lighted windows above the shore, and further off the sprinkled lights of the neighbouring islands.

Another track branches off to the right, into the most desolate part of the island. Once Westside was a populous enough district, with a dozen or so crofts, but within the last decade it has become completely deserted. Life must have been hard for these folk — their fields were so poor that the farmers of Njalsay hadn't thought it worth while to go on cultivating them; all that marks them now are a few crazy fencing stobs and a rusted plough or two in the shelter of a broken wall.

Very bleak the district of Westside looked, athwart those falling curtains of snow.

I reached the ridge. I was glad to see, far below, the light in the window of Riggeridge farm. I had less than a mile to walk from there.

A man I did not know was standing where the road branches. The sight of him startled me — frightened me, I admit, for a second or two. On such a night one expects all the living to be part of a firelit circle.

'Please help us,' the man said. 'I know you're a doctor. My wife is in great pain. You must come.'

'Who are you?' I said. 'Where do you live? What's wrong with her?'

He didn't answer. He gestured vaguely towards the ruined district of Westside. He turned and bent his head into the snow. His feet rose and fell. I followed him.

There was just enough light to see the ditches. The man walked fast. He knew where he was going. I followed in the wake of his black footprints. I saw, with relief, that it was not going to be a solid night of snow. To the north, over the hill, a torn patch of sky appeared with a few stars shining in it.

Then, quite suddenly, there was a lamp shining in the window of what I had always known to be a deserted croft — I even forgot its name. And now the man began to run across the field that separated road from croft. I heard voices inside, bright with welcome and anxiety and reassurance.

I made my way to the croft more slowly. When I was halfway there the man appeared at the door. 'For God's sake,' he shouted, 'hurry! She's near her time!'

I assisted at a birth that night. A short time after I entered the hovel a boy was born. The man had made such preparations as he could. He had kettles on the range. There was adequate clothing for a new-born child airing over a chair that stood back-on to the fire.

The new mother was not much more than seventeen or eighteen years old. The birth had not been easy — the man told me she had been in labour for hours. She took the child with great tenderness into her arms. The shadow of the man fell over them both.

The man and the girl were so wrapped up in the marvel of what had happened that I had a short time to take stock of the situation. The house had patches of damp on one wall. One of the roofing flagstones had shifted — you could see a triangle of sky through it, there was room for a star to shine in.

It was certainly no fit habitation for a family. Yet the man had salved things from the ruin — the kettles, for example, and the paraffin lamp that burned in the window. There were a few plates and cups without handles on the table. The single shelf in the cupboard had a loaf, a basin of potatoes, tins of this and that. A zinc bucket of water made blue tremblings in the corner.

It was over. I had done what I could. The little family was wrapped in their flame of happiness.

I had a great many questions to ask them. Who were they? Where had they come from? What did the man do for a living? Had they got permission to live in the croft? It would be impossible — surely they realized it? — to try to bring up a child in a ruin like this. . . .

Instead I made a quiet exit. I walked home under the wide hemisphere of stars, and my feet crackled through pure silver all the way. I fell asleep almost at once.

*   *   *

'No,' said Tom Selwick. 'Nobody's lived in the croft of Wanhope for seven years now, since old Ezra Sinclair died. Why do you ask?'

'I thought I saw a light in the window late last night,' I said.

'That's impossible,' said Tom. 'It could have been a reflection of the snow or the stars.'

'I saw a lighted paraffin lamp,' I insisted.

Tom shook his head.

'Do you not have tinkers in the island?' I said. 'Wandering folk.'

'There used to be,' said Tom. 'But now the tinkers don't wander any more. The tinkers have houses and cars in the town. They're better off than me.'

I knew, of course, that they weren't tinkers, or anyone who belonged to the islands. It was very hard to say what the man's accent was — he had spoken a good plain English, the kind that anyone from Shetland to the Scillies could understand.

'There's another kind of going-about people,' I said, 'that have recently come into existence. Beatniks they're called, or some name like that. They don't like society, affluence, working to timetables, serving machines. These young folk are beginning to seek out the quietest loneliest places to live in. Sometimes they settle in communities, sometimes a young couple try to make do on their own. They live in poverty. They don't interfere with other people. Some of them seem to exist on vegetables and water. They go in for meditation a lot.'

Tom laughed. 'I've heard of them,' he said. 'In fact some folk like that have come to live in Norday and Selskay. Maybe that's the explanation, doctor. If so, we'll be seeing them soon. They'll have to come down to the store for their provisions.'

I haven't done anything in the way of finding out more about that mysterious family in Wanhope croft. I ought to have gone there this morning to see how it is with the mother and child. I will certainly go before sunset. But I would not be surprised to find myself standing in the door of a cold dripping bare ruin; and to have to turn then and say to myself, 'Clifton, you idiot, it was a snow-dream you had between the manse and the village on Sunday night'; and finally to say to Tom Selwick in the smithy, 'You're right, man, it was the light of snow and stars in the window of Wanhope, no paraffin lamp at all. I was up there this afternoon, just to make sure. I expect I had drunk too much of the minister's brandy.'

We were invited to the Manse on Sunday evening, for dinner. It was a marvellous occasion, as I knew it would be, with Meg the cook: some kind of delicious pheasant soup, then lobster, roast pork and trimmings, a trifle as light as birds, coffee and five-star brandy, two bottles of first-rate burgundy. How does Grantham manage it, on his stipend? The trouble is, we can't compete, even if I could afford it — Isobel is a good plain cook, nothing more. So long as they don't expect too much when we have them for dinner at New Year.

Present were, besides Grantham and his missus and ourselves, Dr Clifton and an extremely witty lawyer friend of Grantham, Robert McCracken, from Glasgow, who's going away later today, I think, if he hasn't left already. I do wish he could have stayed on to see the New Year in — we could do with a leavening of his cleverness and fun in this place.

The problem at the moment is, do we invite the doctor or no? That man is enough to put a damper on any company. There he sat on Sunday night at the manse dinner, only moving his jaw to eat, which he did to some purpose. I expect he's half starved. Why can't he get that Mrs Pegal to cook a mid-day meal for him? He's too mean, I expect — and him with that huge salary! 'I cook for myself. I like cooking,' he said sometime in the course of the evening; and that's about all that he contributed to the conversation, except take issue with Grantham over something or other. I do not like him. I expect we'll just have to go on inviting him occasionally to the schoolhouse for a casual supper, now that the tradition has started. But the New Year dinner — I don't know — I'll have to ask Isobel about it.

In spite of Dr Clifton, then, it was a successful evening. (I hope to God ours goes half as well.) McCracken had an anthology of some of the best stories I've heard since I was at college. The man has a deeper side to his nature, though. He has read a lot of history and anthropology, and he's thought about it. He gave old James quite a run for his money, on the subject of the gospels. Altogether a most interesting man. He says he'll come back in the summer, to fish.

The weakness in my left leg is in general much better since the school closed, thank God, for the Christmas holiday. The rest, I expect, has done it some good. But of course I know all about these improvements — they lift your heart for a day or two, then down comes the shadow again, the foot begins to drag on the floor. And what about this hand I am writing with — my taut sensitive hand? Last night, for a few seconds, it was made of snow. I haven't mentioned the hand to Isobel yet. No sense in adding to her worries.

'Nothing really wrong with you at all.' The sweetest sentence I ever heard, from that specialist in Newcastle, and me thinking that day I was teetering on the brink of the grave; and also the specialist when I went in looking more like an undertaker than a healer. 'It's mostly in your mind. You're a bit of a hypochondriac, don't you know? I can't tell that to everyone, but you're intelligent. It could be that cities are too much for you — city schools — delinquents — all the urban pressures. Would it be possible for you, now, to get some quiet country school, eh? Far from the madding crowd. Think about it seriously. Moors, streams, clouds — that's the kind of place that'll keep the power in your legs, Mr Prinn'. . . .

And that was that. We sold our house and most of our furniture, and read the advertisements in the educational papers, and I wrote a letter or two, and had an interview; and here we are, in a half-dead island between the Atlantic and the North Sea.

"O true apothecarie, thy drugs are quick". . . . It was marvellous, how much my health improved. I didn't exactly leap about the island like a goat, but still I could go where I wanted to be surely and freely. That desolating feeling of no blood or substance below the knee — as if a man were beginning to be a ghost from the instep up — that had vanished. I said to Isobel one midnight, after we had made love, 'There's nothing more to worry about. My sickness — it's gone like the snow. Touch me again.' The second time was a celebration and an act of thankfulness. . . . Next morning, as I was walking from the breakfast table to the classroom, my leg fluttered under me. It was a momentary spasm — but I was terrified, I can tell you. I taught for the rest of that morning seated at my desk. The country children must have wondered why their instruction that day was so disjointed, and why their teacher — usually so masterful — spoke in a chaste vacant voice.

When I got down from my desk at lunch-time the strength had returned to my leg. It had been a momentary relapse — perhaps imagined — perhaps because I was worried that morning about the news from my brother in Australia. (His shop having to close — the shutters up — could it be bankruptcy? And if so. . . .)

Three and a half weeks later the desolation struck again, when I rose to turn the record of that Brahms quintet. It lasted all that night and most of the following day. More of my leg seemed to be involved. The children must have noticed my hirple. Then, again, the substance took over from the shadow, and the blood beat and flowed.

Last night, at supper, the spoon fell out of my hand. It clattered and splashed into the soup plate. 'Sorry,' I said to Isobel. She gave me a white look. Now my right hand is becoming acquainted with the shadows. That never happened before; the weakness was on the left side.

What am I going to do? What will become of me? My imagination is not so strong that it can make a ghost of parts of me. I am dying piecemeal.

I ought, of course, in the first place, to go and have a talk with Clifton; tell him the history of my trouble and the symptoms; ask for a straight diagnosis and prognosis. So that, if need be, I can put my house in order.

But I am terrified to do such a thing. (It's with me like the man in the dock when the black cap is at the judge's elbow and the foreman of the jury gets to his feet.) I won't go to see him. Not yet.

Another thing. If I'm going to die — and die

lingeringly and disgustingly, if the trouble is what I think it is — I can't eke out the remainder of my days, however long is left, in a community of strangers with whom I have absolutely nothing in common. I must get back to my own kind.

Thank goodness Isobel and I agreed before we married that there would be no children, ever.

If the illness were all — but it brings such enormous problems with it. Isobel guesses what it might be, I think, but says nothing. Or next to nothing. This morning, at breakfast, she said, 'Phil, dear, you're white. I think you've got a bit of a cold. You ought to go and see Dr Clifton.'

I said I didn't have a cold, and the less I saw of Clifton the better I liked it.

I must go and see him. My hand is withering. It will be a bitterness to listen to him. He doesn't like me, I know. He has the kind of inverted snobbery that claims to prefer the company of yokels and fishermen to the likes of me and James Grantham. I've wondered sometimes if he isn't "queer", at least by inclination: seeking out the husky silent island men in Selwick's place, after dark, to gossip and laugh among.

He might even like hurting me.

How should I take advice and sympathy from the likes of him?

I began to write the above, after Isobel had gone to bed, in order to spur myself into cheerfulness. For really, in spite of all, I did enjoy Sunday night at the manse. The memory of all that good food and talk has left a glow. I said to myself, 'I'll keep a diary for one day only. I'll write about that good time, and it'll be like a fire that I can come back to whenever I'm in the dumps'. . . . But — I might have known it — the shadow has taken over from the song, the song has become a dirge, a dark whisper. . . . Like the voice of Clifton among the falling snow when I offered him a lift in the car, 'No, thanks. I like walking in the darkness — you never know what you might meet.'

MINISTER

Slow enfolding of darkness. Imagine a man standing
on a headland near the north of Lapland at noon: he
sees glimmers and darkenings on the sea, a grayness
in the south: then night begins to enmesh him again.
At midnight his whole hemisphere is sheathed in
blackness, except where frost and starlight put fugitive
jewelry. The boreal tide is still rising — it washes our
mouths and eyes and spirits. Tomorrow is the solstice,
the last reach of night and winter. Soon we will begin
to feel the first tremor of spring (though usually the
worst weather comes in January and February). The
man who stands on that Scandinavian headland will
see then, far more spectacularly than us, the upsurge
of the fountain of light. He will hunt and fish in a
summer of blond shadowless splendours. The sign of
the sun will be on the window where he sleeps and
prays and makes love.

Certainly such violent alterations of light and darkness must have some effect on the people who live far
in the north. But here quietness is the keynote — "they
keep the level tenor of the way." They are withdrawn
with strangers, until friendship and sincerity are tested
and proved, and then there is no end to their open-
ness and kindness, winter and summer. Meg and I know
this well; we have been in Njalsay island now for
three years. I would like to think that I will end my
days among them, but I expect that won't happen.
Meg is turning her face more and more often to the
south. She wants to be there to satisfy her hunger,

before her palate is too dry and sour for relishing
love.

How pleasant to be here, in my comfortable study,
on a midwinter night. I came up after supper to
write the short Christmas sermon that has been forced
on me. I lit three coloured candles on the desk, and
put a fresh peat on the fire. Outside the window it is
pitch black; the sudden snow of yesterday faded
almost as soon as it fell. I drew the heavy curtains.
Then I put a sheet of paper on the desk and unscrewed
my pen. Instead of a happy little Christmas homily, I
find myself brooding on the mysteries of darkness,
winter, death.

For death keeps high revelry at this time of year —
at least, he did in Njalsay last week. There was the
old ailing man up at Klonbreck for a start. Then, a day
or two after, Miss Lethman, who I'm sure died of
slow starvation at last after pinching and scraping for
twenty lean years. (She would have nothing to do
with the Welfare State.) And last, that poor boy who
killed himself among his creels and oars. How strange,
to stand over three open graves in one week, and
strew earth on the coffin, and say, "All flesh is
grass. . . ."

And now I must confess to this sheet of paper —
for nobody else would be interested — how helpless I
feel in the midst of such suffering. For I visited the
houses of death, and in all three places I felt useless,
a reverend irrelevance. Up at the farm the surviving
Cotts seemed relieved that the good old man was
dead at last, whether in consideration of his long
suffering or their own advantage it would be hard to

say. In Miss Lethman's house there was only her old cat — I think the vet who comes to the island every month will have to do something about the creature. Down at the shore it was awful — the dreadful wailing of the old woman, and the branded face of Ragnar's girl friend. My duty is to administer comfort — I was confused, platitudinous, in a flush and sweat — I'm sure both these women were glad to see the back of me.

No man likes to feel that he is no good at his job, especially when his uselessness in a brutish but necessary function is flung in his face twice or thrice a month. . . . Meg is singing to the piano downstairs, some modern ballad or other. It's time she was in bed; I want her to be asleep when I go up.

One of the candles — the yellow one — has just had its flame drowned in a brimming sea of wax. One of the others is smoking and leaping. I must get this weirdest of meditations finished before I'm left utterly in the dark.

It is not only with the bereaved that I feel my use-lessness. I have felt increasingly since the end of summer that I'm really not needed in the island at all; or rather not wanted, for every community surely needs a lamp-bearer, a bringer of comfort.

Everything seems to point that way. The meagre scatter of faces in the pews on a Sunday morning — that is disconcerting, to say the least. This was once a religious island. Oh, I know what they say — "de-population". . . . "in the old days they *had* to go to the kirk on Sabbath". . . . "better a few sincere believers than a churchful of dumb frightened oxen"

.... What unsettles me is that the islanders who ought
to be there don't come — I mean the young fishermen
and the farm girls, those who are standing at the door
of the future with empty purposeless hands. All I
seem to minister to are the islanders who come to the
church because their Sundays would seem empty if
they didn't come. Do I fill a space in their lives, no
more?

So, this is the darkness that has stolen, shade by
unquiet shade, into the soul of the minister of Njalsay
parish in this bleak midwinter. Last Yule, I remember,
I was happy enough.

There is something even more dispiriting. I see
souls in pain in this island that I can't do a thing for,
because they won't declare their troubles to me. That's
why I sometimes wish I was called Father Grantham,
and had a little dark confession box full of whispers in
a corner of the church. Then they might come and tell
me their troubles, and I would be able to dispense
supernatural comfort. Ragnar Holm, for example,
would he still be alive if he had been able to unburden
himself?

Phil Prinn too, the schoolmaster — what's come
over him this past month or six weeks? Certainly
something is troubling him — his wife knows a little,
but not everything, I think. He's not even putting a
brave face on it any longer. That's the trouble with
these clever mass-produced minds — their foundations
are in the sand. The tremendous dark earth-rooted
courage of old Josh Cott, in comparison!.... What's
wrong? What in God's name is wrong with the man
that he won't tell his friends even? Several dark

threads have been woven this winter into the life of
Philip Prinn, B.A.

Didn't a letter come, ten days ago, from Bert
McCracken in Glasgow? That did nothing to cheer me
up, either. Not that he said anything outright. It was
all hints, confusions, shadows of pain. Barbara left him
six years ago, and took the children — I don't think
that's worrying him now. It's something else, something even more ruinous. "So, old Jim" the letter
ended, "between one thing and another, life is not too
sweet at the moment. Lucky you, with your Meg and
your little flock in that island — no need for you, not
for many a year yet, to flee away and be at rest. . . ."
I showed the letter to Meg — and she agreed, there was
some veiled trouble somewhere — and she agreed further that he must be invited for Christmas. (Though
Meg may have had another kind of mutual therapy in
mind.) He left today, assuring us of his eternal gratitude for a wonderful holiday. But — I might have
known it — I was not able to get near his pain.

Then there's Clifton, the new doctor. That man
intrigues me more than a little. Why has he, a young
eager practitioner, left the cities of the south to waste
his talents among a few healthy islanders? He is a
deeper character than either Prinn or McCracken. I
admit I'm a bit envious of him. There he is, on the
best of terms with everyone in the island, rich and
poor, beggar and laird; whereas I ply my unwanted
trade at only a few orthodox doors. Dr Clifton is well-
liked in Njalsay, no doubt of that, with his easy
pleasant outgoing nature — but there's a mystery
about him — a sense of scars healing but not yet at

peace – and this cruel winter has scratched them open again.

So, after the funeral of Ragnar the fisherman, on Friday – when I was at my lowest – I was struck by a comforting idea. Why not have a dinner – a midwinter feast – and invite all those suffering souls to sit round the one table? I mentioned it to Meg. And of course she agreed; capable creature that she is, she loves planning a dinner, or a picnic, or a concert. Bert was here already; he had arrived on the Wednesday. It only remained to order the goodies from the town, and send out cards to Messrs Prinn and Clifton. And do you know – the thing actually came off – the evening was a success! Old McCracken crackled with cleverness – he even had a go at Christianity, and made out a good case (at least from the standpoint of The Thinkers' Library), but he really of course didn't know what he was talking about. And Phil enjoyed showing how clever he was – what Swiftian insight he had into the life of Njalsay. I let them go on. At least they had put aside their sorrows for an hour or two. With Clifton it was more difficult to know. He smiled, and nodded, and put in a word occasionally. Once or twice I caught him with his mask off – then he looked bored, or contemptuous. He is, as I said, a much more subtle case than my other two guests.

I needn't say how excellent were the food and the drink. Meg can put a great deal of thwarted love into a meal.

Snow was falling when we waved goodbye to them just before midnight – Phil and Isobel in their car, Clifton preferring to walk. 'A Christmas-card Yule,' said Bert as we watched the dark sky-drift and the spectre of the rosebush in the light from the window. . . . (But in fact the snow was all gone next morning.)

There's another candle gone. The third one should last another ten minutes, long enough to unburden my soul of the last winter shadow, if my wrist doesn't seize up first with this torrent of written words. This is what the Christmas sermon has come to: an ill-shaped brooding on the soul's winter, a St Lucy's lament.

There was to be no Christmas sermon, at all. It was the question of the Christmas sermon that dropped the little shadow between me and my session. This too has never happened before.

It was my own fault. I sprang it on those good people too suddenly; it must have been to them like a blow on the face. 'This coming Sunday,' I announced blithely from the pulpit, 'Christmas Sunday, there will be a special service. You will be pleased to know that there will be no sermon at all. Instead, there will be a ceremony of carols, sung by the children of the Sunday School. My wife has been organising this since Hallowe'en, in addition to organising me, the Manse, the Women's Guild, and the Lifeboat committee. There will also be something new. When you enter the church next Sunday you will see, in the choir, the Bethlehem crib — Joseph, the ox and the ass, Mary with the holy child in her arms, angels, shepherds, and kings, and of course the biggest star any of you have ever seen. . . . So, we look forward to a happy festival in the church next Sunday'. . . . I was not prepared, after the service, for the troubled face of Obadiah Smith, of Osgarth farm, my good gentle session clerk. 'Mr Grantham,' he said, 'a word with you. I've been speaking to one or two of the other elders. It's about this service next Sunday. We don't feel all that happy about it. . . .' Other troubled faces gathered about me in the church door; Andrew Sillar looked red and angry. They left most of the speaking to Obadiah, though occasionally one of them would put in a few words in an access of feeling. The crib — that was the trouble, it seemed, at first. They did not want a crib in the church. It smelt of idolatry. Didn't they have these cribs in Catholic churches at Christmas? They would have me know that this was a Presbyterian church, and always had been, and always would be. They would be very pleased if I reconsidered the crib. The last thing they wanted was trouble. . . . I gave in, as graciously as I could. I knew what Meg would say when I told her (and she having spent a month putting the tableau together, and decorating it beautifully). 'Very well,' I said, 'there will be no crib.' And smiled at them. . . . They were still mulish. 'Forbye this crib thing,' said Obadiah, 'there's never been a Sabbath in this kirk that a sermon wasn't preached. Never since the kirk was built. We'd take it ill if there was no sermon.' 'If there's a sermon,' I said, 'there will be no time for the carol-singing. There can't be both'. . . . I was prepared to dig in my heels on this matter. 'Very well,' said Andrew Sillar, 'let there be no carols then. Carols indeed! Carols is papish too. Our kirk is founded on the sermon, the preaching of the word.' 'The carol service will take place,' I said. They must have seen that I was quite determined about it. 'Could you not see your way,' said Obadiah, 'to preach a short sermon — it need be no more than five minutes — half way through the service?'. . . . Andrew Sillar was muttering away in the background about papedom and idols. 'When I was young,' he muttered to Albert MacVicar and George Brinkie, 'we didn't even keep Christmas in this island. That's a fact. "Christ's Mass" — what could be more papish than that!'. . . . 'Now, Andrew, that's enough,' said Obadiah. He turned a troubled face to me. 'Please,' he said. It is because I love this old man that I said, 'Very well, there will be a brief sermon during the service next Sunday'. . . . It was as if the entire deputation gave a sigh of relief in the winter air; they were all smiles, except Mr Sillar, who looked if anything angrier than before. . . .

That little quarrel at the church door last Sunday has troubled me more than I cared to admit to myself at the time; but a white piece of paper has a way of luring the truth out. I was bitterly hurt by it. And Meg's rage, when I told her over the lunch table, did nothing to help. I am more than an inadequate husband; I am a weak pastor. . . . Supposing the midwinter midnight was so wrapped in cloud that the watcher on that boreal cape could see nothing — not a star, not a glim on a passing wave, not his own hand in front of his face? I don't wish to appear more important than I am. I'm not capable of putting my lips to that chalice called by mystics "the dark night of the soul." But last Sunday I was more depressed than I have ever known.

In fact, in the globe of this earth, in the mappamund, there is no place so bewintered and boreal that it cannot cherish the remembered blessing of light, and hope for its certain return.

In the largest island of the Orkneys there's a magnificent stone-age burial chamber. Four thousand years ago the Orkneymen brought their great departed chiefs to this fortress of death, and entombed them in one of the three recesses, and afterwards sealed the opening with a huge cube of stone. Then the hunters and farmers re-emerged into the light.

Surely no house on earth could be as desolate as Maeshowe on a midwinter day, so dark and so drained of the sweetness of existence. But in the midst of this ultimate blackness a small miracle takes place. When the sun sets over Hoy on the afternoon of the solstice, about three o'clock, a single finger of light seeks through the long corridor that leads into the heart of the chamber and touches the opposite wall with a fugitive splash of gold. This never happens all the rest of the bright year. After a minute or two the glow fades. But it is as if a seed of promise had been sown in the womb of death itself.

*   *   *

Meg threw open the study door five minutes ago. 'There's a man down below,' she said. 'He wants to speak to you.' 'Who?' I asked. 'I don't know,' she said coldly — 'He's a stranger. I've never seen him before.' 'Where does he live? Did he say what he wants?' 'He said something about a baby in danger, and would

you come at once please — some place in Westside.'
'Nobody lives in Westside district now — not that I
know of. Tell the man — whoever he is — I'll be
right down'. . . .

Meg had interrupted me in the middle of my
description of Maeshowe and the midwinter sun. I
hastened to finish it before the glow faded; my pen
fairly scurried over the paper. The man could wait
for a couple of minutes.

I heard Meg calling from the stairhead, and a calm
deep voice answering from below. I wrote the last
few words and put the sheets of paper in the desk
drawer and locked it. (I don't want my wife to read
this particular manuscript.) As I did so the last red
candle gulped and went out.

Meg was moving about in our bedroom. I groped
my way downstairs in darkness. No more than five
minutes could have passed since Meg summoned me.
When I reached the open door there was nobody
there. I walked down the path to the end of the
garden. There was sufficient starlight to see that the
road that led to the village and the desolate Westside
district was empty for half a mile of its length.

'Hello, there,' I called, sure that the man must be
somewhere near at hand. 'Who is it? Come on, into
the house.'

I waited for a long time at the garden gate. No-one
answered. Then I went in again out of the darkness
and silence and cold, and locked the door.

SILVER

'You'll never get her', said the skipper of the *Kestrel.* 'She's meant for some rich farmer on the hill.' He shook his head.

The three other fishermen of the *Kestrel* shook their heads. 'You're too poor,' they said.

Bert the cook laughed sarcastically.

I took the three best haddocks I could find from the morning's catch and set out for the farm.

They shook their heads after me. The skipper took his pipe from his mouth and spat — he thought I must have gone out of my mind.

I was astonished at my own resolution. Was I not the shy one of the *Kestrel,* who dodged into the wheelhouse whenever a pretty girl stood on the pier above and asked were there any scallops to spare?

I walked on through the village with my three sklintering haddocks.

For the first time — between the tailor shop and the kirk — I felt a flutter of fear. The farm I was going to — it was said that queer proud cantankerous folk lived on it. What could a shy fisherman say to the likes of them, with their hills of green and yellow and their ancestors going back to the days of King Hakon?

That stern tree had lately burgeoned with Anna.

For the love of Anna I was approaching Muckle Glebe.

Old Check was taking the shutters from the hotel bar as I went past. It was opening time in the village.

I stood in need of a glass of rum to feed my faltering flame.

'Well', said the old landlord, as he set the rum before me and took my silver, 'they're still at it. Belfast. Viet-Nam. The Jews and the Arabs. And now Iceland.'

Poor old Check, I thought to myself, worrying about troubles he can do nothing to put right. How terrible to be old, and your heart as dry as a cork!

'Well,' I said, drinking down the last of the rum, 'but there must be love songs even in places like that.'

He looked at me as if I was mad. One or two villagers came into the bar. I went out.

As I left the last houses of the village the small simple-witted boy called Oik who lives with his mother and three or four illegitimate brothers and sisters in a war-time hut ran after me. The story is that a horse kicked him. If so, that beast set a spark of great innocence adrift on the world.

'O mister,' he said, 'where are you going?'

I said I was going to Anna of Muckle Glebe. No point in dissimulating with a boy like Oik.

'Are you going to give Anna them fish?' he said. He looked at the haddocks with round pellucid hungry eyes.

I said it was a present for Anna.

'Anna's the nicest lass in Norday,' said Oik. 'But she tells terrible lies.'

This mingled estimate of Anna's character, coming from such an innocent mouth, intrigued me. I stopped in my tracks and looked at the boy.

'Besides,' said Oik, 'they don't need fish up at Muckle Glebe.'

The three haddocks flashed in the sun. 'Maybe two would be enough for a place like that,' I said. I loosened the string and freed a jaw and gave the smallest fish to Oik.

'Now tell me,' I said, 'what kind of lies does Anna tell?'

But he was off. He did not even pause to thank me. His bare legs flickered across the field. The dog leapt out of the hut to meet him, barking. 'O mam,' he shouted, 'look what I got! That man from the *Kestrel* has give me a fish!'

I went on till I was out of hearing of the sounds of wonderment and barking.

Quite apart from Anna, I was going to Muckle Glebe to get my silver chain back. Anna had taken it from my neck, between kisses, at the dance on Friday night in the community centre. It was the chain my mother gave me on my seventeenth birthday in January. 'Come up to the farm Thursday morning,' Anna whispered. 'They're all going to the mart in Kirkwall. We'll be alone. You'll get your chain back then. And something to go with it far more precious, precious. You can bring a fish too, if you like' . . . . And she had sealed the bargain with another marvellous kiss.

I knew then that I could marry no other girl in the world but Anna. The very thought of her, all that week, had been enough to set my spirit trembling.

But how could poverty like mine ever fall like a blessing on that proud house?

My feet went on more slowly.

The shop of Mrs Thomasina Skerry — coats, corned

beef, spades, cups, coffee, whisky, salt fish, tobacco, sweets, stamps, newspapers, all in one withered drab hut — stood at the crossroads.

I went in for a packet of fags.

'I like a fish,' said Thomasina, eyeing the couple of slaughtered beauties that swung from my forefinger. I laid them on the floor, out of the way of her all-devouring eye.

'It isn't often we see a Selskay man in this part of the island,' she said. 'I like nothing better than a bit of boiled haddock and butter to my tea.'

I was talking — I knew it — to the most talented gossip in Norday. Certain information about a certain farm could be traded for a firm fresh haddock, I hoped. (The *Kestrel,* I should explain, visits this island only rarely — we come from Selskay, further to the west — about Norday we know only rumours and legends.) But, even from the warped mouth behind the counter the very names "Muckle Glebe" and "Anna" would come like music: whatever she might say about them.

'I have a message,' I said, 'to a big farm a mile further on.'

'Muckle Glebe,' she said. 'Muckle Glebe. The Taings — a proud lot. A cut above the ordinary. O, very hoity-toity — you would think they were gentry, or something. Let me tell you, they have their faults and their failings like everybody else. The great-grand-father of the present Taing was an orra-boy, a dung spreader. O, I could tell you a thing or two. . . . I haven't been keeping well in my health lately — my stomach — "a light diet", Dr Scott says — "fish, for example", he says.'

'Maybe what you say is true,' I said, 'or maybe it isn't, but there's one member of that family that no tongue could ever blacken, and that's Anna Taing'. . . . My lips trembled as I pronounced the blessed name.

Mistress Skerry's eyes widened. 'O, is that so!' she cried. 'Indeed! Anna Taing. I could tell you things about Anna Taing, mister. But I'm saying nothing. It's best to keep silence. In this island the truth isn't welcome. My tongue, it's got me into trouble before now. . . . The great thing with fish is that you can use the water you boil it in for soup, and make patties with the left-over bits. The cat, he generally eats the head.'

'What you say,' I said, 'will go no further'. . . . And I bent down and freed another haddock-jaw from the string and held it up among her sweetie-jars and loaves and fair-isle jerseys.

We admired the beautiful silver-gray shape together for three long seconds.

'Well,' she said. 'I'll tell you. It's general knowledge anyway.'

The fish was hers. She laid it on an old newspaper behind the counter — wiped her hands on her apron — licked her lips — and told me a bad story.

A student from Edinburgh had worked all last summer at Muckle Glebe, from hay-time to harvest. Whenever he got leave to work, that is, for wasn't that little tart of an Anna running after him, from field to byre, and more than running after him once it got dark and the farm work was done. Thomasina had heard it from this customer and that, but she saw the proof of it herself at the Agricultural Show. Hundreds of folk there, going and coming; and there, in the midst of all the people and animals, in the broad light of noon, stood Anna of Muckle Glebe and the student, with their arms tight around one another, and kissing every minute regularly as if to make sure their mouths were still there. Love is for night and the stars. It had been a public disgrace.

But then, Anna Taing was and always had been a man-mad little slut. There was hardly a lad in the island that hadn't been out with her. She would go with any Tom, Dick or Harry. There was that hawker that had been in the island — a right low-looking tyke — wasn't she seen knocking at his caravan door at midnight one night. . . .

But she still wrote to this student. She still kept up with him. And the folk up at Muckle Glebe, they were right pleased whenever the typed letters with the Edinburgh post-mark came. 'Because, you see,' said Mrs Thomasina Skerry, 'they're a nest of snobs up at that place, and what a grand catch it would be for their Anna — somebody who's going to be a lawyer or a doctor.'

Her rapturous narrative over, she counselled me, whatever my business was at Muckle Glebe, not to breathe a syllable of what she had said.

My throat worked on this gall for a full minute.

'You're nothing but a damned old scandal-monger,' I shouted. And picked up the sole remaining haddock. And made haste to shake the dust of bananas and wheat and cloves and tea and wool from my feet. And left a patch of slime on her shop floor.

At the door of the farm of Muckle Glebe I set down
my gift and knocked. No one answered, but I had the
feeling that eyes were watching from curtain edges. I
knocked again. (Surely there was no duplicity in the
true gentle fun-loving heart that had unfolded itself
to me at the dance in the community centre – it was
impossible – and the world was full of evil old hags.)
I knocked again.

This time the door was opened by a young woman
– a sister, obviously, and about six sour years older.

She gave me the coldest of looks.

I asked for Anna.

I felt immediately what impudence it was for a
common fisherman to come enquiring about one of
the daughters of this ancient farm that had a coat-of-
arms carved over the lintel.

'My sister Anna,' she said, 'flew to Kirkwall this
morning. From Kirkwall she will be flying to Edinburgh. In Edinburgh, for your information, she is to
be engaged to Mr. Andrew Blair, a veterinary student.
It will be announced in "The Scotsman".'

I mentioned, trembling, a silver chain. She said she
knew nothing about silver chains.

She shut the door in my face. When I turned to
go, I discovered that the four cats of Muckle Glebe
had reduced the firmest and fattest of my haddocks
to a jagged skeleton.

THE BOOK OF BLACK ARTS

(1)

A foreign ship anchored one day in the harbour of Hamnavoe. A small boat was lowered and half-a-dozen sailors were rowed towards the steps. They bought provisions in this shop and that. They had only a few English words between them.

Gold and silver coins shone between their fingers. The Hamnavoe merchants understood that language well enough.

Finally, with loaded sacks, they went into a tavern.

They had a good time in 'The Leaping Dolphin'. The landlord was no ignorant yokel — he had sailed the seas, he had a smattering of French words and Spanish words and Dutch words. He said "Gotenburg", "Marseilles", "Cadiz", and foreign teeth flashed with delight all along the bar counter.

And dimples of joy appeared in the landlord's cheeks when he saw the silver coins (the gold coins had all gone by this time to pay for the beef, eggs, butter, water, and bread).

In those times half-a-dozen sailors could drink for a long morning on the strength of a few silver kroner.

The foreigners drank whisky and ale. They laughed. They beat their fists on the table. Two of them sang. One lifted a chair and danced round and round with it. The door of the tavern filled up slowly with Hamnavoe faces — men, women, and children. The minister went past on the street with a loud "tut-tut-tut" . . . .

"Archangel", cried the landlord. The sailors gathered round him once again. Their glasses needed refilling, their pewter mugs contained only froth. The last crown piece rang on the bar.

It was time then to see to the ferrying of the provisions from pier to ship.

With much hand-clasping and back-slapping and embracing they took their leave of the landlord, swearing eternal friendship. They would certainly come back, next time a storm blew their ship into Hamnavoe. The whisky had been good — "bon, bon". They made, somewhat unsteadily, for the street. The faces in the tavern door drifted away like snowflakes or butterflies.

"Genoa", shouted the landlord after them. "Amsterdam. Boston".

The landlord returned to the counter. He laughed with joy as he poured Spanish and German coins back into the till. He hadn't done such good business since the day the whalers left for the Arctic in April.

Then he looked up and saw that not all the sailors had gone. The tall dark melancholy one, Luis, was standing in a shadowy corner. He looked more melancholy than ever.

(Sometimes liquor has this effect on a certain type of sailor. He feeds deep upon the sadness of chance and time, and seems to enjoy it. He enjoys it as much as the singing sailor with a mug in his hand likes guitars, or the kissing sailor likes girls.)

'Viski', he said to the landlord.

'No money, no drink', said the landlord. 'Get out'. The landlord knew where joviality begins and ends.

'I vill give you book', said Luis.

'I don't want books', said the landlord. 'Terms cash. It's closing time. Allez out pronto.'

'Much powerful book', said Luis. 'Is magic'.

Something earnest and tragic and appealing in the sailor's demeanour kept the landlord from frog-marching him through the door and into the street.

'I'll see this marvellous book first', he said.

The sailor took out a small black book rather like a bible. He opened it. The spread pages were black and the printed words were in startling white. The effect was like a long scream. Here and there throughout the volume were crude woodcuts. The landlord had been long enough at school to know that the script was in Latin.

In the end, after some haggling, he agreed to take the book in exchange for one flagon of whisky, value a shilling.

Luis handed over the book with the face of a prisoner being relieved of his chains, and at the same time as if his heart was being torn out by the roots.

He groaned, and covered his eyes. On the street outside he laughed.

Then he put the stone flagon under his arm and lurched down the pier in a kind of broken dance.

*   *   *

'Well', said the minister of Hamnavoe to the landlord, 'I have looked at your manuscript. As you correctly guessed, it is in Latin. It appears to be a copy of some book or other.'

'I see', said the landlord.

(The landlord was much too wily a man to take the book itself to the stern autocrat of the spirit who lived in the big manse on the hillside. He sensed that there was something unwholesome, even sinister, about the book he had got hold of. So he had spent a whole evening behind the bar copying it out, page after page, though the white words on the jet-black pages made his skull ache. This was the manuscript that he brought to the minister, with a certain amount of bowings and "beg-pardons" and scrapings of his feet; for he and the minister were not — to put it mildly — on intimate terms. But he knew that the minister took pride in his Latin scholarship.)

'You say one of the foreign sailors left it in your ale-house', said the minister.

'In my tavern', said the landlord. 'That's right, your reverence.'

'It is an extraordinary thing', said the minister. 'It is the product of some perverse imagination. It purports to be the work of one of Satan's minions'.

'Is that so?' said the landlord. (Though he was not sure what "minion" meant.)

'This black angel instructs the owner of the book in ways to twist the course of nature, so that innocent bystanders who see a chair dancing by itself on a floor, for example, or a summertime bush full of icicles, will be struck with wonderment. . . . It is of course the most sheer and utter nonsense'.

'I expect so', said the landlord, nodding and smiling.

'Certain small material benefits will accrue to the owner of the book also, it is claimed', said the minister. . . . . He screwed in his eye-glass and flashed a look at the manuscript and translated slowly. . . . "in so far as this un-important knight of the kingdom of hell — the writer of this work — has power to bestow benefits on the diligent student of it; for the writer is one of the least in that kingdom, and has not seen the Lord of Darkness face to face above three times; and his particular gifts are for mischievousness and pranks, whereby the hearts of men are made merry for a moment. Who but he pulleth away the stool from the old dame when she is minded to sit down? Therefore he which hath this book will be cause of much merriment and wonderment and pain" . . . .'

'So that is what the book is, really', said the landlord. 'About how to work tricks?'

'It seems so', said the minister. 'Dark unseemly pranks. Some poor old woman falling on her backside on the floor, who but fools would laugh at the like of that — and scripture tells us that the laughter of fools is like the crackling of dry thorns under a pot?'

But the landlord was smiling to himself at the image he had of the old hag and the stool that ought to have been there but wasn't. That was the kind of fun that appealed to him most. He was rapidly coming to the conclusion, while that old bore droned away beside the manse fire, that the book would be worth its weight in gold to him.

The minister flicked through the last pages of the manuscript. 'And so on and so on and so on', he said. 'Jokes and japes, to keep fools diverted from the true business of human life, which is the glorification and enjoyment of God'.

'Well', said the landlord. 'Thank you very much. I must be getting back now. Opening-time'.

'It is not *all* light-hearted sinister banter', said the minister as he showed his guest out. 'The last chapter is a black one indeed. Not that it says anything definite. Let me see. "He that possesseth this book, and hath had benefit by it, will not be unwilling to suffer a little for the diversion and merriment that have been his. He will not grudge a little rent to the lowly knight of Lucifer who whiled away one moment of eternity in a nook of hell putting the black pages together. For suffer he must, with his nails and his hair and his withering mortal flesh; as ash and cinder follow flame. And if he should wish it in his heart to be rid of my book, let him do so by all means, but only in the way of vending, or selling, and only for a lesser sum than the sum that he purchased it with. He that buyeth the book for a farthing, I will have that creature for my squire and servitor in the eternal errantries of hell" . . . .'

'What a strange document!' said the landlord to the minister at the manse gate.

'If such a volume exists', said the minister, 'and I pray that it is only the work of some human imagination, but if this writing that you have is the copy of an actual book, I would rather be that dead rat in the ditch there than the man whose library it is in now'.

*   *   *

The tavern in Hamnavoe was the scene of some extraordinary incidents in the weeks and months that followed the visit of the landlord to the minister.

For example, Jock Friskin the ploughman ordered a glass of rum at the counter late one winter afternoon. He had been ploughing all day in the rain and he needed some fire put back in his bones. There were a few fishermen and sailors in the tavern. Jock paid his twopence and the rum was set in front of him. He raised the glass to mouth-level and saw that he was about to swallow a glass of clear liquid, like water. He smelt it − it had the smell of water. The tip of his tongue too told him that it was water.

'Landlord', he shouted, 'I ordered rum, not water!'

The landlord came scurrying from the opposite end of the counter. 'Something wrong?' he said. 'What's the trouble? Water, did you say? It looks like rum to me.'

And like rum it looked to all the other customers, and now also to Jock himself: a glass of dark smouldering Jamaican fire. He gaped at it. 'I'm sorry', he said. 'I must have made some kind of a mistake'.

'That's all right', said the landlord courteously. The customers returned to their card-playing at the tables.

Jock raised his "rum" again, and again all his senses told him it was "water".

He had a temper like a bull. Besides, he was cold and tired. 'Look', he roared, 'water!'

The tavern looked round, startled, at the red-faced man and the glass of dark spice-fuming liquor he was holding up.

'It is my best rum', said the landlord in a quiet

voice, 'out of this barrel of Jamaican'. He turned to some of the sailors, who were experts in rum in all its variety. 'Go and have a look at the gentleman's glass. See what you make of it, please'.

Half a dozen rough characters crowded about the bewildered man from the fields. They smelt, they sipped, they held it up to the lamp.

Finally Amund the Faroese whaler returned their verdict. 'Is very goot rum'.

The sailors all glared at Jock, for wasting their time, and went back to their "vingt-et-un" and aquavit.

Jock made an act of blind faith and threw the liquor against his throat. A lump of cold water settled on his cold stomach.

He left the tavern like a haunted man.

The landlord began to laugh. He laughed till he cried. He laughed till he was so weak that he had to lay his head down on the counter. His fists trembled on each side of his head. He was beside himself with merriment. For five full minutes he could do nothing in the way of serving his astonished customers. 'It worked', he said at last in a weak voice. 'Jock and rum and water. Water and Jock and rum. Rum and —' His face crinkled and his eyes grew narrow and he began to sputter again with uncontrollable mirth.

'Is not funny', said Amund. 'Zat poor man, he works hard all day, he need drink. He pay goot money. He zink he drink vodda. Is very sad'.

He shook his head in a puzzled way.

As for Jock the ploughman, I'm glad to report that he went into the tavern on the opposite side of the street, and ordered a glass of rum, and there the rum

remained good rum all the way down to his wintry
stomach. . . .

That is only one of the hundred astonishing things
that happened in that particular tavern within the
space of a few months.

'The Leaping Dolphin' acquired a reputation for
weird and zany events. Folk came from other islands
and parishes to see the gantry where one night in front
of a score of drinkers the stone jar of brandy turned
into a dog that barked thrice and then flowed back
into its original ceramic form. (The landlord main-
tained that they were all drunk — he hadn't seen any
such thing — it was some kind of collective hallucina-
tion.) Men from the English ships and the American
ships came to see the stool where the mermaid had
sat: a town bailie and two respectable merchants,
having their morning dram, had actually seen a mermaid sitting at the bar. The landlord said no — how
could such august townsmen, members of the kirk
too, have imagined such a nonsense? — he himself
had been in the premises all that day. He was of
opinion that their honours had shared a generous jar
before ever they entered 'The Leaping Dolphin'. . . .
He scratched his head for a long time, furrowed his
brow, tried to imagine the exact circumstances of that
morning. Well yes (he admitted) there had been someone, and a female too, in the tavern that morning —
little Wilma the seamstress with her grannie's pewter
flask to be filled with gin (for the sake of her poor
grannie's bladder, which was frequently upset and
could only be cured by Hollands.) Wilma had sat
down on a stool at the counter. She had been carrying

a cod that one of the Rockall fishermen had given her, a huge fish with its tail swishing the floor. . . . While he was filling Wilma's grannie's flask with gin, the three important townsmen had come in. . . .

The landlord, remembering the scene, began to laugh. He laughed and laughed till he lost his breath and almost choked. One of his customers had to thump him on the back.

From all the islands folk came to have a drink in "the enchanted tavern".

In other ways the landlord prospered. A cousin of his in Virginia that he had never seen, died and left him a thousand dollars.

A deputation of townsfolk waited on him one day and asked him to become a magistrate in place of the mermaid-entranced bailie who was now discredited. He bought a silver-mounted stick and a three-cornered hat and began to walk down the street with a strut and a swagger.

A certain widow, a lady of property, whom he had admired for some time but who had hitherto given him nothing but cold looks, actually smiled at him one morning outside the custom-house. . . .

*　　　*　　　*

It disappeared overnight, all that sudden wealth and promise and fantasy. It was destroyed at a stroke, literally.

A black cloud tumbled over Hamnavoe one summer evening. Out of its heart came such drenchings of rain that all the townsfolk ran indoors. The cloud grumbled

and belched. It sent out a single stroke of lightning.
It tumbled on, diminished, over Graemsay and Hoy.

When the sun came out again, the little town beside
the sea glittered and gleamed — all but one building
in the centre, which stood there, a shattered smoking
cavity. 'The Leaping Dolphin' had been struck by the
thunderbolt.

The landlord lost everything. The lightning had
smashed from roof to cellar, hurtling crazily all the
way down among mirrors and panes and pieces of
polished brass. Alcohol and ashes seethed and reeked
in the foundations. The tin box where all his wealth
was — his bonds and notes and securities — was rup-
tured: a few flakes of ash remained. His newly-tailored
magistrate's robe — even that was fit only for a
scarecrow.

But one thing had not been destroyed, *The Book
of Black Arts.* Every drawer in 'The Leaping Dolphin'
was charred and shattered, except for the drawer
where the book lay.

Next morning, when he came to himself, the landlord gaped at it in terror.

He managed to start up in business again before
winter and the return of the whalers from the Arctic,
but not in the old spacious 'Leaping Dolphin'. It was
a little black hut at the end of a pier that he kept
now, with three bottles on the shelf and an ale-barrel
for a counter. A few old poor folk with small thirsts
drifted in and out. The landlord made a miserable
profit — that is, compared to the profits he had once
made.

And all the fun was out of him.

Nobody heard any more that dark uncontrollable laughter.

One Wednesday afternoon a farmer who had been at the cattle mart in Hamnavoe visited the drink-hut. He had sold two heifers and his circuit of celebratory drinks brought him at last to the hut on the pier.

He bought more than whisky and ale before night-fall. He rode home under the stars with a little black book that the landlord had sold to him for sixpence.

(2)

The new owner of the Book of Black Arts was a surly lazy unpopular man. His name was Rob Skelding. He was resentful of every farmer in the parish, but he kept his worst venom for the neighbour who shared the hill Inglefea with him, a decent hard-working pious farmer whose name was Tammo Groat. Both men were bachelors.

Rob thumbed through the pages of the book he had bought, in the lamplight; his clumsy lips moved; as he read he looked from time to time through the small webbed window to where the lamp of Upgyre (Tammo Groat's farm) sent a glim through the night.

The two farms on Inglefea could not have been more different. On one side lay a fertile burnished slope, with silken-flanked cows and thick-fleeced sheep on the pastures beyond. On the other side of the boundary-stone were lank thin-eared fields, and indifferent stock, and a steading dappled with rot and rust.

Rob studied his sixpenny book every night that autumn. . . .

Next year an astonishing thing happened, as between those two farms on Inglefea Hill. It was as if a great wheel had turned, against the sun.

The good farm of Upgyre withered and sickened. The seed died in the furrows, though Tammo dowered it with dung and seaweed. A few gray shoots broke the earth in June. A few gray ears smouldered like ash.

And the lithe animals dwined among the thin grass. The bull crouched in his field like a broken king. The gander and the ram mourned their lost potencies.

'It is a thing that happens', said Tammo. 'I must have bought poor seed. It is a cross that every farmer must bear now and then. . . .'

But what struck the whole parish as extraordinary, and uncanny, was that the poorly-tilled farm of Stark, across the burn from Upgyre, began that same summer to burgeon mightily.

It seemed that the surly one had sowed the sun in his furrows.

And his cows wore the sun between their horns. Their mouths uttered brightness on the morning. Their udders yielded continual brightness of milk. Rob had to employ a girl to make butter and cheese. And Rob's hundred hens bickered and ran and laid eggs like little moons under every tuft of grass and heather.

His cock announced royally the beginning of each day.

And his dog barked louder that August than all the dogs of the parish.

In the old days, when such a perversity in nature was observed, "witchcraft" would have been whispered fearfully at every hearth and threshold.

But some of this generation of farm-folk had learned to read and count. They had sat at the feet of a dominie, and had received a small measure of enlightenment. They had left forever the dark region of ignorance where witches and fairies breed.

That perverse turn of the wheel, as between Tammo's farm and Rob's, that was — must be — a sheer stroke of chance.

Rob reaped an abundant golden harvest. Tammo helped him to bind the sheaves. His own field was hardly worth putting a scythe to.

And Rob treated his harvesters, once the last scythe was hung up in the barn, with a kind of coarse joviality. There was a mighty supper of beef and bannocks and cheese and whisky. After the women had gone home to see to their fires and cradles a few crude ploughmen's choruses were sung. Rob gave his helpers a half-sovereign each to take home with them; like splinters of the fruitful sun the coins lay in those dark country hands. To his neighbour Tammo he gave as much butter and eggs as he could carry. 'Look, man, my barn will be full to the rafters with oats and barley. There's enough beef and mutton and pork out there to fill the hold of a Balticman. That stone jar on the sideboard, it never lacks for whisky. Your land, Tammo, it's had too much of the sun in its time. Now it's all ashes — burnt-out cinders and dust' . . . .

But Tammo shook his head and returned to his unlucky acres. He had faith that upon cinders a new breath falls — no man knows how — and dead flames rekindle themselves. That is to say, Tammo was a good kirk-going man, and "resurrection" was no empty theological concept to him.

Winter whitened Inglefea. Then spring came back to the hill with birds and ploughs and oxen. Tammo ploughed his field with stubborn patience. Rob ploughed his field carelessly and brutishly. He shouted across the burn to his neighbour, 'It's no use ploughing ashes, man!'

After seedtime a first shadow came about Rob's face.

What he had boasted about was true. In his cupboard beef, pork, ale, eggs, cheese never failed, and his whisky-jar was a well that perpetually renewed itself. But the good things of the earth mean little once the hungering mouth is a shadow.

The crofters waited for the green shoots to break sunward through the furrows.

Tammo's barley came up strong and green. Rob's came up as it always had until last year, sparse and wretched. (Not that the sick man, moving painfully between bed and fire, cared how his fields did.)

Neighbours came and did odd bits of farm work for Rob. Tammo milked his cows and set traps for the rats in the barn of Stark. Tammo had never seen such a plague of rats on a farm. They tarnished, they gnawed at, the hoarded treasures of last summer.

, The servant girl of Stark went home to her mother, frightened by the skull that began to stare through the skin of her master's face.

The kindest man in the parish to the sick farmer

was Swart the blacksmith. Swart sat beside his bed all
night when he had his fever and bad dreams. Swart
kept the fire and the lamp burning for him, and wet
his gray mouth with water.

Swart spelled through the few books (mainly theological) in the kitchen of Stark, to keep himself awake
in his long vigils. One book that he tried to read was a
small black-bound volume with white print on jet
pages.

'Take it away', said Rob when he woke up. 'Take it
away, man. Take it to hell out of here. That book will
give you your heart's desire.'

Swart thought that was a strange way for Rob to
speak. But of course the man was sick and delirious
half the time. He understood this much, that Rob
wanted him to have the book, no doubt as some kind
of reward for his services.

'Well, thank you', said Swart. 'I've never seen such
a droll-like book. Where did you get it now?'

'Never ask,' said Rob. 'Take it away.'

But all the same Rob charged Swart a penny for it.
And Swart put the book in his pocket and went home
to the smithy, yawning, in the early morning. . . .

After that Rob of Stark seemed to get a little
better. He was able to move about and even do a
little work. But the illness — whatever it was — had
put twenty years on him, and the shadows never
left his face until he died, unlamented, two years
later.

That one marvellous year of fertility was never
repeated in the acres of Stark farm.

(3)

Swart the blacksmith was a well-liked man in the parish. The smithy was the parish parliament — all the crofters gathered about the anvil after the day's work was done, and they told stories and listened to theological argument till midnight. And Swart presided over all with kindly tolerance.

Occasionally there were contests of strength in the smithy: harrow-lifting, pressing, wrestling. Some of the young crofters were strong enough, but Swart was king at all these physical contests. He was so modest in his victories that none of his victims bore him a grudge.

But there came a bitter hour in the life of Swart the blacksmith. A man arrived in the island with a famous stallion, a sire of hundreds, which he led from stable to stable around the parish. After his great burnished beast had been suppered one night in the grieve's steading, this stranger was taken to the smithy by some crofters.

The stranger was an agreeable man. He travelled, he told them, all over the north of Scotland with The King of the Glens — that was the name of the stallion. He sang them a Gaelic song. Tammo of Upgyre asked him if he was any good at wrestling or weight-lifting. The stranger said he had done a bit of wrestling in his time, in bothies and barns here and there. The smithy-men asked him if he would care to wrestle with some of them. The stranger agreed, smiling. The men formed themselves into a ring. The stranger threw four of the locals, one after the other, fairly easily. There were no hard feelings. 'But wait', said Tammo of Upgyre who had gone down laughing under the thrust of the stranger, 'wait till Swart here puts his hands on you.'

The stranger and Swart looked at each other. They smiled. Swart tucked up his sleeves. They moved about and grappled and heaved. Then, slowly, Swart went down under the vibrant arm of the stranger.

'Again', said Swart. 'You caught me off balance.'

The crofters nodded. Swart must have been caught off balance. Such a thing had never happened before.

The second bout ended when the stranger pressed his fists into Swart's back and thrust at his shoulder with his powerful chin. Then Swart gave a cry and went down like a felled tree.

When he got to his feet he was red in the face.

'You butted me with your jaw,' he said, gasping. 'That is never done here. You must have different rules in the highlands.'

The stranger said he was sorry. He had not meant to wrestle unfairly. Let them try again. This time he would keep his jaw to himself.

But Swart shook his head. 'It's closing-time,' he said. 'I have work to do in the morning.'

The crofters had never heard the blacksmith speak so peevishly, like a small boy who has been smacked for something he didn't do.

The stranger put on his jacket and thanked them all for a good evening. He said he looked forward to see them again when he next visited the parish with The King of the Glens. He bade them all a good night. (He was to sleep in the grieve's house.)

The blacksmith said goodnight to nobody. He put

the door of the smithy between them and himself with
a great clash.

The crofters looked at each other again on the dark
road outside. Their friend Swart — they had never
seen such an unfriendly look on his face before. What
was wrong?

*   *   *

They asked themselves that question more and
more as the weeks and months went by. What ailed
Swart? What had gone wrong with their good blacksmith?

His defeat in the wrestling match seemed to have
changed him utterly.

The smithy was different too. The old happy winter
evenings were no more, with the story-telling and the
fiddles and the long patient analysis of the minister's
sermon the previous Sabbath. It had suddenly become
a stage for the performance of all sorts of weird and
silly acts, and the only performer on the bill was the
young blacksmith himself, Swart.

A pleasant man had suddenly become a braggart
and a show-off.

One evening, when the smithy was full, he took a
red-hot bar out of the forge and licked it. His tongue
sizzled. Swart smiled and went on licking. The bar
turned gray. He thrust it back into the white heart of
the furnace, and drew it out, and folded his tongue
languorously about the glowing iron.

Once or twice would have been enough. People get
tired of tricks, however clever. But Swart kept

re-kindling and kissing the bar for an hour and more. He was very pleased with his performance, and he showed it. Some of the older men went home before the smithy closed.

'I'll tell you what, men,' said Swart to those who remained. 'You remember that stallion-master who cheated at the wrestling? I'm longing for that man to come back again. Next time I'll kill him.'

He spoke with such venom that the crofters looked at each other and slowly shook their heads.

'He was a fine man,' said the miller.

'I'll break him in two,' said Swart darkly. 'You wait and see.'

Perhaps, the crofters all reasoned with themselves in the following days and weeks, as they worked in their barns and byres and kilns, perhaps all will be well again soon with Swart the blacksmith. Sometimes a cloud passes through the clear spirit and darkens the words and actions of a man. 'That happens to the best of men. The cloud passes. Then we will have our old happy evenings again in the smithy.'

But, if anything, things got more disagreeable in the smithy.

Swart's perpetual obsession was the stranger who had thrown him twice at wrestling. 'That man,' he said, 'God help him when next he comes to this parish! I hate a cheat. You saw how he tripped me. You all saw that with your own eyes. You saw the way he butted me with his head. He will be made to suffer for it. He'll never lead a stallion through the hills again, not after I've seen to him. I hope he comes, and that very soon.'

Tammo of Upgyre said he had heard that The King of the Glens and his master were in Caithness.

'Good, good,' shouted Swart. 'Thank you, Tammo. Thank you for your good news. What chance, I ask you, has the man against strength like this?'. . . . He took a horse-shoe from the wall and snapped it like a barley-stalk. It was truly an impressive performance. Swart had never managed to do *that* before. The previous winter the younger men had all tried their strength on a horse-shoe, without success. At the end of an hour's grunting and sweating Swart had said, 'It's too much for us. We'll have to eat more porridge.' And the inviolate horse-shoe had been hung once more from its nail in the wall.

And now Swart had broken the same horse-shoe with one twist.

A few of the crofters clapped their hands. The oldest one said, 'That was right well done, Swart.'

Their praise went to his head at once. (This had never happened in the old days either — Swart had been all modesty and gentleness.) Horse-shoe after horse-shoe that night he plucked from the wall and snapped as easily as icicles.

'Careful,' said the oldest crofter. 'Careful, man.' It was not so much the waste that he was worried about as the unseemly twist and glint in the blacksmith's face — a kind of diabolical mask. It was Swart's face all right, but darkened and coarsened and rendered grotesque.

The blacksmith snapped the last horse-shoe in the smithy and threw the fragments on the ringing floor.

'That's what I'll do to him,' he said. 'When

will he come, tomorrow? I hope so.'

They called it The Night of the Horse-Shoes in the parish for many a year to come. At midnight Swart said to the three crofters who were still there, 'Listen, boys, have you ever seen anything like this?'

The lamp had burned to a low glim.

Swart felt among the sooty rafters, and brought down what looked to them to be a small bible. But when Swart opened it the white words on the black pages came at them like a scream.

They looked at Swart and shook their heads.

'I tell you what it is, boys,' said Swart. 'So long as I have this book, I can do whatever I like. Nothing and nobody can stand against me. I hope with all my heart that man and his stallion get a good crossing over the Pentland Firth.'

The three crofters walked home on the midnight road without speaking.

*   *   *

The stranger and The King of the Glens arrived in Hamnavoe next day. The man was busy at the farms for a full week. On the Saturday evening he presented himself at the door of the smithy.

The smithy was crowded. Word had got around that there was likely to be a meeting between Swart and his enemy.

'Well, blacksmith,' said the stranger pleasantly, 'I hear you're eager to meet me. I hear the words "Swart" and "wrestling" wherever I go in this parish. We must have another bout, you and I, by all accounts. Well, I'm ready.'

He began to take off his jacket.

'That's true,' said Swart. 'But you see, mister, it isn't every day I have the honour of meeting a famous champion. A smithy is a poor place to wrestle in. We should fight in the fields. Hundreds of people should be there to see. And money should be wagered'. . . . He felt along the rafters and brought down a little bundle of notes tied with tape. 'I, Swart the blacksmith, am willing to bet ten pounds.'

'Ten pounds is a lot of money,' said the stranger. 'Ten pounds is as much as I earn in a whole season with The King of the Glens. I wrestle for fun and good fellowship.'

'So,' said Swart, 'you are afraid of me.'

'No,' said the stranger. 'But I do not have ten pounds to wager.'

The stranger was not smiling any more. He was plainly put out by the open malice of the blacksmith.

'I will fight you in a field on Monday morning,' he said. 'I will fight you under the sun. Then I'll take my horse to the next parish. I see I'm not so welcome here as I was last spring.'

But the men in the smithy crowded round him and shook him by the hand and clapped him on his powerful shoulder. Before the smithy was closed ten pounds had been collected among them to be the stranger's stake money. The twenty pounds were mingled together in a leather purse, and the grieve undertook to keep it and to hand it over to the winner. (More than one of the parish men hoped that their old friend, the braggart at the anvil, would be humiliated.)

The stranger bade them all goodnight. But when, last of all, he turned to Swart, his eyes fell away from a dark devilish smoulder.

*   *   *

The fight on Monday morning, in the field beside the mill, was the greatest that had ever been seen in Orkney.

Hundreds of folk were there, from six or seven parishes, and whalers and fishermen and shopkeepers. The news had gone round like fire on the wind.

Even the laird and his lady watched from the high window of the Hall.

Whoever won the best of three rounds would be the winner. The grieve made that announcement, holding high the heavy prize purse.

Swart won the first round. The stranger was plainly nervous. Not one friend was there to hearten him (though he got plenty of cheers when he appeared out of the crowd.) But the hatred in the face of his opponent put him out more than anything. He went like a man in a dream at Swart. Swart's right arm coiled about his throat, and pressed, and wound. He must choke, or fall. Swart flung him on to the grass. It was all over in two minutes.

A cheer went up from the crowd.

The stranger was more composed at the start of the second bout. He knew now that many of the spectators were on his side.

Swart leapt at him the way a cat goes for a mouse. The stranger side-stepped. Swart blundered on, and was trapped from behind in thew and muscle and sinew. A distracted four-legged beast, the battle staggered here and there. 'Face to face!' cried Swart. 'Face to face! Fight fair!' Then he found his face among the grass and daisies and churned-up mud.

The crowd roared, even louder.

The third bout lasted for half-an-hour. Such rage and cunning and strength had never been seen in the islands. They struck at each other; they kicked; they circled; they enfolded, enwound, threw each other off and away, up and down, right and left. Swart's chest heaved like his bellows − an invisible flame seemed to come from the gape of his mouth. The stranger fought coolly, calmly, as if he trusted that the torrential energy of his opponent must give out soon; and then the exhausted man would be his. Sometimes it seemed that Swart's strength was guttering out indeed. His clinching arms would drop, his legs would tremble. But always new energy came to him, from the sun or the dark earth; and again he turned his baleful power on the stranger. . . . This perpetual renewal of strength seemed unnatural to the stranger − it disconcerted him and discouraged him − the blacksmith should have been his twenty minutes ago. He reasoned with himself that next time Swart showed signs of faltering he would go for him before the devil poured new fire into him. The moment came when the sun stood right over the mill. The stranger thrust Swart from him. Swart groaned and staggered and shook his head. Then the stranger struck him like a thunderbolt, broke through Swart's arms, took him by the shoulders for a final throw. It was a trap he had rushed into. Swart's yielding body grew solid as rock. The stranger was wrapped in ponderous arms. The life-and-death wrestle began and lasted for five tortured minutes. The fighters seemed rooted to the one spot, they swayed as the gale of strength blew itself out. And when it was over the stranger lay on his back. Pale and smiling, he acknowledged defeat. Swart stood astride him, and groaned.

It was then that the crowd saw the blood at his mouth.

Swart turned away from the twenty-pound prize. He went blindly through the cheers and the offered hands. He staggered across the field and in through the door of his cold smithy.

There they found him, an hour later, with his head against the anvil and his beard red-clotted.

They carried him into his bed. And the grieve sent for Teenie Twill, who was the kindest and best nurse in the district.

Swart was grievously injured. Several of his ribs had been cracked in the fight, and he was in continual pain. But that didn't seem to worry him, Teenie Twill reported, so much as something else — a deep wound in the spirit. 'I have been in the flames of hell,' he said to Teenie one morning. 'That man with the stallion,' he said after a time, 'is he still in Orkney?' Teenie said, Yes, the man had gone on into Birsay and Evie, and he seemed none the worse of the fight. In fact, he was continually asking after Swart, and sending him good wishes. Everybody liked him. 'Well,' said Swart, 'I hope I'll get to like him too. For my soul's sake. Meantime, Teenie lass, you see that purse with the twenty pounds in it — that's to be given to him next time he's in the parish. He won, after all. *He* won. He didn't have to fight me *and* the black creature that was inside me that day.'

Teenie didn't know what to make of that kind of talk. Swart still wandered a bit at times. Otherwise he was getting better — his ribs were slowly mending. But it was doubtful if he would ever be able to work in the smithy again. The wrestling match had taken too much out of him. He was a broken man.

One day he wanted Teenie to read the bible to him.

Teenie didn't know whether that was a good sign or not.

She searched the house for a bible. Finally, beside the forge, she found a little black book, and took it in to Swart.

He screamed and covered his eyes when he saw it.

'Take that out from here,' he cried. 'Out and away!'

Teenie, who was a curious little soul, opened the book and saw a picture of a man with a forked tail. Strange exciting white words starred the midnight pages.

'Teenie,' said Swart in a low voice. 'Would you like to have that book?'

'Why, yes,' said Teenie, 'if you don't want it.'

'It will give you anything you want,' said Swart. 'It will give you what you most desire in the world.'

Teenie had a certain heart-hunger; she knew, the poor soul, what most she wanted. But she did not think this weird book would give it to her.

'Well, thank you,' she said.

'You must pay for it,' said Swart. 'It will cost you a farthing.'

Teenie smiled at Swart's wayward words. He was not quite better yet, the poor man. He had just given away twenty pounds and here he was demanding a farthing. 'Well,' she said, 'I think I can manage a farthing.' And there and then she opened her little purse.

(4)

Teenie Twill lived by herself in a small cottage at the roadside.

How did Teenie Twill live?

In the laird's big house, three mornings a week, she polished oak and silver and mirrors and twenty tall windows.

When there was sickness in any house, Teenie Twill was sent for at once. She had kind healing hands.

Teenie Twill stitched pretty designs, with coloured threads, on linen. The Hamnavoe merchants bought these samplers from her, and sold them to foreign skippers.

She was poor, Teenie Twill. But her hearth-stone shone and her doorstep gleamed and the little panes in her window glittered.

Teenie Twill's cat Twork purred and blinked and washed his face beside the fire, or on the doorstep on a summer day.

She had a certain heart-hunger, Teenie Twill.

Often the fishermen, going home with their baskets of fish, left a haddock or a little skate at Teenie's door.

But Sam the ferryman, he left nothing at Teenie's door. He went past her door without one glance. He did not seem to be aware of the little plain hungry face that watched from the end window of the cottage till he was out of sight.

Sam the ferryman was not interested in a plain creature like Teenie. Four or five bonny girls were after Sam, from the hill crofts and the loch-side crofts and the farms down at the shore.

Nobody knew about Teenie's heart-hunger but herself. If they had known they would have laughed.

One day in August Teenie, and a hundred others, went to the agricultural show in Hoy. Five boats ferried the people across Hoy Sound. Teenie enjoyed the show, with its prize rams and cockerels, and the ginger cake and the ginger ale, and all the crowds of folk. Soon it was time to go home. The sun was down. The ferry boats left, one by one. Sam's boat was the last to leave. Teenie waited on the Hoy shore till the very end. Sam the ferryman carried the other girls on his thick shoulder out to his boat. The girls screamed and chortled and kicked. Sam did not come back for the last passenger. Teenie Twill had to wade through cold sea to the boat. She was wet to the knees. Coarse arms hauled her in.

And at the pier of Hamnavoe Sam took sixpence each from the farmers and the grocers and the town wives. From the giggle of girls he took a kiss each. From the one who lingered last on the boat, Teenie Twill, Sam took sixpence.

That night Teenie Twill cried a little beside the fire. Arabella her neighbour came in for the loan of an egg for her man's supper. 'Mercy!' she cried, seeing Teenie's tear-studded face, 'have you not enjoyed yourself at the show?'

Teenie nodded, but went on crying, and put a couple of eggs, blindly, in Arabella's hands. (She would of course never see the eggs again — Arabella forgot about loans at once.)

Arabella reported to her man that Teenie Twill was going a bit queer in the head — first signs of spinster-hood — a pity for the creature.

That same night Teenie opened, idly, the farthing book she had got from Swart the blacksmith. She could make neither head nor tail of it. But there were a few loose pages with elegant writing on them tucked into the back cover. This, Teenie thought, must be the English version of the text. The translation was diffi-cult enough, in all conscience. Teenie sighed. Then she came to a section with this heading — "Concerning the Heart, and the Cold Alien Heart of Another, and How that Heart is to be Aroused, and Hunted Down, and so Won". . . . What on earth did *that* mean? Teenie read on. She read beyond midnight. Her eyes were bright and her cheeks burned. Still she read. Her lamp flared and gulped and went out. Teenie gave a little cry of terror. She left the book on a chair and groped her way to bed. But she did not sleep. Her eyes shone with excitement on the pillow till the sun got up.

The very next morning Teenie was sweeping the ashes from her hearth. The cat licked daintily from his plate of milk. There came a loud thundering at the door that made Teenie and the cat jump on the flagstones.

'Come in,' said Teenie in her small voice.

Sam the ferryman entered. He was in pain. He pointed to his right hand. A splinter from the oar had gone into the palm: not just a little needle of wood either, but a ragged sizeable fragment. He winced with pain. The fishermen had told him to go to Teenie. They said she would get the splinter out and bind up his wound. If anybody could cure it, it was Teenie.

Quietly, without any fuss, Teenie performed the ritual of healing.

Sam the ferryman stayed on for his dinner. He ate the herring and potatoes and butter with his left hand. With his bandaged right hand he stroked the cat.

He said he was in no hurry to get back to the "Swift" (that was the name of his boat.) It was a slack time of year with him.

Teenie brought him a mug of ale. He said it was very good ale. The cat leapt up on his lap. Teenie put more peats on the fire. Then she brought him the full jug of ale and set it on the table before him, so that he could help himself.

Sam the ferryman smiled at Teenie.

Sam stayed all afternoon. He said what a neat clean bit of a place Teenie had. Arabella from next door came in for the loan of a lump of butter. Teenie said, quite sharply, that she had no butter to spare. Arabella had never been sent away empty-handed before. She told Andrew – that was the name of her husband – that Teenie was entertaining a man, none other than Sam the ferryman, in whose company no lass was safe. . . .

The autumn shadows began to cluster in the corners of Teenie's house.

Sam said she must be very comfortable in such a trim bright cosy little place.

Teenie said yes, but for loneliness now and then.

Teenie brought him bannocks with butter and rhubarb jam thick on them; and, of course, more ale. Twork slept on Sam's lap. Sam said he didn't know the time he had enjoyed a day as much; and that in spite of the trouble in his hand.

It grew darker. They crouched, two shadows, at each side of the fire.

Sam said it was a hard and a tiresome life, the life he led: eating coarse ill-cooked food day after day, putting to sea with strangers in all weathers, sleeping under the stars with no cover but a tattered sheepskin. It was not much of a life, when you thought about it.

Teenie went to light the lamp. Sam said there was no need for that. It was cheerier in the firelight. That was another thing he missed in his trade, a good fire to come home to.

Once Teenie thought she saw a face pressed to the window: Arabella's.

Sam said he supposed he would have to be getting back to the boat. He emptied Twork from his lap on to the floor.

Teenie said Sam would be the better of biding for a bite of supper. It was very cold outside. He shouldn't trust his hand to the night frost. It might fester and grow rotten. He wouldn't want to lose his hand! He wouldn't want to end his days with a hook at the end of his arm!

Teenie and Sam laughed, one on each side of the fire.

Sam held out his bandaged hand in the firelight. Teenie took it gently in both her hands. Then she kissed it.

The two shadows leaned towards each other until they made a kind of arch in the firelight, the keystone of which was a red tremulous kiss.

The cat leapt softly on to the bed.

The flames lessened in the hearth. The peats sank through red into gray, with innumerable whisperings. Teenie shivered in the sudden chill. Sam's hand began to hurt. It was time for both to seek another warmth....

Arabella saw Sam going down to the shore before the sun got up, in the twilight before dawn. 'That little hypocrite!' she said to Andrew her man. 'So prim and proper and respectable! I would never have believed it. But I saw it with my own two eyes. I did. It's as sure as I stand here. Sam the ferryman, of all men — a cruel heartless brute if ever there was one. I need the loan of a bottle of ale from her, for your breakfast, but I've a good mind not to go!'

*   *   *

The story of poor Teenie Twill is so painful from here on that I will try to make an end with as few words as possible.

She got her heart's desire. But bitterly she had to pay for it, with sorrow upon sorrow.

Her first sorrow was that Sam the ferryman never visited her again. After a few nights she went down to his hut on the shore. He closed the door in her face. Arabella's estimate of his character was not far wrong — "a cruel heartless brute".

His hand, I'm sorry to say, soon healed.

The second grief that afflicted Teenie was that, after five months or so, once the evidence was plain to be seen, she was haled before the kirk session, and sternly reprimanded for her sin, and ordered to stand for three Sundays in succession, in sackcloth, before the congregation in the parish kirk. And there the minister lashed her with his tongue. And Arabella nodded her entire approval, sitting in the front seat of the gallery. Teenie stood there as cold and still as a statue.

The third grief that fell on Teenie was that the respectable folk of the parish no longer recognized her. The laird's lady dismissed her from her service. Teenie was very poor after that, and very lonely. But still a fisherman here and there left a fish on her doorstep. And such good folk as Tammo of Upgyre saw that she didn't lack for meal and butter and an egg or two. And Swart the blacksmith told her to take as many peats from his stack as she needed.

Arabella never came again to borrow a single thing, for a whole year and more.

Teenie's fourth grief was the birth of a little boy, in that cold house, with much pain, one summer evening. It was a beautiful child. But it drew only a few breaths in this world, and then the surly midwife covered its face, and the sexton carried it to the kirkyard.

After a few blanched days, Teenie was able to rise from her bed. The first thing she did was to take the black book from the drawer where she kept it hidden. 'Sorrow on me,' she said, 'that ever I read in your pages.'

She stoked up the fire and threw the book in. Nothing happened. The flames enwrapped it. Teenie thrust it into a red chasm, the very heart of the fire. It lay there, unconsumed. (It had begun in more terrible fires by far.) Teenie piled on peats and bits of driftwood all day. Next morning the book was there, black and baleful, among the ashes.

Teenie took the book to the top of the hill one very windy morning. She ripped the pages from the binding; she tore the pages across and across. She threw the fragments into the wind. They went whirling away in all directions, a small black blizzard.

When Teenie got home the book was lying intact on the table.

That afternoon Teenie wandered along the edge of the crags. She had weighted the book with the heaviest stone she could carry. She dropped stone and book over the edge. She heard the little plop and splash of the drowning.

When Teenie got home she saw a fish lying on her doorstep, and the black book beside it.

That was the fifth and greatest grief that Teenie had to endure — knowledge of the book's indestructibility. Grief is too mild a word for it. It was more like despair, madness, terror, soul's eclipse. For what had the begetter of the book said:. . . . "if he should wish it in his heart to be rid of my book, let him do so by all means, but only in the way of vending, or selling, and only for a lesser sum than the sum that he purchased it with. He that buyeth the book for a farthing, I will have the creature for my squire and servitor in the eternal errantries of hell". . . .

Teenie decided to make away with herself, and end her life. No-one would miss her except Twork the cat, and a few old folk and bairns and invalids. The parish would not be surprised to learn that her hat had been seen floating in the sea one morning early. Then the tongues would go round the parish like a bell: "Teenie Twill has made away with herself". . . 'Poor Teenie Twill!'. . . . 'The slut, it was the only thing she *could* do!'. . . .

Teenie decided to walk out into the sea one evening after sunset. She wouldn't stop till the waters covered her mouth.

What was she doing then, lingering outside the manse door with a little hard square shape under her shawl? Not much comfort for her there, surely — the minister had lashed her with his tongue in public for her lust and shamelessness; what would he say to her, what *could* he say to her, who had studied wickedness in this tract and manual of hell?

Teenie Twill went up the long path to the manse door, drifting, wavering, once or twice half turning back. Her little fist seized the brass knocker and let it fall. Then the huge house was full of clangings and echoes.

A snippety servant girl opened the door and looked at Teenie Twill like the far end of a fiddle; told her to wait; vanished, came back again, and ushered her into a book-lined room.

The awful man looked at Teenie over his spectacles.

Teenie told her story in a low toneless voice. Then she laid the book on the minister's desk.

The minister flicked through the pages. His eyes

widened. He gave a low whistle.

'So,' he said, 'the book existed after all. The devilish thing has actually been read by mortal eyes, and here, within my pastoral bounds! That drink-pedlar, he was the first Orkneyman to have it. He came here to visit me, with his lies and his unction. He made a poor end, that one – died of his own bad drink. . . . Then, let me see, who had it after him? There were plenty of rumours. I only half believed them. . . . Stop crying, girl, you came to the right place. . . . It was that coarse farmer at Stark. He was supposed to have it for a time. Much good it did him. He wore away to a shadow in a month or two. Robert Skelding of Stark. A great beast of a man – nothing of him but skin and bone in the end. His coffin was as light as an infant's. . . . That ever I should hold in my hands a book hot from the presses of hell!. . . . They will not believe it in the Presbytery when I tell them, a week come Tuesday. . . . Who had it after Rob Skelding? Let me think.'

'It was Swart the blacksmith.'

'Speak up, girl. Don't whisper. I'm an old man, I have wax in my lugs. Swart the blacksmith. I always thought Swart was a decent young fellow. Very generous, very charitable. It only goes to show. There's not one of us but has a chink somewhere in his armour. Not one. And there the great Adversary inserts the point of his sword. A little bit of vanity – that was Swart's trouble – his only weakness, as far as I could see. He couldn't suffer to be beaten, especially when it came to wrestling and lifting gates from hinges and such-like nonsense. Well, well – so he gets a good and a fair promise out of this abomination of a book, and he nearly kills himself (poor Swart!) fulfilling the promise. They say he hobbles about on a stick now, like a man of eighty. A stranger labours at his forge.'

The minister shuffled through the black pages.

'It must have come here on a ship. I suppose that vagabond in 'The Leaping Dolphin' was telling the truth, for once, when he said that. . . . Well now, girl, what do you want with me? If you think I'm going to buy this filth from you, you're very much mistaken. How does it come to be in your hands anyway, a little creature like you, eh? Haven't I seen your face before? Yes, I have. You're the lass I censured in the kirk in April'. . . .

Teenie bowed her head.

'You're in far greater trouble now. I hope you realize that. I don't know if I can help you at all.'

'God have mercy on me then,' whispered Teenie.

'Just go on saying that, *God have mercy,* every morning and every night for a while. Maybe a stray angel will hear you. . . . Old Professor Macdonald in Edinburgh, I mind, gave us three lectures on exorcism and the outwitting of the Devil. But that was a long time ago, and I might have forgot.'

Teenie told how she had thrice tried to destroy the book, in vain.

'So,' said the minister. 'You're the one who bought it for a farthing. You goose. Follow me, girl. We're going for a walk.'

The minister put on a black overcoat and a black hat as big and round as a cartwheel. Together he and Teenie Twill left the Manse and walked a mile through the fields to the kirkyard at the shore. The minister hummed fragments of the psalm tune "Kilmarnock" as they went.

The old gravedigger was busy with his spade. 'Another funeral, is it?' said the minister. 'Who is it this time? Always somebody. Into your shed with you. I have something to do here that isn't for curious eyes. It'll only take two minutes'. . . .

The old gravedigger chuckled and lit his pipe and climbed out of the half-dug grave.

'Leave us your spade,' said the minister. 'I need it.'

The gravedigger wandered away among the tombs.

Spade-flashings, smell of new-delved earth in the late afternoon light. Then the minister threw the spade with a clang against an old tombstone.

Teenie watched with a throbbing heart.

'Creation of evil,' intoned the minister above the thing he held in both his hands, 'put upon this good and godly earth (we know not how) for the destruction of men's bodies and souls, and for the enlargement of the kingdom of hell, know that a limit has been set to thy workings, and that this very hour and day thou shalt melt like a black flake in the holy fires of God, and never be seen more by mortal eyes. And as for the chaste and gentle person that thou thoughtest to bring down into despair and the pit of hell – for that there is no coin of less value in this realm of Britain than a farthing, or fourth part of a penny, and that farthing she paid for thee (and also for a farthing, scripture saith, two sparrows are bought, creatures from the hand of God, throbbing jewels compared to thee, thou trash of hell) – as for this girl, I say, she hath fully and frankly confessed, and hath repented her of her folly, and now her face is Godward set as ever it was in the time of her innocency. Begone now, and for ever, out of time and beyond the forbidden yearnings of the children of time.'

The minister threw the book into the earth. The swart pages fluttered.

The minister wielded the spade again. He scattered earth over the book. As soon as the first clod hit it The Book of Black Arts flared, shrivelled, curled; and was a cluster of ashes in the rich last light flooding in from the west.

'Begone, like a dream, into nothingness,' said the minister. 'Amen.'

Teenie sighed deeply. At that moment two birds chirped at her from a bush in the kirkyard. Teenie Twill had never heard such beautiful sounds.

'Bless you,' said the minister. 'That's it. Nothing more to worry about. We'd better be getting back now. I have a sermon to write.'

Together they moved among the tombstones to the gate. Behind one stone the gravedigger was smoking, his pipe upside down in his mouth.

BRIG—O—DREAD

When thou from hence away art past
Every nighte and alle
To Whinny-muir thou com'st at last
And Christe receive thy saule

From Whinny-muir when thou may'st pass
Every nighte and all
To Brig-o-Dread thou com'st at last
And Christe receive thy saule

From Brig-o-Dread when thou may'st pass
Every nighte and all
To Purgatory fire thou com'st at last
And Christe receive thy saule

'I should say at once who I am, in case it is necessary for me to make a statement soon. My name is Arkol Andersvik. I have been married for twelve years to my dear good wife Freya. We have a son, aged 11, called Thord, a clever fair-haired boy whose craze, at the moment, is science fiction. His school reports are promising – I will say no more. We live in a fine old house in Hamnavoe, and I have a garden that slopes down from the hill to the street. My shop is in the town centre. Out of whalebone we – my brother and I – carve souvenirs and mementos and I deal in a variety of sealskin articles. We do a fair business in summer, when the islands are filled with tourists. I am a councillor. I am fifty years old.

'I try not to neglect the cultural side. For the past ten years I have imposed a discipline on myself. I have striven to acquaint myself with the best that has been sung and thought and written. You might call it a quest for truth and beauty. At the moment I am engaged on reading *Hamlet* for the third time. A poem that I chanced on last week really delighted me – the *Ode on a Grecian Urn* by Keats. It gave me a feeling of great purity and peace.

'My brother says this pursuit of culture is a substitute for the kirk pew. He may be right. I am not a religious man.

'Something strange has happened to me. That is why I am preparing this statement. I am not at home, nor in the shop. I don't know where I am, that's the truth. I am sitting on a bench in a bare room, like a prison cell. (But that is impossible.) Or it could be like a room where witnesses wait until they are called to give their evidence. It is worrying. I have never been involved in any kind of legal process. I intend to get to the bottom of it. It is a waste of my time, to put it mildly. I have a business to attend to. I have council work to see to this very evening. Freya will be very worried indeed.

'I have just discovered, with a certain relief, that I am not in prison; they have not removed my tie and bootlaces. I will go on writing in my notebook. That might help to clarify the situation in my mind.

'Wistan and I went seal-shooting yesterday afternoon, it being early closing day in the town. (Wistan is my younger brother.) We took our guns and motored four miles along the coast to a certain skerry where the seals come and go all summer. Some people wax sentimental over these animals. They invoke all the old legends about the selkie folk, half man and half seal, and their fondness for music. They denounce those who slaughter them, forgetting that they are voracious beasts that eat half the fish in the sea. The legends are charming, but most of that kind of talk is slush. Every man has his living to make. (What about the beasts that are slaughtered for our Sunday joints?)

'Wistan and I got out of the van at the cliff top and, carrying our guns, made our way carefully down salt broken ledges to the sea, only to find that the skerry was bare. The seals were away at their fishing. That was disappointing. We decided to wait for an hour or so, seeing that it was a fine afternoon and still early. I laid my gun along a ledge of rock. Wistan said he would take a walk round the coast, to see if he could find some shells or stones that – properly decorated — might tempt the tourists in search of souvenirs. He offered me his whisky flask. I declined, of course.

'A word or two about Wistan. He helps me in the business. I might have made him a partner but the truth is that there is a certain waywardness about him, an unreliability. He went to sea as a lad — came home after two years. My father used his influence to get Wistan work in a lawyer's office in Kirkwall, but he left, saying he couldn't bear the thought of scribbling and copying all day and every day, maybe for the rest of his life. For the next year or two he was a ne'er-do-well, spending his mornings in the pub, his afternoons in the billiard hall. Most evenings he would take his flute to dances in this parish and that. Wistan's conduct clouded our father's last years — I am certain of that.

'In the end I employed him in the shop. What else could I do? He is my brother. I did not want to see him wasting his life entirely. Wistan has talents. No-one can make more handsome sealskin bags and slippers than him, and the way he paints birds and flowers on stone is masterly. He, not I, is the whalebone carver. I pay him twelve pounds a week. He has a small house on a pier and lives there alone. (In case somebody should say, "That is a poor wage to give a man", I reply, "That is all the business will stand. Give him more, he would simply squander it. . . ." Besides, who but myself would employ him?)

'Poor Wistan! He is not highly regarded in the community. He was a delightful child, but some kind of raffishness entered into him at adolescence. It has never left him — the dreams, the deviousness. He drinks too much. Freya does not like him. I inflict him on her all the same — I insist that he comes to dinner every Sunday. In that way I can be sure that he gets at least one good meal in the week. He lounges about in the house all Sunday afternoon while I retire upstairs to my books and gramophone records.

'I thought to myself, between the crag and the skerry, "How on earth can Wistan afford whisky, on his wage?" I am not a skinflint, I hope, and I have nothing against a dram in the evening — but to booze in the middle of a summer afternoon! So I shook my head at the offered whisky flask. Still holding his gun in the crook of his arm, Wistan took a sip or two.

'A sleek head broke the surface fifty yards out. Large liquid eyes looked at the hunters. I whistled. Wistan whistled, farther off. The creature stirred and eddied towards us. "Come on, my beauty", I remember saying. The water was suddenly alive with seals. And this is all I remember, until I found myself an hour ago in this cell-like room.

'It is very strange. Where am I? Where is Wistan? Where is the seal, the shore, the gun?'

*   *   *

Mr. Andersvik had no sooner closed his notebook than he saw that the door of the mysterious room now stood open. It was a summer day: there was blue sky and white clouds. He was free to go, it seemed.

Outside a signpost pointed: TO THE MOOR.

The landscape was strange to Mr Andersvik. The

moor stretched, a wine-red emptiness, from horizon
to horizon. It was eerie, to say the least. "Well," he
thought, "I'm bound to meet somebody who can tell
me the way to Hamnavoe." Indeed, when he took the
track that wound into the moor, he saw a few people
and they too, like the landscape, had a remote
dreamlike quality. They moved like somnambulists.
Every heath-farer was solitary and did not appear to
be going anywhere. The moor was a slow soundless
dance of intersections and turnings. The faces were
down-tilted and preoccupied. It was soon obvious
that the moor-dwellers wanted nothing to do with
Mr Andersvik. As soon as he tried to approach one or
other of these lonely ones, to ask the direction, they
held out preventive hands — they had nothing to say
to him, they did not want to hear anything that he
had to say to them. Mr Andersvik was a bit hurt to
begin with at these rebuffs. But after he had walked a
mile or two a kind of contentment crept through him.
It was quite pleasant out here on the moor. What
contented Mr Andersvik particularly was the account
he had written in his notebook in "the court-room"
— he had set it down defensively (as if he was actually
going to be charged with some offence) in order to
put a good face on things, to cover up certain shames
and deficiencies in his life that were, after all, his
own concern. But here, on this moor, the images and
rhythms of his prose pleased him very much indeed;
he could savour them with extraordinary vividness
in the solitude and silence. The remembrance was all
pleasant, a flattering unction. He began the cycle of his
life again — Freya and love and the garden, Thord and

promise, Wistan and irresponsibility, the shop and sealskins and money, the council and honour, the temple of culture where he was a regular devoted worshipper. . . . The second round of meditation was if anything sweeter than the first. . . . This delight, he thought, might go on for a long time. He very much hoped that it would.

Mr Andersvik discovered, by certain rocks and a certain gorse bush in the moor, that he had drifted round in two wide circles. He was learning to behave in the manner of the moor-dwellers. He halted.

"This will never do", said Mr Andersvik to himself, breaking the lovely idyll. "I must get back. These memories are not entirely true, I'm afraid. I must open the shop. There is this council meeting tonight."

He turned. He strode on across the moor, frowning and purposeful. He was aware that his ankles had been rather badly scratched with gorse-thorns — he had not noticed the pain till now.

One of the moor people loomed close, with a tranced preoccupied face, drifting on, smiling, in a wide arc across the path of Mr Andersvik.

"Please", said Mr Andersvik. "One moment. I'm wanting to get to Hamnovoe. Could you tell me if i'm going in the right direction?"

"What's wrong with this place?" said the dancer on the moor. "What greater happiness could there be than this solitude? If you leave the moor you'll never get back. Beware, man. Your journey will end in ashes and smoke". . . . The man drifted on, smiling, feeding deep on the honey of his past.

A finger of fear touched Mr Andersvik. To go on

like that for ever, nourished on delusions! He was
sure of one thing now, he wanted to break out of
these endless self-flattering circles. He hurried on.
Gorse tore at his ankles. Once he fell in a blazing
bush — his hands bled and burned. He picked himself
up and went on. Clumps of gorse blossomed here and
there on the moor — it was impossible to avoid them
entirely. Freya would have to put some disinfectant
on a multitude of scratches.

He came over a ridge and saw with relief that the
track gave on to a road.

It was strange. Mr Andersvik thought he knew every
road in the island, but he had never been on this
particular one. He came after a mile or so to a crossroads. The signpost said: TO THE BRIDGE. He
walked on. Soon familiar hills and waters came about
him. He recognized Kringlafiold and the twin lochs
with the prehistoric stone circle. And over there was
the farm where his sister Anne had gone to live and
toil when she married Jock Onness thirty years before.
Alas, Anne had been dead for four years. That death
had been a blow to Mr Andersvik; Anne was one of
the few folk he had ever had affection for. He felt a
pang as he looked at the widowed farm. Should he
call in and have a word with old Jock? He thought,
not today. The shop — souvenirs, sealskin — he was
losing pounds. Besides, he did not feel in a mood to
explain to the old man all the strange things that had
happened to him. Jock was very deaf, and not too
bright.

He walked on. Ahead was the little stone bridge
that divides sea from loch, parish from parish. Under

the triple arch salt water mingles with sweet water twice a day. A woman was standing at the hither end of the bridge. She beckoned to Mr Andersvik. Her face was tranquil, as if a quiet flame had passed through it.

It was his sister Anne.

He tried to speak, but his mouth locked on the words.

"Arkol", she said, "I've been expecting you. You've been on the moor a long time."

"An hour or two", he whispered.

"Longer than that", said the dead woman. "Oh, much longer. Well done, Arkol, all the same. Only a few folk have the strength to tear themselves away from that moor."

Mr Andersvik took his first dark taste of death.

"I had to come and meet you", said Anne, "before you cross the bridge. Otherwise the pain would be too sudden and terrible."

The half-ghost understood nothing of this. Death, in his understanding, was a three-day feast of grief, a slow graining and seepage among roots, the last lonely splendour of the skeleton — but all enacted within a realm of oblivion (except for a few fading fragrances in the memory of friends). An eternity of harps, or flames, had always seemed to Mr Andersvik an insult to the human intelligence.

He could not by any means accept his present situation. Yet here he was, in dialogue with a solicitous riddling ghost.

"Arkol, you've chosen the truth", said Anne. "That's splendid. But the truth is cruel, Arkol. A poor naked truth-bound ghost has a terrible journey to go."

"What happened to me?" said Mr Andersvik after a time.

"A gun-shot wound. In the head. The court said 'Death by misadventure.' Poor Arkol."

"My gun was six yards away on a ledge of rock!" cried Mr Andersvik. "That's impossible!"

"Poor Arkol," she said again. "But that's only the start. Are you willing to be dead?"

"No," he cried. "I don't believe it. Don't touch me. I can't be dead! I have years of work in front of me. Thord must be given a good start. Freya must be provided for. There's the housing committee and the graveyard committee. I am going to extend the business. I haven't made a will."

His sister soothed him. She spoke to him with all the tenderness and kindness that in the old days had persuaded Mr Andersvik that, for example, he must really not be so pompous, he must learn to laugh at himself a little; that he must give Freya a more generous house-keeping allowance, she was having to pinch here and patch there — it was a shame, him with all that money and all these pretensions. . . . Now Mr Andersvik sensed a new depth in his sister's concern. He bowed his head. He yielded to her wisdom, there on the bridge between the dead and the living. Anne kissed him on the mouth, and so sealed his death for him.

Arkol crossed over the bridge then.

In darkness the dead man returned to the dimension he had left. Time is a slow banked smoulder to the living. To the dead it is an august merciless

ordering of flames, in which the tormented one, in
Eliot's words, must learn at last to be a dancer.

*   *   *

His fellow-councillors were sitting in the council
chamber. There was a new member seated in the chair
he normally occupied — his brother Wistan. The pro-
vost was making some kind of formal speech. . . .
"welcome our new councillor, Mr Wistan Andersvik,
to this chamber. We welcome him doubly in that he is
the brother of the late councillor Arkol Andersvik,
who died in such tragic circumstances a month ago.
The late councillor was a highly valued member of
this assembly. His wisdom and his humanity will be
greatly missed. Some said that maybe he was over-
cautious in this matter and that, but my reply to that
was always, "Arkol Andersvik is a true custodian of
the public purse". . . . A more prudent man never
walked the streets of this burgh. We trust, indeed we
know, that his brother will be in all respects a worthy
successor. He will bring imagination to our debates
where the lamented elder brother gave us abundant
practical sense. I will ask you, fellow-councillors,
to be upstanding as a token of our respect for that
good man who was taken so suddenly from our
midst". . . .
They stood there, a lugubrious circle, and Wistan
stood among them. Arkol felt for the first time
the pain of the wound in his head. He cried out
that they had taken a murderer into their fold,
a brother-killer; but no-one heard him. They passed

on to the next business on the agenda. . . .

* * *

Arkol shook himself clear of that flame. Darkness beset him again for a while (he did not know how long);
then, far on, a new flame summoned, a white splash of
time. He eddied like a moth towards it. . . . What shuttered place was he standing in? Light sifted through
slatted window blinds. Of course he soon recognized it:
it was his shop. The clock ticked on the shelf, spilling
busy seconds into his timelessness. It was a quarter past
ten in the morning, and still the door hadn't been opened to the public. So, it had come to this. How had Freya
ever allowed it! She ought to have sold the business as
a going concern. It had been a small gold-mine. Plenty
of folk would have given a handsome price for 'A.
Andersvik — Novelties, Presents, and Souvenirs'.

The key shrieked in the lock. The street-door
opened. A familiar shadow stood there, carrying a
heavy bucket.

Arkol saw in the new light from the street that there
were no longer any painted pebbles or sealskin on the
shelves. In their place were pieces of baked hollowed-
out clay, garishly decorated. So Wistan had set himself
up as a potter? The shop was a shambles — it reeked of
burnt earth.

"You killed me", he said sternly. "But you're too
loutish and lazy to enjoy the fruits of murder. How
dare you ruin a good business! Filthying my shop
with your mud and fire!"

Wistan set his bucket of clay beside the warm kiln.

He moved over to the bench. He began to knead a
lump of clay with knuckles and fingers. He was
humming happily to himself. . . .

Arkol came out of that flame singed and trembling,
and glad of darkness.

*   *   *

He stood on Celia's pier in the first light of morning. . . . (Time here was, as always, surely, a limpid
invisible burning.) The old women arrived with their
cats and basins while the fishermen (just back from
the west) handed up the steps baskets of haddocks.
It was a famous place for gossip and opinion and elegy.
Gulls, savage naked hungers, wheeled between the
boat and the pier.

They were speaking about a death.

"Accident", Maisie Ness was saying. "That makes
me laugh. You can't shoot yourself by accident. He
was in trouble, if you ask me. He was on the verge of
bankruptcy. So I heard. There was nothing else for
him to do but shoot himself."

"Well", said Andrina Moar, "he isn't that much of
a miss. The swank of him! The strut of the creature
along the street!"

Not one face on Celia's pier stilled with sorrow for
the dead man. Instead, the women, old and young, began to tear at Arkol's death like gulls among fish guts.

The haddocks gulped and shrugged in their baskets:
dying gleams. Cats mewed. Sea and sky and stone was
an asylum of gulls. The voices went on and on in the
sunlight. . . .

The darkness wrapped him away, trembling, from the slanders of the living.

*   *   *

He emerged into fragrance and sweetness. A peaceful green rectangle sloped down from the hill to the clustered roofs of Hamnavoe: his garden. What man was that sitting on the bench under the sycamore tree? It was, again, Wistan. Years had passed. Wistan's face was thin and sick and gray. Was he perhaps on the point of accomplishing his suicide by alcohol (an end that Arkol had more than once prophesied)? Then Arkol saw that Wistan was somehow injured — his right hand (the one that had pulled the trigger) was white and thick with bandaging. Wistan looked very seedy indeed in that net of green wavering shadows. (So Freya, out of the foolish kindness of her heart, had taken the creature into her house, for cure or for death.)

Freya came out of the kitchen into the sunlight. There was an extra decade of flesh and capability on her now. She was carrying a tray with salves and bandages on it. Wistan looked up. Blackbirds sang here and there in the bushes. It was a marvellous summer morning. The man and the woman smiled at each other. But immediately the shadow fell on Wistan's face again.

Freya set down the tray on the bench. She bent forward and kissed him on the forehead.

The ghost stirred in its flame.

"So, dearest", said Freya, "this is one of your

black days, is it?". . . . She knelt on the grass and began to undo the bandage on Wistan's hand.

There was a passionate outpouring of song from the rosebush at the bottom of the lawn.

"It *was* an accident", said Wistan in the shivering silence that followed. "The gun went off in my hands. But, dear, he'd done such terrible things, anything he could think of – you know – to make me eat dirt, that sometimes I think". . . .

"We've been through all that before", said Freya the comforter. "I know. You've told me hundreds of times". . . . She kissed the scarred hand. "There, if it helps you. Of course it was an accident. Just as you didn't mean to put your hand in the kiln last Friday. You were aiming for the seal that day. You might as well argue that *I* killed Arkol. If I didn't particularly want him to die, that was just because I'd got used to him. I realize that now. . . . You wedged the gun into his arms – that's all you have to reproach yourself with, love. It was nothing. It was clever of you, in fact. It saved a lot of trouble, a lot of fuss and anger and suspicion."

Wistan closed his eyes. Freya began to spread the unguent over his charred palm.

Freya said, after another blackbird interlude, "I don't think now, looking back, that I ever really liked Arkol. The meanness of him, the arrogance! That horrible flesh lying beside me all night and every night! But you, dear, the first time I ever saw you. . . ."

The ghost smouldered in the garden, among the sievings of birdsong. It glowed. It reeked. It longed to be anywhere, in any darkness, away from this incestuous place. Then it remembered, and acquiesced in the stake. The flames thickened. The ghost burned terribly. Yet it forced itself to look while Freya wrapped Wistan's wound in new bandages, swiftly, delicately, tenderly; and even afterwards, when the man and the woman enfolded each other on the long bench.

If only a ghost could die. . . . It bore into the darkness terrible new scorchings.

*   *   *

Arkol came to a room that had a stale smell in it. It was the study where he had sought to improve his mind with good music and books. A reproduction of Van Gogh's "Sunflowers" hung over the mantelpiece. Freya, it seemed, had sealed the place off like a mausoleum. The dust whispered to him from shelf and record-player, "What good was it to you, after all? You went through life blind and dense and hoodwinked. Here we are, Chopin and Jane Austen and Shelley, and we tried to tell you many a wise and many a true thing, but it only served to bolster your self-importance. Go and look for some peace now, poor ghost, if you can. . . ." No-one ever entered the study. *Hamlet* was lying on the table, just as he had left it the day before his murder, and *The Oxford Book of English Verse*, open at 'The Grecian Urn'. The ghost bent over the gray page. The poem was, as never before, a cold pure round of silence; a fold; a chalice where, having tasted, a man may understand and rejoice.

*   *   *

Arkol passed deeper into the charred ruins of his life. In another room a youth was sitting at a table, making notes of some kind. Thord had grown into a pleasant-looking young man. Bits of *Hamlet* drifted through the ghost: 'Thy father's spirit'. . . . 'He took me grossly full of bread'. . . . 'Avenge his foul and most unnatural murder'. . . . The ghost smiled, in spite of its pain. As if this ordinary youth could ever be roused to such eagle-heights of rage, assoilment, passion! What had Thord done with his life? Arkol had had high hopes of the shy eager boy with his pile of science fiction books on his bedside table. Thord, he had thought, might well become a physicist, or a writer, or even a seeker among the stars. The ghost bent over the warm shoulder. Thord was filling up a football pools coupon. On the door-hook hung a postman's cap. To this favour the clever little boy had come: knocking at doors with white squares of gossip, propaganda, trivia. It did not matter. The ghost drank the beauty of his son's face — and saw, without rage, how like his mother he was now. He longed to linger out his time in this flame. But, shadow by slow shadow, he was folded in oblivion once more. . . .

*   *   *

This was the rock, right enough. Coldness and heaviness and poise lay across the ghost, a gun-shape. It oppressed him. He wished he were free of it. Another man was walking on the loose stones of the beach fifty yards away. The man stooped and picked up a stone or a shell every now and again. The man uncorked a flask and tilted it towards his mouth. A sleek head broke the gray surface — a seal, with large dark brimming eyes. The ghost whistled, but no smallest sound was added to the wash of the waves, the sliding of stones, the click of a bolt. There was another louder whistle farther along the shore. Suddenly the bay was musical with seals; they clustered about the off-shore rock; their sea-dance was over, they clambered awkwardly on to the stone. "Come on, my beauties" .... Whitman's song came on the wind:

>   I think I could turn and live with animals,
>   They are so placid and self-contained.

A line of Coleridge flowered: "he blessed them in his heart". . . . The ghost raised an invisible hand seaward. He greeted the clean swift beautiful creatures of the ocean. He acknowledged the long wars of man against that innocent kingdom. He whispered for forgiveness. Then he turned calmly to face the blaze and the roar.

*   *   *

The day began with streams of blood. All the village followed the white-robed priest and the heifer whose horns were hidden under wreaths and clusters of blossom. Children danced and shouted. The throng of people disappeared beyond the last house of the village.

The only man who did not go to the ceremony sat in his cell and waited. The door had been open since first light.

He heard, after a long loaded silence, a whisper on

the hillside, a fierce flailing of hooves, a surge and a spattering; then a wild ecstatic cry.

Presently the folk returned to the village. The lonely celebrant went with his red arms into a small house at the shore. The village street was soon empty. Family by family, purified, was eating its morning meal.

Not long afterwards the prisoner was summoned out to the village square.

A court of some kind was assembled and waiting. The square brimmed like a well with light. People of all ages sat here and there. Arkol was invited to station himself beside a sun-warmed stone.

The interrogator faced Arkol. Four people sat apart from the others, against the wall of the pottery-maker. Arkol took them to be a panel of judges. They consulted together. Occasionally one looked across at him and smiled.

The interrogator began with a reading out of the statement that Arkol had originally made: "trust of the townsfolk". . . . "quest for truth and beauty". . . . "intend to get to the bottom of this". . . . The interrogator was interrupted every now and again by wondering laughter.

The older men and women sat in their doorsteps. Children — hidden voices — shouted in the gardens behind the street. The sound of the sea was everywhere. A young man went round the people in the square carrying a tray with a pitcher and tankards. An old man nodded approval over the white blown fleece of foam. An old woman shook her head reprovingly at all the raised tankards.

The voice of the interrogator — austere, measured, and melodious — reached into the bright morning. The villagers were rather bored with the proceedings, on the whole. Arkol could tell by their faces that they would much rather have been down at the fishing boats, or on the hill with their sheep, than wasting the day with such a trivial case. But at the end, he supposed, the villagers would have to give some kind of a verdict in the square.

Some young folk had got out of it by bathing. Arkol could hear shouts along the beach and the splash of bodies in the surf. There were mocking harp-like cries, then a sudden silence. A young man, gleaming with sun and water, passed hurriedly through the square and entered a small steep alley. Children shrieked at the sea drops that shivered and showered over them. Voices from the rocks called for the insulted one to come back. A girl with wet hair appeared at the mouth of a seaward close. "We're sorry, Adon," she called. "Please come back. Please."

"Silence," said the interrogator sternly. "Go back to the sea. We are considering an important case."

The girl withdrew bright hair, bright shoulders.

The case suffered no more interruptions. The interrogator paused upon this phrase and that: . . . 'a word or two about Wistan' . . . . 'I am not a skinflint, I hope'. An old man laughed above his ale. Arkol smiled ruefully.

A boy called from a hidden garden that he had caught a butterfly — he had — but it had wriggled out of his fingers and was free in the wind once more.

What intrigued Arkol more than anything that

morning were the faces of the four judges who, he supposed, would finally decide whether his application should be granted or no. They sat on a long bench in front of the interrogator. It was as if old woodcuts and frontispieces and dead music had trembled and quickened. These were the jurors: a man with wild hair and a wild mouth — a young woman who in spite of merry mischievous eyes looked rather prim — a man with a russet beard and a scar at one ear — long lank hair over a lank dark cheek, a velvet jacket, lank fingers: the hollows and shadows scattered whenever the man smiled, which was often.

There was silence in the square. The reading of the statement was over.

The cup-bearer had spread a white cloth on a long trestle table. He reappeared in the square now, carrying a tray with steaming fish on it, and bread. He set the tray on the table. He began to arrange seats.

"The statement, it is a tissue of lies," said the hollow-cheeked juror in a foreign accent. All the jurors nodded. They looked at Arkol and smiled.

"The wonder is how he ever managed to escape," said Van Gogh. "I took him for a typical moor-dweller as soon as he arrived here last night."

"He is a hero," said a girl in a doorway who was feeding a baby at her breast.

The bathers came up from the sea, white-shrouded and shivering. The girl whose face had been glimpsed for a moment between the houses looked anxious now. Her companions tried to reassure her. They went in an agitated troop up one of the alleys.

The cup-bearer carried from the inn a huge pitcher —

both his arms were round it — some wine slurped over on to the cobble-stones. An old man cried out in alarm. But the pitcher was safely deposited at last among the fish and the bread.

"As one of the villagers," said a man who was leaning against a wall smoking a pipe, "I think he must at least do this before we give him the stones to build a house — he must alter the account of his life so that it comes a bit nearer the truth."

The villagers shouted their approval.

"You can't eat or drink with us, you understand," said the interrogator to Arkol, "or stay here in this village, until you have paid your debt to the truth. You must revise your statement in certain important respects. You will be given pen and paper. Now that you've crossed the bridge and been through the fire, I think you may enjoy doing it."

The villagers turned away from Arkol. They began to gather round the table. The bathers, all but two, came down the alley and joined the others. Mugs and pieces of bread were passed round — there was a mingling of courtesy and banter. Three seats were empty.

Arkol sat on a sunlit step. He poised his pen over the paper. He wondered how to begin.

The children's voices drifted down from the hillside. They were filling baskets with blackberries. Pure echoes fell into the square. The children shouted that they would not be home till sunset.

The lovers who had quarrelled on the sea verge stood in the mouth of the close. They were tranquil and smiling now. They moved into sunlight. Folk rose up at the table to let them pass on to their places.

Arkol wrote. Phrases with some beauty and truth in them began to come, with difficulty. He longed to sit among the villagers, and share their meal. But the feast was eternal. He hoped that he might be able, before it was over, to present to the elders the poem of his life.

PERILOUS SEAS

On the afternoon of 5 November 1724 a merchant ship *Caroline* of Guernsay dipped gently northwards through the Mediterranean. She had weighed anchor at Santa Cruz that morning with a cargo of Turkish leather, woollen cloth, and beeswax, bound for Genoa. The *Caroline* mounted twelve guns. She carried a crew of twenty-three, including five officers; the crew was a mixture of Swedes, Scotsmen, Irishmen, Danes, Englishmen, Welshmen. She was under charter to a company of Dutch merchants. In that year the Netherlands were at war with the Dey of Algiers, and so the Dutch were glad to charter neutral ships to carry on their rich Mediterranean trade. The master and owner of the galley was a middle-aged Channel Islander, Oliver Ferneau.

To Captain Ferneau on the quarter-deck that afternoon came the first officer, Bonadventure Jelfs, who asked with all deference but some unease when he expected that the *Caroline* should reach Genoa.

Captain Ferneau, speaking English that had only a slight foreign spice to it, answered that they should see the coast of Italy before nightfall. He put his hand on the bright hair of the cabin-boy who was standing beside him. They should reach the harbour of Genoa, he said, sometime the next day; it depended on wind and weather, and also of course on God's will.

The skipper told his cabin-boy, a Swedish child ten years old called Peter Hanson, to fetch his snuff-horn from the cabin; he had forgotten it. The angelic-looking messenger went off at once.

As soon as they were alone, Mr. Jelfs said, 'If I'm not mistaken, it depends even more on the intentions of Mister Williams.'

'What do you mean?' said Ferneau sharply, but he spoke as if Jelfs' remark had reverberated from a private doubt of his own.

'There is a bad element in the crew,' said Jelfs. 'That Welshman, he is the worst of all. He is the ringleader.'

'What are you afraid of, Jelfs? Tell me, please,' said Ferneau.

'I am not easy in my mind, that is all, captain,' said Jelfs.

'Allow me to say what is in *my* mind,' said Ferneau. 'You are troubling yourself unnecessarily. You have bad imaginings. This happens when one has been at sea for too long a time.'

'I hope so, indeed,' said Jelfs.

'Sailors were never angels,' said Ferneau. 'I have sailed with worse than this crew. I can control them. I have been a shipmaster twenty years. I can handle men well enough. You spoke of Williams.'

'Yes,' said Jelfs.

'He *is* a bad one, that Williams,' said Ferneau. 'You are right about him. We have a rat with sharp teeth in our hold.'

'There are others,' said Jelfs gloomily. 'Winter, Macaulay, Melvin.'

'Silly loud-mouthed boys,' said Ferneau. 'Card-players with knives. They rant and rave in their rum cans. There is also on board this ship, fortunately for us, I am glad to say, John Gow.'

Mr. Jelfs, with a coldness about his mouth, said nothing. He put a steady look on the cold gray heave of water in the west. The coast of Africa was a thin line on the horizon behind.

'So,' said Ferneau, 'you do not trust Mr. Gow either, Jelfs?'

'It is my opinion,' said Jelfs, 'since you ask, that it was not a good thing you did, to advance Gow from the crew.'

'I did right,' said Ferneau. 'John Gow is a good sailor. He is an honest open lad, well-educated too. I will not have you say anything against him. I trust him very much.'

Peter Hanson stood between the two officers with the silver-mounted snuff-horn in his hand.

Again, Mr. Jelfs made no reply. He took the snuff-horn from Peter Hanson, and sent the boy away with a curt sweep of his hand. He passed the horn wordlessly to Captain Ferneau.

'There is something more,' said Ferneau. 'Gow is well-liked by all the crew. He has a way with him. I am not well-liked, I am what you call a Frog, a Frenchman. You are not popular either, Jelfs – you have been too free with that ropes-end since we left the Texel. You are meagre with the rum also. But Gow is very much respected. Let there be any kind of trouble, I will send Gow to speak with them. He will stamp it out. That is a young sailor who will go far.'

'Winter threw his plate of beef at the cook,' said Jelfs. 'That is why I am here. I have come to report the incident.'

'Who did?' said Ferneau.

'Winter,' said Jelfs. 'The Swede.'

'I don't like that,' said Ferneau. 'This is the first food complaint since Santa Cruz. Did anyone else refuse?'

'No, sir,' said Jelfs. 'Only Winter.'

'The complaints at Santa Cruz, they were without cause,' said Ferneau. 'It was good food, plenty of fruit, wine, new bread. I did not like that then. I do not like this now. It was only Winter, you say?'

'Winter,' said Jelfs, 'the Swede. At Santa Cruz, as you say, sir, they complained of the food without reason. If there had been scurvy, or scab, or bowel flux. But there was nothing. They ate with both hands. Someone is putting them up to it. There is an evil intelligence at work on this ship.'

'That in Santa Cruz was indeed a shameful thing,' said Ferneau. 'The gentlemen merchants of Santa Cruz on board, drinking my brandy, so pleasant, black men and white men mingling, as in a courteous game of chess. Then three sailors from the hold with their caps on their heads — who, again? — yes, Winter, Petersen, Macaulay. Winter says, *The food we get to eat, Captain, it is bad, it is rotten, it is not fit for beasts.* Winter shouts this at me, in front of the merchants of Santa Cruz, my guests! My dear Jelfs, I am red in the face at this moment, only thinking of it.'

'That is why I will be thankful,' said Jelfs, 'when this voyage is over.'

They were aware that a third presence had been on the quarterdeck for some time. They turned. It was

John Gow, the sailor from Hamnavoe in the Orkneys that Ferneau had promoted to second mate in the Bay of Biscay. He stood smiling at them with his hat under his arm. Captain Ferneau raised his hand in welcome; but the new officer lured no respondent smile from Bonadventure Jelfs.

'Never wish that, Mr. Jelfs,' said Gow. 'We will have a good prosperous voyage. I know it.'

'All is quiet below, John, yes?' said Ferneau.

'Dice, cards, bible-reading,' said Gow. 'Winter is in his hammock. There is a request, sir. One of the sailors, James Williams, is wanting to see you. I made so bold as to bring him with me.'

'Again, Williams,' said Ferneau. 'What does Mister Williams want?'

'O, I couldn't say, sir,' said Gow. 'He's always on his high horse about something. I took the liberty of bidding him follow me. He's standing below. I knew you would wish to grant him a hearing.'

'Show him up, John,' said Ferneau.

Gow turned and called for the man to take off his cap and enter.

James Williams, a sailor with a dark vivid restless face, entered. He bowed and said, 'Your pardon, Captain Ferneau.' Under the pleasant sing-song of his speech there might have been, for those who are attuned to the music of fate, a whine and a snarl.

'You desire to see me, man?' said Captain Ferneau.

'Indeed yes, captain, if you will allow it,' said Williams.

'It is another complaint, like in Santa Cruz?' said Ferneau.

'No indeed, captain,' said Williams. 'I would not dream of complaining at all.'

'What is it, the food?' said Ferneau. 'No? You cannot stomach the food?'

'Goodness, captain,' said Williams, 'the food is excellent food. I have not tasted better on any voyage.'

'State your business then, as briefly as possible,' said Ferneau. 'I have work to do.'

'It is, look you, the matter of my wages,' said Williams.

'You are not paid enough?' said Ferneau. 'Is that what it is? You signed on for so much in Amsterdam.'

'More than enough I am paid,' said Williams.

'Well?' said Ferneau.

'I would like, as it were,' said Williams, 'to be paid in English money, captain, considering as it were that I am to spend the money in London in all likelihood at the end of the voyage.'

'That is impossible,' said Ferneau.

'I would like it paid so,' said Williams, 'in English money, however.'

'Look here, man,' said Ferneau. 'This ship, the *Caroline*, is under charter to a Dutch company. Do you understand that?'

'I understand nothing, captain,' said Williams, 'except that I serve you to the best of my ability.'

'I was given the currency of the Netherlands to pay the crew,' said Ferneau. 'Not the currency of France, England, Ethiopia, or the Eskimos, but the currency of the Netherlands. Do you understand that?'

'Indeed I am not caring —,' said Williams.

'God damn you, man,' cried Ferneau, 'what do you take me for, a high-sea banker? When you reach London take your Netherlands money to any merchant and he will give you English equivalent money. Dutch currency is in good standing in the exchanges. I am telling you so. Is that plain?'

'It is not plain to me at all, captain,' said Williams. 'There is many grumbles among the sailors about this wrong money.'

'Let me speak to him, captain,' said Jelfs, stepping forward.

'Very well, Mr. Jelfs,' said Ferneau. 'I lose my temper. Netherlands silver — what could be better!'

Mr. Jelfs put his thin white face close to the flashing face of the Welshman.

'It is to the captain alone I wish to speak,' cried Williams, 'not to his subordinate.'

'You will do what you are told,' said Jelfs.

'Always I have done that,' said Williams. 'I know my station. I am a simple sailor. It is just, look you, that I am uneasy in my mind about my wages.'

'You are a bad influence in this ship,' said Jelfs.

'I would not have that said,' said Williams. 'You do not like me, Mr. Jelfs. Mr. Gow here, Jack Gow, he may have another opinion of my character.'

'Speak civilly to your officers,' said Gow in a low voice. 'Don't drag me into this.'

'It is my own private opinion,' said Jelfs, 'that you would be none the worse of a good flogging.'

'That is another matter,' cried Williams. 'You are too fond of the ropes-end, Mr. Jelfs. All the sailors think this. The sailors will not endure it for ever, no indeed. They will stand only so much. We are not animals to be beaten and kicked.'

'That's enough, Williams,' said Gow. 'You'd better go now before you say anything else.'

'Between your floggings and your pig-swill and your bad money, look you, there will be funny things done on board this ship,' chanted Williams. 'We are on the open sea. We have thoughts and we have whisperings. Make of that what you will. We have teeth. We have knives.'

Gow came between Jelfs and Williams. He took Williams roughly by the shoulder. He whispered intensely to him, 'Be quiet, for God's sake! You'll ruin everything.'

The vivid possessed face of the seaman went from Jelfs to Gow to Ferneau. It shivered with rage and impotence.

'What did you say then, Mr. Gow?' said Ferneau.

'The man's tongue ran away with him, sir,' said Gow. 'He is a Welshman. He gets drunk on words.'

'He has said too much,' said Ferneau. He turned on Williams. 'Get out of here,' he cried. 'Get back where you came from. I will consider what should be done with you.'

'Don't let him go, sir,' cried Jelfs. 'Teeth, knives — that was mutiny. Put the irons on him now. There are other bad characters down below. It is like a candle-flame among gunpowder, to let him go now.'

'No, no, let him go,' said Gow. 'He's one of those windbags, brave enough with his tongue, but a poor thing really. I know him. He's neither liked nor trusted by the other men. A sniveller, a bad loser. He has no influence over them.'

'But you have influence, Mr. Gow,' said Jelfs.

'You're quite right, Mr. Jelfs,' said Gow. 'And I
don't use the ropes-end either.'

'Mr. Jelfs, Mr. Gow,' said Ferneau, 'that's enough.'
He turned once more to Williams. 'Get out,' he said.
'I will consider your case. Perhaps it will be necessary
to put you ashore in Genoa. You are a bad influence.
Mr. Jelfs is correct.'

Williams, five steps down, turned to say, 'It is a
long way to Genoa.' Then his dark head disappeared.

'There again!' cried Jelfs. 'What did he mean by
that? – *It's a long way to Genoa....* '

'He meant nothing,' said Gow. 'A fool with a hot
loose tongue, that's what he is. I intend to say a thing
or two to Williams before nightfall.'

'Nevertheless I did not like what he said,' said
Ferneau. 'Mr. Jelfs, you will tell the supercargo, the
surgeon, and the boatswain to come here at once. Say
it is important. Say it is a question of the safety of this
ship.'

Jelfs left the quarter-deck at one.

'Sir, I assure you, nothing is amiss,' said Gow.

Ferneau held up his hand. 'You are too trustful,
John,' he said. 'Mr. Jelfs is right. I have set my mind
against it for a long time, but now I know. There is a
wicked element on board my ship. We must stamp on
the smoulder before it takes hold. You are our gunner,
John. I have appointed you to that position in Santa
Cruz.'

'Yes, sir,' said Gow. 'Thank you.'

'See that the small-arms are cleaned and loaded

immediately,' said Ferneau. 'They have not been used for a long time. I will give you the key of the arms chest presently. It is in my cabin. So long as we have the pistols they can do nothing. The pistols must be ready at a moment's notice. I know the stink of evil.'

'Mr. Ferneau!' cried Jelfs from below.

'I will give you the key presently,' said Ferneau. He shouted over the rail, 'I am coming.' He said to Gow in a low voice, 'Yes, good. Our lives may depend upon it.' He tugged his hat over his troubled brow, and turned, and left Gow alone on the quarter-deck.

'The pistols will be cocked,' said Gow.

The prow smashed gently through the sea. The sails creaked. The voices of the officers below sounded like remote empty echoes. . . .'arms chest'. . . .'Genoa' . . . .'complaints'. . . . Someone came running up from below, a rapid tattoo of feet on the ladder, random violent words; there appeared again on the quarter-deck the livid face of Williams.

'And here's something else I forgot to tell you, Captain Ferneau' he yelled. He saw Gow standing there alone. 'You, is it, Jack,' he said. 'Tell me, where is the frogging scum of a Frenchman? Where is Jelfs? I'll —'

Gow gathered the filthy blouse-front into his fist. 'You've done enough howling and singing for one day,' he said quietly. 'O, you poor damned idiot, you nearly let everything out.'

'Me, Jack?' said Williams. 'I was very discreet, I thought. Only —'

'Shut your bloody gab, and do as I say,' said Gow.

'You've turned them all into watch-dogs.' He let go of
the excited man in front of him, and dropped his
voice to a whisper. 'Listen, James, do exactly what I
say. We are to go for them tonight. Tomorrow might
be too late. Melvin, Macaulay, Moore, Petersen, Winter,
Rollson — tell them the operation is to be advanced
by twenty-four hours. They are to go to their hammocks but they are not to sleep. The pistols will be
ready. I will give you the word.'

'Whatever you say, Jack,' said Williams.

'Only the men whose names I gave you. Tell them
at once, in whispers, one after the other,' said Gow.

'Tell the men what?' said Jelfs' voice behind them.

'Tell the men to obey their orders,' said Gow
sternly to Williams, 'or they'll find they've lost a good
friend in Jack Gow. Now get out of here.'

'I'm sorry, sir. Yes,' said Williams humbly and
thankfully, like one who has been given absolution,
and left the quarter-deck.

'I'll help you with the firearms, Gow,' said Jelfs.
'Algier and I will be only too glad to help you.'

'I'll manage very well by myself,' said Gow. 'It's a
part of my duties to see to the firearms. No-one is to
handle them but me.'

There entered the quarter-deck Captain Ferneau
with his arm about Peter Hanson's shoulder; Mr.
Algier the supercargo; Mr. Guy the ship's surgeon.

'So, gentlemen,' Ferneau was saying, 'that's the
situation. It may be the fartings of a windbag. It may
be nothing at all. John here thinks so. On the other
hand, we may be on the brink of great danger. Do
be very careful. John here is to get the firearms

ready immediately. You will all be issued with a
pistol. You will keep it by you always. You are to
sleep with the pistols under your pillows.'

Gow bowed and smiled to the group of officers.

'With our pistols we will quickly put a stop to any
nonsense,' said Ferneau. 'We will blow them to pieces.'

Peter Hanson pointed his hand at Mr. Jelfs and
cocked his forefinger and made a violent noise with
his mouth.

'If there should chance to be any trouble,' said
Ferneau, 'the child is to be put in my cabin out of
harm's way.'

Gently the wind shook the shrouds, and the winter
sun slid from behind a cloud and made the water all
blue and silver about them.

A three-quarter moon had risen over Sardinia, and
dimmed a little the light of the stars. The *Caroline*
sailed slowly northwards through a sea that was
roughened only occasionally by a breath of wind.
Captain Oliver Ferneau stood alone on the quarter-
deck. He heard a step coming up from below, a
laboured breath, a creak of leather. He laid a finger on
the pistol on the table, then turned to face the intruder.
It was James Belbin the boatswain.

'Nothing to report, sir,' said Belbin.

'All is quiet, yes?' said the skipper.

'They're mostly asleep in their hammocks, sir,' said
Belbin. 'Mr. Jelfs, Mr. Algier, and the surgeon are in
their hammocks too, but their eyes are open.'

'Where is Mr. Gow?' said Ferneau.

'I haven't seen him, sir,' said Belbin.

The night was so still that their voices were keyed

to whispering; as if a fuller articulation might sully the purity and silence.

'That's good, Belbin,' said Ferneau. 'I think all might be well, after all.'

'Nothing else you want, sir?' said Belbin.

'Nothing,' said Ferneau. 'We are all, I'm sure, in the hand of God.'

'Beg pardon, sir?' said Belbin.

'Do you believe in evil, Belbin?' said Ferneau earnestly. 'Do you believe in the power of evil?'

'Why, sir,' said Belbin. 'I've never rightly thought about that. I leave that kind of thing to the parsons.'

'But there is light and darkness, Belbin,' said Ferneau. 'There is a virtuous power, and also there is a wicked power that goes about in the night time.'

Belbin bent his head. He passed his hand lightly over his brow once or twice. 'I look at it this way, sir,' he said. 'Power is good in itself, whatever colour it comes in. Them that has power — kings and captains and bishops — they decide what's good and virtuous, and everybody else has got to toe the line whatever they feel about it. Excuse me, sir, I'm just an ignorant fellow.'

'No, go on,' said Ferneau.

'Well, sir,' said Belbin, 'the kings and captains are hard to put down. But sometimes the virtue goes out of them, and then somebody else has got to take over. My grandfather now, he was a trooper under Fairfax, when there was the civil wars in England.'

'Was he, Belbin?' said Ferneau: 'I am very interested in what you say. You must have thought deeply on these matters.'

'O no, sir,' said Belbin. 'I never went to school. My father shipped me on board a whaler in Hull when I was twelve.'

'All right, Belbin,' said Ferneau. 'Goodnight.'

'Goodnight to you, sir,' said Belbin.

The blunt moon rose higher between Sardinia and Corsica. There was no sound on the ship but the creaking of canvas and the rhythmic plangent wash of the sea from her bow.

Captain Ferneau, noting the sluggish heave of the *Caroline* through the water, considered that she must be careened and caulked as soon as they were back in Amsterdam; at any rate before the winter was over. The ship was old and must soon be broken up; he doubted if anyone would be interested in buying her. She had been a good fast vessel in his grandfather's time.

The worry of the past day, the contention of the officers, his conversation with the boatswain, led him to think of the solid secure stock he had sprung from — those merchants and sailors of Guernsey — and further back to the Breton countryside that had bred them. Ancient and magnificent and secure seemed the establishment in France, firmly built into history. Yet there were clever men, lawyers and philosophers, who saw mildew and decay everywhere. Belbin the Englishman was perhaps right: it was all a flux, a rooting and a ripening and a rotting. Nothing held. If one could look on those stars that shine in order nightly across the heavens like the implements laid up in some barn for the winter, symbols of the careful husbandry of heaven — men think of them as eternal —

yet if one could look on the firmament with the eye
of God, one would know that yesterday they were
a chaos of fire, and tomorrow they will be cold rust
and ashes; and then, perhaps, the great Harvester might
turn his energies to another seedtime.

He felt very old and tired. This ship now — perhaps
with some young cruel master in command, she
would once more leap over the waves like a dolphin.

There was a single cold scream from below.

Ferneau went to the rail. He leaned over and called,
'What is wrong down there?'

There was running, scuffling, a confusion and babble
and outcry, another terrible scream.

'Belbin,' cried Ferneau, 'please say what is wrong!'

'I think, sir,' came Belbin's drowsy voice from
below, 'there's a man overboard.'

'Lower the boat, then,' cried Ferneau. 'What hinders
you?'

Hands gripped him from behind, thrust his head out
and forward. He was staring down into the water, all
torn silk, and the moon's gently breaking and reform-
ing image. His hat fell into the sea. Hands seized his
thighs and tried to lever him off his feet.

Captain Ferneau turned his head round on his thick
neck; he recognized the two Swedes Rollson and
Winter and the Scotsman Melvin. He flung his hands at
the shrouds and clutched and hung on there, swaying.

'Jelfs!' he cried. 'Algier!'

Winter crooked his arm round the skipper's neck
and forced the head down into the chest. He levered
down, grimacing, waiting for the neck-bone to break.
'Is very strong,' he said, gasping.

Melvin let go of the captain's thigh and took a knife out of his belt.

'Jelfs, captain?' he said. 'Is it Jelfs you're shouting for? His throat is cut. The surgeon's throat is cut. Algier's throat is cut. Your turn now, my bonny man.'

Melvin thrust the blade under Winter's lock-grip into the fat white neck; his hand was laved with warmth; he drew the dulled knife out.

Ferneau whispered, 'You will be shot like dogs when Mr. Gow comes.'

Blood came out of his neck in quick short gushes. His knuckles shone white among the ropes.

Gow said behind them, 'I *am* here, monsieur.'

Winter took his arm from Ferneau's head. His arm was stiff. He shook the numbness out of it. 'Is sticking to his ship like limpets,' he said.

Rollson put his foot in the small of Ferneau's back and wound his hands through his hair and tried to drag him from the shrouds. The wound at the skipper's neck gaped. There was a dark growing stain down his jacket.

They heard a frantic familiar voice down below, saying the same thing over and over.

'I think Mr. Jelfs is speaking,' said John Gow. 'That's strange. Someone told me his throat was cut.'

It was a terrified intense quavering whisper: 'For God's sake, please, time to pray, please, I will do anything, please God, no, not yet'. . . . Then Williams' sing-song, 'Indeed to goodness, Mr. Jelfs, this is all the prayers I'll let you pray,' followed immediately by a shot.

John Gow examined his pistol carefully. He cocked

it. He held it straight out, pointed to the back of Ferneau's head.

The boy Peter Hanson came running in bare feet and grabbed Gow by the jacket. 'Jack, save me,' said the boy. 'Williams says he'll kill us all.'

'You'll be all right with me,' said Gow to the boy. 'Just stand over there till I finish what I'm doing'. . . . To Rollson he said, 'You would oblige me by removing your hands from Monsieur Ferneau's hair.'

The boy recognized his master through the blood and dazzle of moonlight. 'What are they doing to you, sir?' he said.

Ferneau looked round at him. 'God bless you, boy,' he said. 'You have new masters now.'

'But I don't want any other master but you,' said Peter Hanson, and began to cry.

'Don't you, boy?' said Ferneau. 'Well then, Belbin was wrong after all.'

Peter Hanson stuck his fist into his mouth.

Ferneau said in a loud voice, 'Have you no strength, you evil men, to throw your old captain from his ship?'

Gow immediately shot him in the nape of the neck; and reloaded at once and put a second ball into his head higher up. There was a brief smell of burnt hair and flesh.

The dying hands relaxed in the shroud. The large body sagged slowly and slithered and fell face down on the deck. The head was a dark clot.

Gow blew a wisp of smoke from his pistol and reloaded it.

Peter Hanson said, 'Why are you angry with

Mr. Ferneau, Jack?'

There were random shouts and cries from below —
a slither, a shot, paddings and flutterings of bare feet
here and there. 'Wake up, you scum,' Williams shouted
among the hammocks.

Winter took the dead skipper by the shoulders and
Rollson took him by the ankles. He was hardly easier
to manoeuvre dead than alive. They levered the body
up with their knees and forearms, balanced it awkwardly, staggered, heaved it overboard, and staggered
back splotched with red. The body went into the sea
with a small splash.

'You'll go home to your mother with your pockets
full of gold,' said Gow to the boy who was dredging
sobs now deep out of his body.

Williams came rushing up from below. He seemed
to be half insane from the night's work, dancing and
laughing and leaping here and there like a clown.
Across his hands lay Ferneau's sword, and Ferneau's
silver watch dangled between his fingers. (He had been
rifling the skipper's cabin.) After him, more quietly,
came MacAulay and Moore and Petersen. They were
like men who had drunk a lot and were tired.

Williams went up to Gow and kissed him. 'Give you
joy, Captain Jack!' he cried. He handed over the
sword and watch.

'God keep you, Captain Gow,' said MacAulay in
his soft Hebridean voice.

The boy had stopped crying. He stood and looked
the other way, at no-one. A spasm went through him
from time to time: silent wondering gasps.

The boatswain, James Belbin, came up from below.

'Belbin,' said Gow quietly, 'and whose side are you on?'

Belbin said, 'I'm disappointed.'

'We had debates about you,' said Gow. 'We balanced your life anxiously. Disappointed, are you? Your throat's uncut — you should be pleased enough about that.'

'I'm very disappointed,' said Belbin. 'Why did you not tell me that this was brewing? I can cut a throat as well as the next man. Give me leave now to pledge my support to the mutiny.'

'Mr. Belbin,' said Gow gravely, 'you will continue as boatswain.'

Williams took Belbin by the lapel. 'Realize, Belbin,' he sang, 'that you are inferior to me. I am lieutenant.'

'Very good, lieutenant,' said Belbin, smiling. He turned once more to Gow. 'I have rounded up the crew,' he said. 'I have spoken to them. I have reassured one or two doubters. There will be no trouble.'

'I will speak to them now,' said Gow.

Belbin herded up from below a dozen bewildered sailors. They stood about the quarter-deck like sheep in the vicinity of a shambles, eyeing the knives and the pistols, eyeing with little starts and whisperings the dark clots and splashes and runnels everywhere.

'Be quiet there,' said Williams. 'The captain is speaking.'

'Men,' said Gow, 'this ship has a new name. She is no longer the *Caroline*. She is called the *Revenge*. We are no longer bound on errands from port to port. We are not any more the slaves of merchants or bankers. We are a free brotherhood of the sea. We are winged and strong as the albatross. Life on board this ship will be different from now on. There will be no ropes-end. There will be no beef with maggots in it. If you don't want to join us, just say the word and we'll think of some place to put you ashore — Senegal, maybe, or Greenland. We'll think of something to do with you, never fear. But if you decide to be free men, there will be adventure and excitement aplenty, full flagons of it. Mr. Williams here will sign you on in the morning; it's just a matter of taking a drop of blood from your wrists and making your mark in the book. You know me, Jack Gow. I'm not a hard man to work with, so long as you do what you're told. This is a democratic ship. We're all equal. We all work along with each other for the good of all. If in the days to come I let you down in any way — such as, stint you of women and rum, or navigate wrong, or turn out to be an unlucky man, a Jonah — you have the right and the power in such a case to put me down. The plunder we take we will divide equally among us. We on the *Revenge* are all comrades together. If one of you should in the course of duty meet with an injury — lose a leg or an eye for example — he will be compensated in the recognized sum of five hundred pieces-of-eight. If on the other hand you get poxed up you get nothing — that's your own private affair. That's all I have to say meantime.'

'Well spoken, captain,' said Williams.

An Irish sailor called Phinnes said gloomily, 'What if we're captured?'

'In that case, Paddy,' said Gow, 'we'll all jig for five minutes or so at Wapping Steps. That's where they hang pirates.' He laughed. 'But I assure you, a lot of silver and gold will run through our fingers before that.'

'Speak when you're spoken to,' said Williams to Phinnes.

'Now then,' said Gow, 'does anyone object to sailing on the *Revenge*?'

'We have no choice, do we?' said James Newport, another Irish sailor. 'We have to go along with you willy-nilly.'

'You're a clever salt, James,' said Gow, 'You've grasped the essence of the situation. . . . You, Booth, what about you?'

'I'm with you,' said Booth.

'And you, Milne?' said Gow to a tall flame-headed freckle-faced sailor.

Milne said, in a Scottish lowland voice, 'I'm like the bosun, Jack, I'm just sorry you didn't break this to us before.'

'Well spoken,' said Gow. 'I'm sure we'll all get on together well. Thank you. Now then, if you don't mind, I want to be left alone for a while. There's a lot of things to be thought of before morning: such as, how are we going to break out of this bloody sea into the Atlantic. Westwards, that's where the gold and the wine-barrels are. Mr. Williams, in order to celebrate this new brotherhood of the sea, I request you to let every sailor have a double tapping of rum. Then back to your hammocks, men. There'll be work for all of us in the morning.'

There were a few ragged cheers. Then the sailors dispersed in groups, whispering, until only Gow and Peter Hanson were left on the quarter-deck.

'You'd better go and get some shut-eye,' said Gow to the boy. 'It's all right. Nobody's going to hurt you.'

'Yes, Jack,' said Peter Hanson.

'That's a good boy,' said Gow. 'But you mustn't call me Jack any more. I'm your skipper now. This is a new ship. The *Revenge*, that's her name. I'm Captain Gow.'

'It must be cold for Mr. Ferneau in the sea,' said Peter Hanson. 'Not a drop of rum to warm him at all.'

'He isn't feeling a thing, Peter,' said Gow.

'Mr. Ferneau was a kind man to me,' said Peter Hanson. 'Could you not have kept him? He could have scrubbed the decks. He could have peeled potatoes with me in the galley.'

'No, boy. The laws of change are too quick and too cruel,' said Gow.

THE PIRATE'S GHOST

Gow the pirate. . . . was born near the house of Clestron, and afterwards commenced buccaneer. He came to his native country about 1725 with a "snow" which he commanded; carried off two women from one of the islands, and committed other enormities. At length, while he was dining in a house in the island of Eda, the islanders. . . . made him prisoner and sent him to London, where he was hanged. While at Stromness he made love to a Miss Gordon, who pledged her faith to him by shaking hands, an engagement which, in her idea, could not be dissolved without her going to London to seek back again her faith and troth by shaking hands with him again after execution.

—*Memoirs of the Life of Sir Walter Scott,*
by J G Lockhart.

Thora Gordon, only daughter of Mr James Gordon, merchant in Hamnavoe, Orkney, first made acquaintance with Captain John Gow of the galley *George* at the house of her father on an evening in early January 1725.

Captain Gow had been invited to the Gordon house with the other officers of the *George,* but he had arrived at the door alone, and had at once made excuses on behalf of his men. They were indisposed, he said, with a mild sickness, a bowel flux.

Mr Gordon led Captain Gow into his best upstairs chamber, where his wife and daughter were waiting. 'My dear wife,' said Mr Gordon, 'it is surely a great pleasure for us to have Captain Gow for a guest in our house, even though he comes alone. There's a sickness on board ship, Captain Gow tells me, but nothing serious.'

Mrs Martha Gordon came forward and took Captain Gow by the hand. 'It would be an untruth,' she said, 'to say that I remember you as a lad running about these streets and closes of Hamnavoe. It is a dozen years since you left us, sir. An ageing woman has blurred memories. But I remember well your father, William Gow, and his ships, and the fine house he built over there on the far side of the bay. And now forgive my runaway tongue. Let me say only how honoured I am to have you in this house.'

Captain Gow stooped over her hand and kissed it, and murmured a greeting.

'Come forward, Thora,' said Mr Gordon, smiling. The girl stepped forward, shyly, and without a word held out her hand to be kissed. 'I hope,' said Captain

Gow, 'that I will have the honour of a better acquaintance.'

The girl flushed. Her mother took her by the arm and led her back to the dining room. The two men were alone. 'Now, sir,' said Mr Gordon, 'you have done uncommonly well, uncommonly well indeed, to be master of such a fine ship at the age of — is it? — twenty-five. May I ask, what cargo do you carry, and what ports you sail between?' All this he said while he poured from a decanter two goblets of brandy.

Captain Gow seemed to hesitate for a few seconds, while Mr Gordon put the stopper back into the decanter and held his glass to the candlelight.

At last Captain Gow said, 'That must remain something of a secret, sir. It concerns, if you understand, the government. What we are — where we are going — is a business of admiralty.'

'Enough!' cried Mr Gordon. 'Forgive an inquisitive old man. I had no right to ask such a question. Now I can see that Captain Gow — the boy from Hamnavoe — is an even more important man than I thought. The government — the admiralty — indeed — who would ever have thought so! I warrant, matters are working towards another war with the French.'

An unseen gong was struck, and sent soft reverberations into the room where the two men, master mariner and merchant, were lipping, appreciatively, the brandy.

'Understand,' said Mr Gordon, laying his hand on the forearm of his guest, 'I am by no means prying into your business. I will say not another word about it. Yet I cannot help but speculate and marvel.

Come now, Mistress Gordon has ladled the broth.'

'It is indeed a dark hidden business,' said Captain Gow. 'But you are right — we will speak no more about it. Tonight there are other things to occupy my mind. Sir, I congratulate you on a most beautiful daughter.'

'Thora,' said Mr Gordon, pleased. 'She is a comfort and a joy to me. She has a will of her own, though. Come now. You will sit opposite her at the table.'

*   *   *

The supper was a complete success. The ardent conversation of Captain Gow soon thawed the reserve of the daughter of the house. To begin with, she had been very shy. Going round with the flagon, she had in her nervousness even spilled some wine on the linen table-cloth beside Captain Gow's plate; the gout fell and burst and spread a quick scarlet stain.

'What's wrong with that girl tonight?' cried Mrs Gordon. 'It seems she can do nothing right! Captain Gow, a hundred pardons — I think there's a drop or two on your waistcoat.'

But Captain Gow had risen to his feet, laughing, and had taken Thora's hand in his. 'That was nothing,' he said. 'A splash of blood between two people — a good omen, that — a bond, a sign, a seal — a heart's thirling. Think no more of it.'

Thereafter the honoured guest and the girl showed unreserved friendliness and regard for each other; and the old ones looked on with silent approval.

After the supper, they played a few hands of whist

beside the open fire. While Captain Gow was dealing the cards, the servant-girl Anna came in and told Mr Gordon that Mr Jacob Beaton, who was a local magistrate and merchant, was at the door, and wished to speak urgently with him.

While Mr Gordon was absent his wife saw a thing she could hardly credit. Captain Gow laid down the cards, and he bent his sun-dark face to Thora across the whist table. The girl kissed him openly and shamelessly on the mouth.

Mr Gordon returned at that moment to say that Mr Beaton's store had been broken into earlier in the evening. The thieves had taken a keg of rum, tobacco, a cured ham, and some money out of Mr Beaton's desk. Roused by the dog's barking, Mr Beaton and his two sons had gone round to the store, but only in time to see the flight of a few burdened shadows. These they had pursued down to the shore. The thieves had gotten into a small boat and pushed off. Once a safe distance out, they had cursed Mr Beaton — a very decent upright man — and put all manner of the most violent abuse on him.

They had rowed towards the only ship in the harbour.

At this, Captain Gow excused himself. The Gordon family had never seen so great a change in a man within the space of a few seconds. 'The fools!' he muttered. 'God damn them!' Anna brought his coat. He buttoned it about his throat and left the house without a thank-you or a goodnight.

The old pair, beside the fire, were very much disturbed.

Thora crept downstairs. She watched from the open door the cloaked figure making for the landing-steps with long strides.

*   *   *

That was the beginning of a month of lawlessness in the little port of Hamnavoe.

The townsfolk had been pleased in their quiet way to welcome home a local man who had done well for himself. The morning after Gow had been entertained at the Gordons' house he made himself known to the humbler townsmen standing here and there about the main pier. The ship's boat, manned by half a dozen sailors, had landed their skipper at the steps from the ship anchored out in the bay beyond the two holms. 'Well now, Tom, I sat beside you in the school at Hellihole. Didn't the same tawse lash our two back-sides? You're coming up now with me, Tom Watson, to have a glass of rum in "The Straitsman". . . . . 'Albert Swann, I know you, man — you sailed in the *Pearl*, my father's coal boat'. . . . They could see then, beneath the sun-dark mask and the sculptings of a hundred foreign voyages, the boy who had suddenly left Hamnavoe at the age of fourteen — the reckless one — the one who had laughed a great deal — the one who had been cruel to birds and dogs — the frequent truant and Sabbath-breaker.

They responded, shy and smiling, to his heartiness. A dozen townsmen followed Gow and his sailors into "The Straitsman".

One thing caused them to wonder, as the day wore

on: Captain Gow was not getting the respect from his crew that was normal as between seamen and master mariner. They called him 'Jack' more often than not. One or other of them would go up to him and laugh in his face and clap him familiarly on the shoulder. The Hamnavoe men knew all about ships and sailors and discipline; they concluded that this was a most unusual crew. As the rum flowed faster, the patrons of "The Straitsman", and the landlord, became uneasy. They were all well used to whalers and their wild drunken homecomings at the end of a season, but there was a wholesomeness at the heart of the whalemen's celebrations. With this crew there was something sinister — dangerous gleams — the snarl and the knife were just under the surface. At mid-day a fight broke out. The Hamnavoe drinkers were appalled by the furious fists and the vivid violent obscene mouths. In the end John Gow came between the Swede and the Irishman — the crew was a patchwork of nationalities — and pulled them apart. 'For God's sake,' he whispered to them in a voice that was a mixture of rage, appeal, anxiety, 'you must try to behave yourselves for a week or two! This is the short way to the gallows!'. . . . The Irishman said, 'True for you, Jack. I'm sorry. I've had a sup too much of the sugar-cane. . . .' But the Swede was half-insane with rage still. He called Gow a bastard. He turned on the local drinkers and gave them, in his tortured English, as much abuse as they were likely to get in all the rest of their days — "rats" and "worms" and "shit" and "spewings of men". . . . At last the landlord, a huge good-natured man called Ward Seatter, took the spitting, raging creature by cuff and waistband and threw him out, still blaspheming, into the darkening street.

A girl was watching and listening from the opposite wall: Thora Gordon.

'Ward Seatter,' said John Gow, 'and everybody, I am sorry for this.'

'You are not welcome here,' said Ward Seatter, 'you nor any of your scum, ever again.'

Sailors and townsmen, they trooped out into the street. It was a quiet day. Here and there, heads appeared at windows and doors. The fracas had disturbed the whole street.

Gow's voice came from the shore below. 'That was a good beginning! Put a gag in Rollson's mouth! A few more performances like that and the hangman will be busy! Listen, men, we're all brothers in this — we stand or fall together'. . . . There was the sound of a keel over stones then; of oars in water; disturbed seagulls. The townsfolk could hear no more; but they had never heard a captain pleading with his crew in that way before.

And at the shore, as the small boat drew away, they observed Thora Gordon standing, and shading her eyes against the harbour gleam.

*   *   *

Among growing disapproval, suspicion, violence, villainies, the love story of John Gow, master of the *George,* and Thora Gordon, daughter of the Hamnavoe merchant, was enacted. Their meetings took place in

secret and in darkness: at the shore, on the hill behind
the town, even (it was said) among the tombstones of
the kirkyard. Twice or thrice a furtive ship's boat
uplifted a shrouded figure from the pier steps and
rowed her out to the dark vessel lying at anchor in the
bay; and returned again before dawn. Then Anna the
servant girl would be wakened by a fistful of gravel at
her window-pane; and there would be tearful scenes
at the breakfast table. 'Daughter, you are breaking my
heart'. . . . 'Your father — not I — will speak to you'.
. . . 'You are not too old for a whipping, rest assured'.
. . . 'Thora, dear child, promise me you will never see
that Gow man again. The rumours about that ship
and the crew! The hen-houses at Wardhill were rifled
last night — who was it but them! And the great stone
sent crashing through the minister's window — that
poor Mistress Gillies! Worst of all — how can I mention this — think of the danger you stand in — the
two girls from Graemsay island forced aboard the
ship, and kept there, willy-nilly — the heart blanches
to think of it!'. . . .

To these appeals and reproaches the daughter kept
silence. She did not say a thing either, when James
Gordon came in and took his seat for breakfast.
'Well, my girl, what's the white face for? Didn't you
sleep? Well, you have an excuse, with all the wickedness abroad in the islands! Thank God we found out
about Gow in time. An imposter, a bandit. I have it
for a fact — are you listening, Thora? — his men broke
into the Hall of Clestrain the night before last. They
carried knives. Gow was there too — oh, yes, he was.
They demanded the family valuables. Mrs Honeyman —

a brave woman that — she refused to say where they were hidden. They tore the house apart, but found nothing. Mrs Honeyman had hidden the heirlooms, such as they were, under a pile of feathers in the attic — she told the villains the feathers were for stuffing pillows. . . . It won't be long now. The magistrates in Kirkwall are informed. Word has been sent to Edinburgh. There will come an end to this bad time. . . . My dear child, I know how well you thought of Gow on that first evening. I thank God we found out in time. . . .'

The kindly old man — it will be seen — had no notion of how things had been developing between his daughter and the master of the sinister ship out in the bay. No-one, not even his wife, had the courage to tell him of the terrible web in which Thora was enmeshing herself.

*   *   *

That same week another merchant ship, the *Margaret,* dropped anchor in the bay. In the afternoon the captain of the *Margaret* was rowed ashore. He asked at once, and urgently, to be taken to a magistrate. Mr Jacob Beaton, Mr James Gordon, and the Rev Aeneas Gillies went to meet Captain Watt in the parlour of Login's Inn, the most respectable establishment of that kind in Hamnavoe. Captain Watt, in the brusque clipped way of some skippers, asked those leading townsmen what they knew about the ship *George,* to which they were giving the hospitality of their harbour. A babble of voices answered him.

Finally, the minister spoke for all of them, and indeed for the whole community. He described, in some detail, the abominations which that ship had perpetrated on the town and on the neighbouring islands and parishes: the thievings, the insults, the fighting with knives, the rapes. The like outrages had never been known in Orkney before! The whale-men and their carry-on — disgraceful though it was from time to time, no doubt — was the innocent gambolling of children in comparison to this dark villainy!. . . . Captain Watt listened gravely. He informed them that as soon as he had entered the roadstead from Hoy Sound he had recognized the ship. She had not always been called the *George:* by no means. When first he had the acquaintance of that ship, her name had been the *Caroline,* and her master had been a friend of his — a somewhat voluble but kindly Channel Islander called Oliver Ferneau. Well, then, in the winter of the previous year, 1724, this ship and her crew had disappeared utterly. She had been on a voyage from Santa Cruz in Morocco to Genoa in Italy with a cargo of beeswax, Turkish leather, etc. She had never reached Genoa. Soon afterwards, however, a strange vessel, with the bloodthirsty name of *Revenge,* had "commenced pirate" in the North Atlantic; had attacked and robbed and sunk ship after ship, without however finding any of the rare precious cargoes the crew were hoping for — what they found mostly was timber, salt fish; once they had taken a cargo of French wine. . . . That was all the desperate raven had managed to snatch from the dove-seekings of legitimate trade. Soon enough, news of the *Revenge* and her depredations

was being signalled back and fore on the great ocean.
The ships of King George's navy were vigilant and
ready to pounce. Winter was coming on, she would
have to find some haven. Then they would have her.
But like another ship earlier that year, the *Revenge*
suddenly disappeared. . . . Captain Watt looked each
man earnestly in the face, one after the other, as he
said, 'Gentlemen, I must tell you that the *Caroline* is
the *Revenge,* and the *Revenge* is the *George* – all
three are one ship, and she is lying out there in the
sanctuary of your harbour!'. . . . He went on to say
that the suspicion – nay, the certainty, – was that the
crew of the *Caroline* had mutinied in the Mediterranean, had murdered Captain Ferneau and his four
officers, and had seized the ship for unlawful pur-
poses. 'And I must tell you further,' he went on, 'that
there was a certain member of that crew that Ferneau
cherished in particular, a young man by the name of
Gow. He had put particular trust in him. In fact,
knowing that it was a cosmopolitan half-criminal crew
he had under him, recruited from the sewers of
Amsterdam, he had confided his anxieties to Gow, and
had even given him the key to the arms-chest. This
Gow, at all events, was recognized in the Atlantic as
the chief villain on board the *Revenge.* These pirates,
you must know, regard themselves as a kind of brotherhood where all men are equal; and though a
skipper is necessary to a pirate ship, he is only *primus
inter pares,* a first among equals.'

'I am sorry to say,' said Mr Gordon after a time,
'that this same Gow was decently brought up in that
house you see across the bay. His father was a

good honest man'. . . .

'Time is running out for him fast,' said Captain Watt.

It was sensational news the merchant brought to the supper table that evening.

'A mutineer!' he said. 'A murderer! A pirate! He killed his own skipper, a man that had treated him with all kindness. He shot him in the neck, then dumped him in the sea. So Captain Watt of the *Margaret* assured us this afternoon. To think the creature sat at this same table and took supper with us! To think that you, Thora!. . . .'

The mother wept, over by the fire. She had not been able to eat a bite of food.

Thora had nothing to say. Her face glimmered between the candle-flames on the table.

'Thora, you should go to your bed,' said her father. 'Thank God, there will be peace again in our islands soon.'

Thora rose to her feet. 'I am going to meet Jack now,' she said. She left the house. She went unhindered into the night.

*   *   *

Nobody knows what happened at the last meeting of Gow and Thora. Lockhart speaks of a 'pledging of faith' by a handshake — surely the most insipid declaration of love in all literature. Country legends of Gow and Thora speak of a handclasp through the Stone of Odin, one of the huge neolithic monuments beside the loch five miles from Hamnavoe. The symbolism is true, for the phallic stone had a hole in the centre of it, and when country lovers clasped hands there the fires of procreation were seen as cold meaningful images; the whole man-woman relationship was encompassed; a lifetime of fecundity (furrow and cornstalk) was fore-enacted. This is the safe kind of love-in-marriage that, though it renews the generations, is of small interest to poets. They are fascinated by the passion that is illicit and forbidden: Romeo and Juliet, Abelard and Eloise, Clerk Saunders and May Margaret. In those lovers the coals of procreation, that were ordained for the kindly warming and fostering of the seed, are kindled selfishly; they make a beautiful barren burning; they may leave scorch-marks on the living and the dead that can only be healed by an "ave et vale" across the grave, a kiss of peace.

John Gow and Thora Gordon had only one night for the mingling of their fires.

*   *   *

Five hours after she had left the house, Thora threw a scatter of small stones at Anna's window. But there were other listeners in the house than Anna; and they rose out of their bed too.

The bearers of the three lamps in the steep stair saw one who had been in flames and darkness they had never experienced themselves. The Gordons hardly recognized their daughter. Thora stood still, in a triangle of anxious smoking flames. Her cloak gleamed from the rain outside; it was soiled too with the earth of the fields. She looked from one to the other, coldly; then she pushed through the lamps and faces, and came to her own room. She entered it alone.

*   *   *

When the folk of Hamnavoe woke that morning and looked seaward, they saw that the pirate ship was no longer in the bay.

*   *   *

The galley *George* (alias *Revenge,* alias *Caroline*) never got clear of the islands. She went aground on a small islet called Calf-of-Eday in the northern Orkneys. There, by a sound stratagem, the laird of the large island of Eday — a Mr James Fea — captured the entire crew, including John Gow.

In due course a government man-of-war, *Grayhound,* called at Eday and removed the prisoners to London. There were twenty-nine of them in all.

Their trial, for murder and piracy on the high seas, took place at the Old Bailey during the last days of May 1725. The novelist Daniel Defoe was present; he afterwards wrote an account of the proceedings.

Gow refused to plead. He was threatened with the thumb-screw. Being still silent, both joints of both his thumbs were broken by the public executioner. Being still silent, he was ordered to be pressed to death:. . . . "that he be put into a mean house stopped from any light, and he be laid upon his back, with his body bare; that his arms be stretched forth with cord, the one to one side, the other to the other side of the prison, and in like manner his legs be used, and that upon his body be laid as much iron and stone as he can bear and more. The first day he shall have three morsels of barley bread, and the next he shall drink thrice of the water in the next channel to the prison door but of no spring and fountain water; and this shall be his punishment till he die."

Faced with this imminent horror, Gow relented, and pleaded "not guilty."

Ten of the prisoners were convicted and sentenced to death by public hanging. Nineteen were acquitted, as being forced or unwilling seamen on board the pirate ship.

Gow's end was particularly cruel. After he had been hanging for four minutes, the executioner pulled on his legs to make a quick end of him. The rope broke, Gow fell to the ground. Defoe, who was present, says: "he was still alive and sensible, tho' he had hung four minutes, and able to go up the ladder the second time, which he did with very little concern."

Later Gow's body was tarred, and arrayed in chains, and left to be a public spectacle.

*   *   *

In Orkney Thora Gordon fell into a sickness. She ate and slept little, and had none of the relish for life that a seventeen-year-old girl ought to have. Chiefly it was her mind that ailed; she began to be troubled by strange images, intrusions into her waking consciousness, appearances that were palpable to no-one but herself.

She looked up from her place at the supper-table one summer evening — it was the day of Gow's execution, but she was not to know that — and there he was, sitting opposite her in his lace cuffs and silver buttons. The sun-dark face smiled at her, the mouth opened to speak. 'Jack!' she cried, but it wavered, melted, was nothing. . . . 'Never mention that villain's name in this house!' cried her mother. 'Jack, indeed! — The shame of it!'. . . But her father leaned over and took her kindly by the hand.

She saw the ghost another time at the mouth of a Hamnavoe close. There Gow lingered, as if troubled, and walked once or twice back and fore in front of "The Straitsman" ale-house. He paused, and listened at the door, as if half afraid to enter. But there was no row or disorder inside — only Ward arranging the bottles on his shelf — the place was empty, the townsmen were all at their work. As Thora hurried along the street to greet him, he faded into the gray air.

The ghost entered into her dreams. He was smiling, he held a smoking pistol in his hand, there was a splash of new blood on the sleeve of his shirt. He looked like an animal that had just torn another mild creature and had then glutted itself on blood and flesh. The dreamer had never seen a face so cruel and handsome. She woke — the face was still there, hovering over her bed, satiated with love, smiling. . . . Her mouth and hands yearned towards the face; which at once crumbled and dissolved.

She was haunted by Gow wherever she went, indoors and outdoors, incessantly. She had gone to the rockpools of the beach to gather whelks one afternoon and was kneeling there beside the cold broken mirror when she saw a boy at the edge of the sea. He was naked; he had been bathing; he laughed and shouted in the high plangent tones of children who have been in the water. She was taken with the whiteness and beauty of him — she had never seen such a lovely boy. He came up the beach towards her. She saw the face of John Gow before time had forged and beaten on his skull the cruel mask. The boy smiled; then was as lucent as the water her fingers lay in; then was nothing.

Another night she stood at the counter of Bab Simison's little shop, and asked for a pound of Jamaican sugar; her mother was going to make a dumpling before bedtime. The shop began to heave and creak about her — it was a ship, it was plunging through a cold sea. Someone lay against the bulkhead — no, he was manacled hand and foot. John Gow's fine shirt was all stained, and he stank with his own fouling. The ship lurched, and trundled the prisoner. But the candle flame on the counter burned tranquil, and the old shopwife was saying, 'Your mam was aye good at the dumplings, indeed,' and scooping soft brown sugar on to the scale. Thora bent in pity to the sea-prisoner and the next wave flung her down into coldness and emptiness. 'Poor lass,' Babs was saying above her, 'thi mother shouldna sent thee oot on a caald night like this, a delicate cratur like thee.'

The next time Gow came to her he was a wandering wailing cry about the houses. 'Release me,' he pleaded, 'give me peace. I can't go out into the healing torment. Your love holds me back. Let me go.' It went on for hours, that voice, in the chimney, under the

door − it whispered from the wind-shaken curtains.
. . . Outside, from the street, she could hear the
voices of townsfolk passing − 'A stormy day indeed'. . . . 'This is the worst gale of the year'. . . .
'God help any ship out in this!'. . . . In the evening
the west wind dropped. Thora, before she fell into
unquiet sleep, heard a last few echoes in the chimney,
'Let me go. . . .cold. . . .into my torment. . . .'

In her sleep that night the girl dreamed that she
was walking on the beach of Hamnavoe harbour, a
thing it was possible to do only at very low tide,
when the shrunken sea leaves a wide desolation of
seaweed and slippery stone. She walked uncertainly
across the ebb. At first the houses above seemed to
be deserted, as on the Sabbath. But when she looked
again every seaward window was crammed with faces.
The silent faces were looking at something other than
her. She turned, and saw that there was a pole stuck
in the foreshore, and something hanging from it. She
took it to be a large fish − a shark or a monster
halibut − that some fisherman had caught in earliest
summer and had fixed here to dry in the wind and
sun. It was a stiff hard shape, it creaked against the
post with every freshet of wind. Then she saw that
the thing was wrapped in manacles and locks. From
some disgusting orifice sifted out syllables, 'Re. . . .
lease me. . . .eee. . . .' She shrank from it. Then the
piers of the town behind her erupted with mockery
and hatred. She turned again − the faces of the townsfolk were twisted with rage and glee. The drinkers had
come out of "The Straitsman" − they dashed their
mugs together.

When she woke from that dream, she knew that Gow was dead; and also that there was something she had to do.

Next morning she spoke urgently to a young fisherman who occasionally brought a cargo of lobsters from Orkney to London. Aaron Folster demurred; it wouldn't be easy, on board his small boat *Hope,* with a passenger, especially a woman passenger. All the way to London? What would her father and mother say? He didn't want there to be any trouble. Mr James Gordon was a very important man in the town. . . . But in the end, in consideration of the sovereign Miss Gordon flashed under his nose, Aaron agreed to give her a passage.

*   *   *

Thora found her way, somehow, to Wapping. The pirates were still there, creaking and clanking in their chains. They dangled so idly in the air, they were so clotted with tar, that they hardly looked like human bodies. She recognized Gow, among the others, by his shattered thumbs, by his strong teeth, even by the shape of his cheekbone under its flap of skin.

The old barge-man who had, for a small fee, taken her to Execution Dock, said 'Sweethearts don't usually come when they're as rotten as this. . . . Are you sure this is the man? Well, my dear, he was the bravest of them all, this one. I saw the hangings. You would have been proud of him.'

Thora clasped the tarred and salted right hand. She said, 'The fires are out. There's nothing left for you here, Jack. Farewell. This is the last mingling of our flesh — a touch only — but it gives us both peace'. . . . A wind coming up Thames took the body and set it creaking like a stiff sack. The wind increased — the chain about the pirate rang. The chains round all ten of the pirates rang.

The girl turned her face to the north.

STONE, SALT, AND ROSE

A ROMANCE

I was captured by two Scottish foot soldiers on the afternoon of midsummer day in the year of God thirteen hundred and fourteen. My horse collapsed under me, and screamed and threshed. I flung this way and that in a pit of spikes and bracken. Then hands dragged me out into the light. I saw blood oozing from a deep gash in my wrist. A maniacal face above screamed at me. A fist trembled in the circle of the sun, then fell on my face. And again. The inside of my mouth was warmth and saltness and slack teeth. 'Mordaunt', I shouted, and the name sounded thin and sweet as a bell in a wood. (Mordaunt is my squire.) Three horns blew to the right of me. The fist fell on me again, but I threw my head aside, and my armour rang with the blow. I saw horses going away from me, going raggedly back over the cornfield, some without riders. My hired horse Rose, still weltering in the pit, gave utterance in a way I had not heard before, a cluster of deep sighs ending in a terrible croak. I had two men to deal with, the madman who screamed and struck and a quiet smiling man. I saw my king far off on the ridge, mounted, his hand raised; then he turned and vanished. Three arrows fell near us; one after the other they swooshed down and stuck quivering in the mud. That was the last thing I saw that day. The smiling Scotsman drew a scarf over my eyes and tied the knot at the back of my head. I could not understand the rapid words that passed between my captors. I was thrust forward by the shoulders. I found that I could hardly walk. The weight of my armour, and my wound, had so weakened me. They dragged me through ditch and stones and mire, for a great distance it seemed. A voice spoke heartily in the strange tongue of those people; then the same voice uttered English words I could understand. 'Well, my lad, and where does your father have his estate? Your father will have to pay a shilling or two to get you back. I think he can well afford it, by the stylish metal you wear on your body. Finn and Angus here, your captors, will need to be paid too. You'll have to content yourself, here in the land of King Bruce, for a month or two. By the end of summer, maybe, my lord your father will have squeezed enough sweat and silver out of his peasants for the ransom. What's your name, now? Where do you come from? Angus, put a stirrup on that horse. I have never seen the famous English archers shooting so thin and wild.'

*　　　　*　　　　*

I was brought, still hooded, to a cobbled courtyard that was fretted continually with a cold rhythmic sound I had never heard before. I found out soon enough what it was – the sea. (My days had been spent among downs and woods.) Many voices, bitter and wondering, gathered about me. A man laughed. A hound-tongue folded the fingers of my wounded hand. My armour was lifted from me. It fell with a clang on the stones. Then, after a time, I was taken inside

by my two captors, and made to mount a circling
stone stair. Up and around we went for scores of
steps. At last we stopped. A door was unlocked and
thrown open with a screeching of rust like a hundred
rats. A hand drew me inside. Then Angus, the quiet
one, took the bandage from my face. Glorious and
hurtful was the light. I saw a bleak room, and a square
barred window level with my face. The only furnish-
ing was a bench against one wall, and on the floor
under it two earthen pitchers, and a stool in a corner.
Angus departed. I was left alone with the brutish one
Finn. 'Well, Englishman,' says he, 'and you thought to
come to our land and take the silver from our kirks
and halls and make harlots of our women. Did you
then? Is that what you thought? Yes, and to live off
the honey and the venison of Scotland. It hasn't turned
out that way. You would have done better to bide at
home and to daff and dally with the woodman's
lasses'. . . . Angus appeared again, his arms loaded
with accoutrements. Finn took two deerskins from
Angus and draped them across the bench. Then Angus
set beside one of the earthen vessels, carefully, a jug
of water. On the window ledge he set a quill and a
ragged scrap of parchment. 'Now, lad,' he said, 'this
is the way it is with you, for the present at any rate.
The floor will be your bed. I hear the English are
great for washing themselves — you have a jar of
water and a basin. The other vessel is for the calls of
nature. Now lad, are you tired? I warrant you're sore
and sad with the things that have happened this day.
You're too young for defeats and woundings. Rest
is a sweet restorer. Youth blossoms in the poorest

circumstances. So take heart. Tomorrow lad, you are to write a letter to your father. (I take it you were taught writing, and Latin and music forby, I wouldn't wonder, by the monks.) You will tell your father that you are a prisoner of a Scottish knight. You will mention the name of this prison and fortress, Castle Wyvis. Also the name of the lord of Castle Wyvis, Sir Andrew de Ross. Also (which is the most important matter of all) the sum of one hundred crowns'. . . . 'Yes,' said Finn, 'or it will be the worse for you.' Then they left me, with more grating of metal within metal. I stood for a long while near the window. It was a fine summer evening, with late roseate light in the sky. The keep was built on a low crag on the verge of a cliff. I have mentioned the sound I had heard that day for the first time — the sea. Since the blindfold had been taken from me, I could see wavering gleams on the ceiling and walls of my cell, green and blue, a light different from the steadfast gold of the sun. Now, alone, I went to the cell window and looked at the sea for the first time. I was shaken with wonder and excitement. I had not imagined that our good earth was so beautifully and perilously girdled. The new element stretched to the horizon, all gleam and serenity and peace. Directly under my prison it had other sounds — it lapped the rocks, it spent itself with whispers and sighs and bell-like tinklings on the sand, it made a strange sound under the neighbouring cliff like a hungry beast glutting itself. . . . I stood at the window, entranced, until the gleam left the horizon. I felt the coming of night in my bones. The stones of the cell exuded coldness. I crossed myself, and crept under the skins, and the rhythms of the sea wove a dreamless sleep about me.

*   *   *

Next morning, at first light, I wrote the ransom letter.

'Father, know by this that your son Geoffrey is a captive of the Scots. It is Geoffrey's hand that writes this. There is blood on my hand where a dagger trenched it in the battle. Andrew de Ross, my captor, takes you to be a wealthy knight, and has mentioned a ransom of one hundred English crowns. Remember me with all kindliness to my lady the Mistress Rosalind. Remember me to my brother Richard and my young sister Ruth. May God keep all your house in safety and in charity. My dear father, this Castle Wyvis where I am kept is a cold and a bleak place. I would that I might see your faces again soon, and my horse Gareth and Nell my falcon. How the battle went I have no means of knowing. It was fought under a great castle on a rock. I saw but a small part of it. All morning I was at the armourer's booth, then late in the day I was put on a strange horse called Rose and pricked on with a score of other young knights. We surged on with a bravery of trumpets and banners. I found myself on a sudden wallowing in a foul pit, and there I was taken. The Scots will keep me in this durance until the ransom is paid. I cannot write more now. The sea under my window is a great wonderment and distraction to me. My wounded hand is sore with the labour of holding the pen.'

On an impulse, seeing that the ink pot was dry, I opened with the quill point the red scab on my wrist, and wrote *Geoffrey* with a seeping of my own blood.

Soon Finn clanked my door open with his key. He looked fiercely at the parchment, then at me. He rolled it up without a word and left the cell.

*   *   *

Five days passed. The only faces that came about my cell were Finn and Angus. They brought me each morning coarse oaten bread and cheese and water, and they removed my body's ordure. Angus did all these tasks cheerfully, as if he had served me since my childhood, and had a good regard for me. 'Now,' he said one day, 'I see you haven't eaten the cheese. It is the best goat cheese, I assure you. Molly Fergusson made it. She makes the sweetest cheese, that old woman, in all this coast. But like enough you are more used to the mild cow-cheese of England. . . .' Another day he said, 'Well, now, your letter is despatched into England. We will be hearing from your father soon enough'. . . . The next day after, in the evening, he brought me a little wine, because (said he) it was the feast day of S. Peter and S. Paul. 'Now', I said to this warder, 'you show me much considera-tion, Angus, and I am thankful for that. But I too, though a prisoner, ought to have been at Mass today, for the ceremonies of the church have always been

delightful to me. Indeed my father has more than once
spoken to the bishop, so that I might at least take the
first orders of priesthood. Would you therefore ask
the lord of this castle if I may not be allowed into his
chapel for Mass on Sunday next, and every Sunday
until I am ransomed?' Angus said that he would
certainly make that request on my behalf, and smiled
heartily, and clapped me on the shoulder. There could
have been a kind of friendship between us, in spite of
our different stations. I felt a warmth about my heart
whenever Angus came to my cell, on this business or
that. How different it was with my other keeper,
Finn. The creature smelt of leather and straw and
horse-dung. He seemed to take a delight in casting my
spirits down. Even his silences were lacerating. My
meat and drink he set down on the window ledge in
a violent way, so that always some water spilled out
of the cup or the hard goat cheese leapt on the plate.
The face of the man when he took away my body's
waste — how he screwed up his mouth and his nose,
and made as if he would be sick! 'I did not think such a
delicate creature had such dews and droppings,' he
sneered at me once. Later that same day, he came
storming in at the door. 'What's this I hear?' he
said. 'You want to see Sir Andrew? About con-
fessions and shrivings and masses? Sir Andrew has
more to do than answer the requests of a young
English dog. The war is not yet over, let me tell you.
The English were defeated, but they are like to return.
If that happens, God help you — the men in the
castle will cut your throat. When the hundred crowns
come, that will be time enough to make requests. Sir

Andrew is too busy. Sir Andrew is getting his men in order for the next campaign. Let me hear no more of such nonsense!' So he ranted at me, before taking my plate and water-jug away. I had hours of misery that night, under the deer skins, before I fell asleep, and then it was only to trudge through desolate dreams. The next morning it was — thank God! — my kindly jailer that roused me. 'Angus,' I said, 'that man Finn doesn't like me. I would be glad if his duties were done by someone else, I'm sure it can be no pleasure to him to wait on someone he hates so bitterly.' Angus smiled. 'You are not to take it to heart,' he said. 'Finn wants to be in the stable all the time, with his horses. He doesn't like this turnkey job.' I asked Angus if he had made my request for spiritual comfort to the lord of the castle. No (said he) for Sir Andrew was busy with affairs of the kingdom; he had had to ride to Perth three days after the battle, and had not yet returned. And as for masses, there was no resident chaplain in Wyvis — it was too small a place — but a monk came on Sundays and holy days from the abbey higher up the river. Then Angus examined my wrist. 'It is healing,' he said. 'There will be nothing there in a year but a little silver scar. You'll be able to say to your sweetheart, *Look how fiercely I fought in the Scottish wars*. And your grandchildren will finger it in your old age, and think what a hero their grandsire was.' Angus and I laughed together in the cell, I standing with a piece of oat bread in my hand. Then there was the sound of horses in the courtyard below. Angus listened with tilted head. 'That's him!' he said. 'Sir Andrew is back from seeing the king

and the nobles in Perth. Now we will know what
is to happen.'

*   *   *

The good weather continued; day after day of it.
The sun shone from early morning into my cell. I
took to rising from my hard bed as soon as the sun
rose out of the North Sea, so that not an hour of that
marvellous sea-fretted light should be wasted. I would
follow the square of wavering brightness as it moved
round my cell; placing my stool here and there, and
letting its warmth lave my still-throbbing wound. At
noon a narrow shaft entered from the south. After
that I could only enjoy the glitter of the vanished
sun on the sea; my cell began to fill with gray shadows.
I kept warmth in me then by walking from this wall to
that, and from that corner to this. By early evening
I was glad enough to creep under my deerskins, and
to sleep until birdsong once more.

So, as the days passed, I was up an hour before
either Finn or Angus unlocked my cell door and took
in my breakfast.

These mornings were beautiful, and touched me
with the happiness that all young men feel at the
vernal bounty of nature. 'Truly the light is sweet, and
a pleasant thing it is for the eyes to behold the sun.'
Yet mixed with my joy was a regret and a sadness.
At this time of the year, if I was at home, I would
be much of the day in the company of Madge or
Jane, the forester's daughters. Both of them I had
enjoyed in the weeks before I had joined the other

men of the estate for the march into Scotland. To
Jane, with her russet hair and fine dark eyes, I had
given the first flowerings of my manhood, but after
that night of pain and sweetness I enjoyed more the
kissings and allurings and sighings of Madge her sister.
No wonder I slept late in the mornings then, so that
my father would come and shake me out of bed!
'Come, now, there's more to a man's days than daff-
ing in the forest with hot little hussies! The sheep
are dropping lambs all over the hill. I'm not a prince
or a duke. My sons must work as well as the hired
men'. . . . For my father knew well how it was with
me in those delicious spring days; he was not so far
away from his own youth. He was a lusty widower,
and certain women here and there on the estate —
apart from Rosalind his mistress — waited for a night
summons from him. He knew how it was between
myself and the forester's girls. There was no question
of me marrying either of them, of course. Other
arrangements were being made. I was given to understand that Beatrice, the fourth daughter of Thomas
Spencer, esquire, of The Knolls, was, if not affianced
to me, at least the centre of a web of delicate
negotiations. A little pretty portrait of this girl had
been brought to the hall, and passed round the table
at dinner one night. 'And, by God', said my father,
'this promises to be a good and a capable woman.' 'It
is not like her,' said my elder brother Richard. 'She's
an ugly little creature. The artist has been well paid
to put roses in her cheeks and that snow on her bosom,'
'Beauty,' cried my father then, 'what is that? Roses
and snow indeed, and as quick to go. I will tell you

this too, beauty puts power into a woman's hands that she wields, more often than not, for evil ends. A man can't do better than marry with a plain hard-working healthy little thing. Then when love suddenly blossoms between them — it may be after a month, or after a year, or after five years — then it is the kind of love that lasts till death and beyond'. . . . My little sister Ruth listened demurely to all this talk, and put bits of white chicken into her dog's mouth. . . .

I sat on my low stool one morning, in my cell, in a square of sunlight, sifting all those memories with a mingling of happiness and regret. Would I ever see Madge or Jane again? Would I ever put the gold ring on the finger of the squire's plain-looking fourth daughter? I half drowsed, and dreamed, as I sat there. Then I heard voices, and for a second or two these voices seemed to be a part of my dream, until I realized that they were real: thin cold Scottish sea-voices, and coming from the beach under my window.

I rose to my feet and looked out. A woman was standing on the verge, holding a cloak over one arm, and looking seaward. There was a disturbance in the water six or seven yards out, and presently a girl rose through it, laughing with coldness and delight, and shaking salt drops from her. Then down again she went, and let the water close over her for a second or two, only to rise again, gasping and laughing and gleaming in the light. 'Come now, Maud,' said the old woman. 'That's enough of that. The seal-men will get you. Ashore with you now!' Then the girl came splashing ashore, and the old one quenched her nakedness in the gray coat she carried over her arm. Whether it was my hunger, or my pain, or my delight that compelled it, I do not know, but the girl, shivering on the beach, suddenly looked up at the cell window. Then she stopped, and continued to look up at me, and the old woman, a step or two away, followed the girl's eyes up to the barred window. The girl, her hair and her feet still glittering from the sea, did not move. The old one spoke sharply to her. 'Come now, do you want your death? Up to the fire with you.' The girl raised her fingers to her lips, still looking up at my window. She left the kiss in the air, and followed the old one up the sea-path and out of sight.

An hour later, or thereby, the lock rattled and the door squealed open. The bearer of my bread and milk this morning was Finn. Not even the surliness of him could daunt me. 'Well, friend,' I cried, 'do you have to look so miserable on such a fine morning? You should be glad to be alive like every other living thing in the world.'

He looked at me as if I was some kind of a toad, or worm. 'A fat lot you have to be thankful about,' he said. 'There's still no word from your father in England. You ought to know what that means, if word doesn't come soon.' He drew his filthy forefinger across his throat.

I ate my breakfast in a trance of happiness. I washed myself for the first time for a week, and thoroughly, drawing off my jerkin and splashing my shoulders in the cold water. The sun progressed, a square of golden sea-splendours, from station to

station round my cell. Most of the rest of that morning
I spent remembering verses and fragments of country
songs that I thought I had forgotten, silly carefree
words about springtime and birds and maidenheads.

My warder that evening was Angus. He was tired,
he had bits of grass stuck here and there on his coat,
he smelt of light and wind. He told me he had been
out in the hayfield all day with a dozen other workers.

'Now, Angus,' I said, 'I'm getting weary of this
place. Could I not work in the hayfield too?'

He shook his head.

'Why not?' I said. 'I couldn't escape. Where would
I go to? I don't know this countryside. They would
hunt me down in an hour. Besides, I don't want to
escape. I intend to stay here until I am honourably
ransomed.'

'It can't be done,' said Angus. 'I'm sorry. It's a
strict order from Sir Andrew.'

'Surely,' I said, 'I could walk in the courtyard,
with a guard beside me. Or better still, stretch my
legs some morning along the sea verge.'

'Sir Andrew says you must be confined here,' said
Angus.

'Well, he's a hard man, this Sir Andrew de Ross,'
I said. 'I know what it is, he is an old bachelor, with
a dried-up miserly heart.'

'Not so,' said Angus, 'he is a widower. His sweet
wife Alysoun died last winter. But a beautiful daughter
is left to cheer him. It's true, he's rather poor as far
as money goes. He knows that the nobles of England
pay well to ransom their sons. That's why you're
being kept here so straitly.'

I forbore to tell Angus that neither was my father a wealthy squire. He would be hard put to it to gather those hundred crowns.

'This daughter of the castle,' I said, 'I expect she's called Maud, or some silly name like that. And she might be fifteen years old or thereabouts, all giggles and blushings. And her hair will be yellowish.'

Angus's eyes widened, and he laughed. 'Well,' he said, 'you must be a sorcerer. Nearly everything you've said is true about the girl, except that her hair is golden and she is the most sweet innocent creature that ever my eyes beheld.'

'I expect this Maud is betrothed to some squire farther up the valley. She'll be married after harvest.' This I said with a catch in my breath.

'He would be a lucky laird that got her,' said Angus. 'But as I told you, the castellan is far from wealthy. The dowry will be small. In the end I think Sir Andrew will have to marry her off to some merchant from Fife, or Aberdeen. Or he might have her placed in a convent of nuns.'

We had spoken so long, Angus and I, that my broth had grown cold. Indeed the whole cell was drowned in cold gray shadows, though there was a last gleam on the sea beyond the headland. I found myself trembling, standing there at the window.

'Now,' said Angus, 'I've kept you from your broth with all my blether. You're shaking with cold. Go to bed, as soon as you've eaten your supper. There's a chill in the nights now. Your wound isn't quite healed yet. I'll speak for an extra blanket for you.'

*   *   *

For two mornings yet the dawn came out of a cloudless horizon. I was out of my hard bed even before the sun began to squander its silent treasury over the waves. Eagerly I went then to my station at the barred window, hoping that the girl of the castle would go down for her morning bathe, and greet me again secretly and deliciously from the waves.

I waited, a cold shadow, at the window. The sun rose. Birds with long thin legs waded in the ebbing water. The sun rose higher. From courtyard and hidden fields and from kitchen came stirrings of the awakened household. Then I knew that the girl would not come today, and probably never again. Soon, heavy at heart, I heard the squeak of key in lock. On the first bereaved morning Angus came in, with a greeting in his mouth, and set my breakfast plate on the ledge, and took away (as cheerfully as could be) my ordure bucket. On the second barren morning it was Finn — the wonder is the earthen plate did not crack across when he set it down. Not a word from him. He took the waste bucket away, holding his nose betwixt the thumb and forefinger of his other hand. 'God, how they stink, the English,' he mumbled as he went.

Next afternoon the weather broke. Clouds drove, herds-long, out of the north, bringing wind and rain. I saw the ocean then drained of all its beauty. The sea was like lead. Waves fell sluggishly on the stones below. It was intolerably cold in my cell. (I wore only the jerkin and breeches I had been captured in.) Swiftly I walked here and there about the floor, and swung my arms, and stamped my feet. But I could not keep the weather from entering the place. The stone immediately under the window sill shone like a dark mirror with rain; each corner stirred with gray gusts.

'Well,' I thought, to comfort myself, 'Angus will be here in a short while. It's his turn to bring my supper. He will have that extra blanket for my bed. Some kind of shelter must be nailed over the window — a shutter, perhaps, or thick sacking. Of course that means the cell will be darker. But then Angus will see that I get a candle, or a small lamp'.

It wasn't Angus that brought my supper — it was him who smelt of leather and horse-dung, my enemy. I decided to speak. 'The weather has broken,' I said. 'You must see how inclement it is in this cell. I'm not asking for a fire — there's no fireplace, so I can't have one. But I would be glad if the window was shuttered in some way, and also if I could be given a candle and flint.'. . . . Finn looked at me as if I had uttered some blasphemy in church. 'A fire!' cried he. 'Candles! A shutter! What are you, some great lord come to be a guest here in Castle Wyvis? And we are to scurry here and there and everywhere to satisfy your lordship's whims! God, what is this world coming to, when the worm imagines itself to be the rose! If your lordship is so cold, your lordship can wrap himself in his blankets and go to sleep for the winter. Such impudent askings, all because there has been a shower of rain! What will your lordship be wanting tomorrow, a flagon of wine, a lass from the kitchen to keep you company at nights! Here is your supper. Eat it and be thankful.' I was hard put to it not to strike the rascal. Instead I said, as quietly as possible, 'It is Angus's turn to bring me my supper.' 'O', he cried, 'so his

lordship has the ordering of the castle too, who is to
do this and who is to do that! Let me tell your
lordship, Angus is not here. Angus has gone far away,
on business.' That was the bitterest blow in all this
long cold day. 'Where has Angus gone?' I said — 'at
least tell me that.' His lip curled for another taunt.
But then, seeing perhaps how wretched I stood there,
he said, 'Angus is sent away on estate business.' He
eased the door open. Had he been too kind to me,
with that last remark? He turned and said, 'You will
have me to deal with in future, no-one but me.' And,
after he had turned the key, he shouted from outside
through the lock, 'There is no word yet from my
lord your father. I do not like that.'

I had no heart to eat the bread and bit of fish he
had brought. I had no heart to pray. I merely crossed
myself, and lay down on the floor under the deerskins, and swooned wretchedly into sleep.

*   *   *

Some kind of a sickness took hold of me that
night while I slept. I had been all my life a strong
lusty lad. Sickness was for old men, and for the lepers
and cripples that begged about my father's gates. I
opened my eyes and knew at once that I had slept
late — the sun was half-way up the sky. The door
shrieked; that sound must have awaked me. There was
that ill-favoured face against the light. 'What's this!'
cried Finn. 'His lordship isn't up yet? His lordship
hasn't eaten his last night's supper? Was the fish not
to his lordship's taste? Let me tell you this, the fish

that swim in the Forth and Tay are the best fish in
the world. The cat shall have it. Would his lordship
oblige me now by stirring out of that fart-pit?'

What was the great weariness that was in my bones?
Nothing mattered to me. The cheerfulness of Angus —
who had gone away — and the insults of this creature
were all one to me. I flung the skins from me and
got to my feet, but at once I had to put a hand to
the wall to keep my legs from folding. It was a strange
feeling, the onset of this sickness — it was not entirely dreadful; the heaviness was in some curious
way comforting, as though life were made much
simpler, as though all my difficulties and troubles and
desires were gathered into one great need, simply to
lie down and to sleep. I felt my way over to the stool
by the window, and sank down on it, and laid my
head in my hands. My wounded wrist flashed with
pain, but my whole body was suffused with a most
kindly heat; and yet I was shivering, and suddenly
my face masked itself in sweat. Even Finn, the
breakfast platter still in his hands, could see that
nothing was feigned in my performance. I observed,
with a kind of detached weary amusement, how his
mouth fell open and his eyes widened. 'What's this?'
he said. 'Sick, are you? Give me your arm. You must
get back on your bed.' He eased me off the stool,
and (not too roughly) led me back to the corner,
and spread the skins over me. He looked genuinely
concerned, but I did not flatter myself that he
worried one whit on my behalf, but only lest some
chastisement be visited on his own skin. If the young
English knight were to die, and no ransom were to

be paid, and he, through neglect, was held to be blameworthy! I whispered, 'You can give my breakfast cheese to the mice in the kitchen'. . . . These were the last words I remember speaking for a long time — I don't know how many days. And the last thing I heard, before I entered the cave of oblivion, were the slippers of Finn my warder flip-flapping down the spiral steps as if some burning horseman out of hell were after him.

*   *   *

I do not know how long the sickness lasted. Time ceased to have any meaning. I had measured my days as a prisoner by the rhythms of sleep and wakefulness, and the ebb and flow of the sea, and the arc of the sun from dawn to noon. 'I am hungry,' my body had said. 'I am satisfied.' 'I am tired.' 'I am refreshed.' 'I am lonely.' 'I am content.' 'I wish to pray.' 'God is not here.' 'The ransom is surely on the counting-house table.' 'My father has turned a bankrupt face to my captor'. . . . On that narrow loom my hopes and fears had been woven, day after day, monotonously. Now the loom was suddenly removed from the weaver. My body began to be clothed with fevers and hectic dreams.

Memories out of my childhood enfolded me, sometimes grotesque and hideous, sometimes of great sweetness, but always of the utmost lucency. I saw the face of my mother who had died when I was a child giving birth to Ruth my sister. I had forgotten the face, but there it was, solicitous and tender, with a scar on her cheek where the pet parakeet had once nipped her. I saw the boar's head on the Yule spit, and my father (his beard frosted) cursing a scullion for some negligence: another image that had gone clean out of my mind. The silly thing cringed away, her forearm covering her face, and I — a seven-year-old — was both appalled and delighted with the drama. . . . These and a hundred other memories I strove to hold on to, but the fabrics vanished at the very moment of their bodying forth on the looms of sickness. Then that first wild fever must have died. I became more aware — but only fleetingly and in a confused dreamlike way — of my actual circumstances. A monotonous presence came and went, and came and went. I whispered darkly, 'Finn'. And others apart from him stooped over me: faces I had glimpsed in the courtyard on the day of my taking. Was I given extreme unction? I have a dark memory of a priestlike figure between me and the light, and the dabbings of oil to my face and hands. Andrew de Ross came, very solemn, and left. Once, when Finn was trying to put some disgusting broth into my mouth, I said in a low distinct voice, 'Where is my friend Angus?' And immediately, as if I had uttered a spell, nurture and nurse vanished. But those actual happenings were mingled with fantasies. Surely it was impossible that one day I saw my father standing against the wall? And one night I woke up to find a candle burning on a small table beside my bed, and a curtain shutting out the stars. 'So,' I said to myself, 'I am to have those small comforts now, at last, when I'm dying'. . . . There was a presence in the room —

the flame of the candle wavered — I suddenly cried
out with joy and gratitude. Fair and beautiful the
face of Maud de Ross, the castellan's daughter, shone
beside the flame, then bowed over my scarred wrist,
and she kissed it. Her mouth moved again, but only
to blow the candle out; and with it my consciousness.
But when I woke up, the sweetness of that moment
was still in my mind, and it lingered most of the day,
even when Finn came to perform the offices of washing and feeding (which he did, I must say, efficiently
and with less overt surliness than hitherto). I was
still too sick to separate dreams from actuality. I
began to feel, too, for the first time, the ravages that
the sickness had wrought in me — pain and weakness,
and a vivid sense of the vanity of things. The spirit
of youth had ebbed far out and left a desolate foreshore, strewn with stinking rocks and pools, broken
wings, bones, crab husks, the wreckage of lost years.
There are moments then when the soul may look
deathward, and whisper 'Very well then, you're
welcome.' I said, at one such time, 'I think that priest
was here indeed with the last oil. My feet are heaven-
bound. What hinders me?' And then, in that last reach
of ebb, I felt strength returning. The clear tides of
youth began, slowly and imperceptibly, to advance
over wrack-strewn wastes. The loom had been set up
once more in a secret corner of time, to take the
rhythms of fate and chance, joy and sorrow, building
and breaking. 'I will not die,' I said on the first day
that I could properly distinguish night from light.
And with those words I turned my back on the burning wardrobes of sickness, and on the last black coat

of dreamlessness that had seemed about to enfold me. I came and sat once more, trembling, before the quiet loom of life.

*   *   *

I was given my freedom soon afterwards, but it was the freedom of the bound man, the serf. Harvest was beginning on the estate when I was let out of my cell and led down the winding stair into the courtyard. The first face I saw there was Angus. I threw my arms round him and laughed with joy. 'Well, sir,' he said, 'what's this I hear about you, while I was away? They tell me you were dallying with death. You're still gray in the face, and thin. A few days in the sunshine and you'll be strong again'. . . .

'What is to happen to me?' I asked Angus.

'You must work like everybody else,' said Finn from the stable door. 'You've eaten and slept since midsummer and never done a stroke of work for it. Your holiday is over.'

'I wasn't speaking to you, sour-face,' I said.

Angus said, 'I have news for you, Geoffrey. Your father couldn't find the hundred crowns to ransom you. I must tell you that plainly. He tried here and there, and this way and that. He pleaded with earl and abbot. He even went to the Jews in their counting house in the seaport. Nobody was willing to risk the hundred crowns. At last your father said, "I never had a son called Geoffrey. Do with him what you will." '

The news was no great surprise to me.

'Did you ever learn to reap?' said Finn. 'Give him
a scythe. The field's half cut'.

I knew how to reap after a fashion. My father had
never allowed us to eat the bread of idleness. Angus
brought me to a teeming yellow hillside beyond the
keep.

For three days I toiled among the harvesters. At
the end of the first day I was so weary I could hardly
hold myself up. I wandered away at sunset with my
scythe over my shoulder in the direction of the castle.
'Where do you think you're going?' cried Finn.

'To my cell, to sleep,' I managed to say.

'You'll sleep in the barn with the other harvesters,'
said Finn. 'The castle is only for folk of importance.'

Saturated with sun and air and ripeness, I slept
among a score of other harvesters in the barn. It was
the deepest most delicious sleep of my life.

I was shaken into wakefulness by a rough hand at
sunrise. I took my sore heavy body into the oatfield
once more. But gradually, as the sun rose higher, the
rhythm of the harvest toil took hold of me. Eagerly
I strode and swung my scythe, and the sunripened
rustling oats fell before me. Other serfs marched
across the harvest field abreast of me, their blades
flashing in the sun. Girls and women came after,
stooping and binding the cut corn. It was like a solemn
ritual, except that the children put gaiety into the day,
running here and there, chasing rabbits and birds and
butterflies, and laughing in the bronze light. Angus
moved about the field and directed operations.

About noon Angus called a halt to the work. We
ate oatbread and cheese, and drank ale, in a shady

corner of the field. The other harvesters looked
curiously at the stranger in their midst. Some glared
at me, but most of them shrugged their shoulders
and paid no attention after a time. It was a dark girl
called Morag who brought the food and drink to me;
and she was so attentive and kind that my cup never
got empty.

'Now,' cried Angus, 'that's enough. You can't work
with full bellies. Back to the rabbit-hunt with you!'
(For bolt-eyed rabbits had been leaping and loping
out of the oats before the advance of the scythes all
morning.)

Never had food or drink entered more deliciously
into a king's mouth.

Till the sun went down we toiled monotonously
across the bright broken field. I turned once and saw
that it was Morag who was gathering and binding my
swathes. She looked up at me, and smiled.

Then, in the cool of the evening, we had supper
of rabbit pie and beer outside the barn. Morag saw
to it that I was well supplied.

While I was still at the last lordly mouthful, Angus
came and sat down beside me. 'Well, Geoffrey,' said
he, 'I've been watching you at work, and you seem to
have got the hang of it well enough. But there's more
to farming, lad, than swinging a merry scythe. Listen
now, I'm going to tell you something of Castle Wyvis
and all the mouths it feeds, and all its barterings and
earnings and spendings, summer and winter. It's good
that you should understand all that. Now, this oatfield that we're cutting, it isn't, you understand,
always an oatfield. By no means. Next year it'll

grow grass. And that patch of heather further up the hill — look over there — we have other plans for that. Listen, Geoffrey.'

What possessed my good warder? He must have seen that I was weighed down with a great golden weariness, yet on and on he went, urgently, lecturing me on the economy of this estate. I heard him in a half-dream. Seven hundred sheep. Forty-one horses. A hundred and fifty cattle. New byres to be built. Bad seed one year from such-and-such a dealer in the Border country. Pitchforks. Peasants. Cartloads of dung. It might be possible to keep pigs, though there had never been styes at Castle Wyvis before. . . .

Then Angus must have seen my head nodding on my breast, for he shook my arm, pleasantly exasperated, and said 'Goodnight, lad. We'll speak more about this tomorrow.' He walked off in the direction of the keep.

I had a second night of dark dreamless sleep. It seemed that only a minute passed before the cock began to shrill from the barnyard. Then the door opened, and Finn entered to summon us to another day of labour.

This was the last day of the oat harvest. The marvellous monotonics of the two previous days went on until, late in the afternoon, the last of the oats went down with whispers of fulfilment. The ritual was over. My scythe flashed idly at nothingness. I did not realize it till Morag came up behind me, smiling, and took me by the wrist. (There was no pain in the wound any more — it had begun to silver over.) At the end of the field the harvesters laughed to each other, and Angus cried from the middle of the stooks, 'Well done, well done!' Then some of the men and women began to dance in and out of the stooks while a young man blew scrannel music on a pipe. Morag tugged my arm. We made a few steps and circles and crosses over the bright stubble, with fingers interlaced, while the crude music went on and on and the old peasants clapped their hands.

Soon the dancing ended and it was time to eat. Morag and I shared a wedge of white cheese, and passed the ale mug between us.

What strange thing had happened to me? I ought to have been the most wretched of men. My father had disowned me. I, a young English squire, had been degraded to a serf in a hostile land. I was not likely to see the pleasant gardens and spires of home again. Yet I never had been so happy as during those three days. I had felt health flowing back into my prison-shadowed body. I knew a fierce delight in sun and wind and the earth's abundance.

'The barley field tomorrow,' said Finn darkly among the laughing harvesters. They had begun their rejoicing too early, he implied.

That night as I lay on the heavy verge of sleep against the barn wall, with a dozen snorers all about me, I felt a stirring in the straw, and a long cold finger touched my mouth.

'Who's there?' I whispered. (But I knew it was Morag in the darkness.) I took her hands and pushed her gently away. 'No, please,' I said. 'You must go away. This can never be. I'm a prisoner in this place, and a serf. What would they do to me if they thought I was a nuisance to their women?'

'Take me in beside you,' she whispered. 'It must be.'

'No,' I said sharply. 'Go away. I need my strength for the barley harvest tomorrow.'

'I have been given orders,' she whispered, and laid her arms about my neck. 'I was told to come in to you.'

'Now, Morag,' I said in the darkness, 'I like you well enough. But I have two sweethearts at home in England, and there is another most precious girl I have set my heart on. You must go away. If Finn were to find you here in the morning!'

She wept a little. Then she said with a firmness I had not heard before, 'I haven't told you a lie, stranger. The greatest one of all has ordered me to lie with you. My master, Sir Andrew de Ross. He spoke to me not an hour ago.'

The tide of desire was stirring in me. Was this ordinance a girl's sweet lie, to satisfy her private lust, or was it some deep plot for my ruin? The current began to swirl and surge and rampage. I no longer cared. I took my harvest-helper in my arms and drew her down into the straw. Our lips touched each other. It was a long time before they parted.

'I have never done this before,' Morag whispered. 'Be gentle with me, stranger'.

*   *   *

The barley harvest began next morning. In the afternoon rain fell. The harvesters swarmed into the shelter of the barn. There was some half-hearted singing, and a wrestling contest, and stories were told. A youth and a girl drifted into a dark corner. Where was Morag? She had left me before morning, and I had not seen her again since the tryst. Rain throbbed on the thatch. 'This rain,' said Finn, 'it has the makings of a long black deluge. The barley will be all a mush. It will not be fit to put scythes to'. . . . I said to Angus, 'That girl Morag, you know, the one that helped me in the oatfield. She came after me and bound my sheaves.' 'I know Morag,' said Angus, 'a bonny hard-working lass.' 'Well,' said I, 'it's just that I'm curious. I don't see Morag. Where is she today?' 'No,' said Angus, 'nor will you be seeing the lass again. Morag has been sent home to her mother. Her mother lives ten miles away.' 'Why has she been sent away?' I asked. 'How should I know?' said Angus. 'It isn't for the likes of me to question the decisions of Sir Andrew.'

In spite of Finn's gloomy predictions, late in the afternoon the black clouds rolled away over the hills to the west, with last mutterings of thunder, and the sun came out. The barley-field glittered. The harvesters cheered and ran out into the light. 'It's still too wet to cut,' said Finn. 'Back to the barn with you. We might be able to cut in the morning, that's to say, if there's no more rain.'

I did not go back to the barn.

What drew my feet, instead, down to the shore, and to that very fringe of pebbles and shifting sea under my cell? I walked back and fore, intrigued by the marks my feet left in the sand. I even dipped

my finger in the sea, and (for the first time) touched
the salt to my mouth. Suddenly, I heard my name
called from above. It was Angus. 'You're to come at
once,' he cried. 'Sir Andrew is holding an assize.'

When I had climbed up the rocks to the gate, my
face must have been blanched. Angus laughed and
clapped me on the shoulder. 'What,' he cried — 'do
you think you're going to be tried and hanged? You're
skin's safe enough, lad. It's just that Sir Andrew
wants an Englishman to see that we have law, and
good law, in Scotland.'

Angus led me into a part of Castle Wyvis where
I had not been before. We walked through a corridor
and came at last to a big stone chamber that had
torches stuck here and there along one wall. At a
table on a low dais sat the castellan, Sir Andrew de
Ross. It was only the second time I had seen him.
'You are to sit down here,' whispered Angus. The
great man did not once look at me.

I found myself sitting beside a monk and a man
who looked like a scribe or a notary; at least he had
a parchment and quill in front of him. On the
parchment was written what appeared to be a list of
names. Three or four guards moved round a door at
the other end of the chamber.

'Call the first prisoner,' said Sir Andrew de Ross.

A man whose head was lost in russet shagginess —
only his eyes and nose were to be seen — was
summoned from the corridor outside and led by two
of the guards to within six feet of Sir Andrew, where
they halted him.

'William Rand, for sheep-theft,' said the scribe,

and made a mark against the first name on the list.

The castellan looked very stern. 'Now, man,' he said, 'look me in the eye — there's a shiftiness in you — tell me did you steal my lord the abbot's sheep or not?'

The man mumbled something.

'You're a liar,' cried Sir Andrew. 'You did not mistake the markings at all. The abbey has different markings entirely to your markings. This is a pitiful excuse for you to make.'

The man shuffled his feet. Then his head dropped on his chest. 'Don't snivel,' cried his judge. 'I can't abide snivelling in a man. How many sheep do you keep this year?'

The man mumbled a figure.

'A hundred,' said Sir Andrew. 'That's enough for any man in your station. A hundred good healthy sheep. And, suddenly, last week, you are found to have a hundred and three sheep, three with the lugs half torn off so that the marks of the true owner, my lord abbot, might not be seen. Were you in need of them? No. Were your wife and your bairn starving and naked, that you had to do such a bad thing? They were not. Why then did you do it?'

More low mumblings from the accused man.

'Let me hear no more,' Sir Andrew cried passionately, 'about a mistake! There was no mistake, other than this mistake, that you departed culpably and shamelessly from the laws of this kingdom. It is this just law, not I, that will pronounce upon you now. You are to be hanged from a gibbet in the courtyard at noon tomorrow.'

I expected the condemned man to grovel on his knees for pardon, seeing that he had made such a wretched appearance. But no: when the guards turned him round to march him out, there was for the first time a look of some dignity on his hirsute face.

'Amen,' said the monk. 'And may the Lord have mercy on your soul!'

The scribe wrote rapidly on his parchment, then strewed sand upon the wet ink.

'Next prisoner,' said Sir Andrew de Ross.

What old creature was this that the guards ushered into the court-room? She had a shrunken mouth and webs about her eyes, and she advanced upon Sir Andrew with a slow pained hirple.

'Molly Fergusson,' said the scribe. 'Indicted for the practice of witchcraft, to the harm of sundry lieges.'

'Well, woman,' said Sir Andrew, 'and what was an old body like you doing, to make a pact with the devil, eh?'

I don't think Mistress Fergusson realized what the proceedings were about. 'Eh, sirs,' she said in a faded voice, 'if this isn't the grand place you've taken me to!'

'Molly Fergusson,' said Sir Andrew, 'is it true what is said about you in this sworn testimony I have here — that you made a clay image of Mistress Anne Gray, sempstress in Castle Wyvis, and bored it through with a gimlet, and so did imagine and compass the death by sorcery of the said Anne Gray?'

'Don't mention that name,' cried the old woman. 'The thief that she is! Trying to take my old Gavin from me. Yes, I did it, and I'll do it again. The wicked slut that she is. Kissing my old Gavin at the castle wall in the moonlight.'

'Mistress Fergusson,' said Sir Andrew, 'listen carefully to me. I have examined Anne Gray and gotten trustworthy reports on her, and I find her an honest chaste good-intentioned woman.'

'Don't say her name!' wheezed the old one. 'The slut!'

'Hear me out,' said Sir Andrew. 'I will ask you a question. How old is your spouse Gavin Fergusson?'

The old woman shook her head.

'No one rightly knows,' said Sir Andrew. 'But this is certain, he is a white-thatched old man, and if he isn't as old as Methusalem he's very much older than the age the psalmist sets for the limits of mortal life, seventy years. He has long been unfit for labour, and I doubt if there is a spark in his eye nowadays from the visitations of lust. Now Mistress Gray —'

'The bissom,' said the old woman.

'Mistress Gray is a woman not yet thirty, with a loving husband and five bonny bairns. Do you think, now, that Mistress Anne Gray would fash herself with a poor old done creature like your Gavin?'

'Yes,' said Molly Fergusson, 'for I saw them at it with my own eyes, at the castle wall, in the full moon, three nights together.'

'Mistress Fergusson,' said the judge, 'I think you dreamed it.'

'Maybe I did, and maybe I didn't,' said she, 'but the world would be well rid of the red-faced randy slut that she is, trying to take that old man from me who's the only creature left to me, out of seven.'

'Will you believe me,' said Sir Andrew, 'that you have imagined all this?'

'If you say so,' said she. 'For I know, Sir Andrew, that you would never tell a lie to an old woman like me.'

'I wouldn't, Molly,' said Sir Andrew. 'I want you to believe this too, that it's a very wicked thing to make spells and enchantments in the name of Satan to harm another person.'

'Well, sir, I'm sorry,' she said. 'I won't do it again.'

'Thank you,' said Sir Andrew. 'Now go away and be good and say your prayers.'

'Sir Andrew,' she said, 'it does my heart the world of good whenever I speak with you.'

They smiled to each other. One guardsman turned her about, the other took her by the elbow and led her out. At the door she turned and cried, 'But I'll never speak to that Gray woman for as long as I live!'

The scribe made another mark on his parchment. Another name was called.

A young man was brought in. He was charged with killing a swan at a bend of the river two mornings since. I saw that he was one of the harvesters who had worked beside me in the oat-field — one of the few who went out of their way to sneer at my Englishness and my fall from fortune. But today he looked frightened.

'Kill a swan, did you?' said Sir Andrew. 'Why did you kill the swan, sir? Was the bird pestering you? Did it fly in your face? Or did you want the whole castle to feast on swan pie next holy day?'

The young man said he thought there could be small harm in killing a swan.

'God knows,' said Sir Andrew, 'there's little enough of loveliness and grace in this world, that an oaf like you should destroy a swan. What did you kill the beautiful bird with?'

'With an oar,' said the man.

'Now,' said Sir Andrew, 'I will tell you a thing. Do you know who that bird belongs to? It belongs to the king. You have killed the king's bird. What have you to say to that?'

The man's face blanched. He said, 'Sir, I swear I did not know that.'

'I could have you hanged for it,' said Sir Andrew. 'Instead you will sit in the stocks tomorrow, in the yard, from sunrise to sunset, without food or drink.'

'I am a harvester, sir,' said the bird-slayer.

'What moves with more grace and power, in water and in air, than the swan? You have made that beautiful swift creature a heap of bloody feathers in the stream. Tomorrow you will sit in a wooden frame for ten hours or thereby. And whoever lists can give you a spit or a kick in passing. Take him away.'

A young man I had not seen before was the next to stand trial. 'John Rankine,' intoned the clerk, 'in that he has gotten Alice Chisholm with child, and will not marry the lass.'

'Is this true?' said Sir Andrew.

'It is,' said the debaucher of innocence, proud and defiant.

'Do you love Alice?' said Sir Andrew. 'I know

her. Her father is the thatcher, Rob Chisholm. She used to be a sweet child about the castle.'

'I love her,' said the accused man. 'And what's more, Sir Andrew, Alice likes me well enough too.'

'What keeps you then from taking her to the priest?' said Sir Andrew. 'Are you too poor to keep a wife?'

The man spoke low and hesitant. 'It's my mother,' he said. 'She cannot thole Alice. She will not have Alice about the house.'

There was a silence in the court for some seconds. Sir Andrew narrowed his eyes and stroked his beard. 'Pray,' he said quietly, 'who or what is your mother?'

'She is Griselda Rankine, a widow.'

'I know these mothers,' Sir Andrew said. 'I know them to the bone. Their precious darling sons, will they let them into the clutches of ruthless girls? Their paragons, that they fed at their breasts. I know them well. I have not sat on this bench since I grew the first hair on my chin, and not grown acquainted with those dames. They are shaken with jealousy and rage and pride. Those harpies were ever the enemies of love.'

'Please,' said the lad, 'don't speak that way about my mother. I cannot abide it.'

'I am here to speak the truth,' said Sir Andrew, 'whether you can abide it or not, sir. Listen now to my sentence.'

'I will pay for the child's fostering, after it's born,' said the young man.

'You will do no such thing,' said Sir Andrew. 'You will cleave to the wife of your bosom. You will shake the dust of your mother's door from your feet. This is the sentence: that you, John Rankine, enter into a state of matrimony with Alice Chisholm before sunset.' To the monk he said, 'You can see to that, Agnellus.'

The monk bowed his head gravely.

A look of fear came on the young man's face, and was followed at once by a glance of happiness; and then those two emotions contended together for possession of his mouth and eyes. A guard tapped him on the shoulder.

'One bold, true word to your mother and you're free,' said Sir Andrew. 'Be happy then with your wife for ever. Love is the sweetest gift of heaven to the creatures of this earth.'

As if the castellan had uttered a spell, the little door behind him opened and a girl came in. I saw, with a wild sudden leap of the heart, that it was the daughter, Maud, whom I had thought immured in some convent in the hills. She came up to her father, and stooped and whispered in his ear. He nodded, gravely.

My heart beat joyously and erratically. I longed for one thing, that Maud de Ross would turn again and smile at me. Her attentions were entirely for her father. She continued to whisper urgently in his ear. She turned, with that flowing pure movement, and made for the door. Once there she turned again and faced the courtroom. Her eyes went quickly from the guardsmen at the door to the monk to the scribe, and fell on my face for as long as a butterfly hangs on a blossom. Then she nodded her head, and turned, and closed the door softly behind her.

I heard Sir Andrew de Ross say, 'I am called away on a sudden business. The *Maria* has made landfall, my ship. There are two cases yet to try. What are they, Piers?'

'Quentin Bell, of the Mill, for not paying his taxes. Sander Douglas and Archibald Grant, ploughmen, for drunkenness and fighting in the alehouse on Saturday night,' said the scribe.

'I will hear them tomorrow,' said the castellan, and rose to his feet.

Angus leaned over and said to me, 'You must be stirring too, Geoffrey. There are preparations to be made. I think I did not tell you, Geoffrey, but you are going on a sea voyage.'

*   *   *

'We will not!' said Walter Glendinning. 'We dare not do it! I have a care of the lives of all this crew. He is a murderous barbarian. Let me hear no more of Schvein.'

The ship *Maria* of Leith, Scotland, lay at the mouth of the Oder, having discharged at a small Allemand seaport — whose name I forget — a hundred sacks of Scottish meal, and seventy-eight wolf pelts, and fifty barrels of salted herrings. There, in his warehouse, the merchant Heinrich Holl had happened to remark that one Schvein ruled a stretch of the coast fifty-three miles further east, in the territory of Latvia. This Schvein was a nuisance to all the Baltic traders. He lived in a very old castle. Sometimes he claimed that he owed allegiance to the prince of Muscovy, at other times he said he was the king of Poland's man. But in fact, said Holl, this Schvein was a robber baron, who did what he pleased with impunity. He had ships that sometimes traded as far as Norway, but as often these vessels laid aside their legitimate trappings and appeared nakedly as pirates. And yet no one, it seemed, could do a thing about it. Schvein sat serene in his castle. One summer four of the German ports had entered into a league against Schvein, and besieged him by sea in his castle till the first storms of October. Schvein appeared at his seaward battlement from time to time and threw down on the bored sailors below mingled insults and courtesies. How delighted he was to have the honour of harbouring so many fine ships! — they were welcome to stay for as long as they liked — unfortunately at the moment he had nothing to barter for the treasures they had in their holds. . . . Another day he would call them "scum", "sea-rats", "sons of whores". But, insult or mockery, this Schvein was always laughing; there was no end to his good humour. He could not be starved out, that was the truth, because he owned a huge fertile tract of land along the river and a thousand men laboured in those immense wheat-fields. The strangest thing about this extraordinary pirate chief was that he owned a collection of the weirdest animals that could be seen — huge creatures with long curling hollow noses and ears like flags, and lions and leopards, and birds in cages that spoke the languages of men.

I had picked up my ears as soon as the merchant

Holl had said that name, Schvein. Had not my
master, Sir Andrew de Ross, uttered the same name,
casually, on the quay at Leith, just before we had
last weighed anchor? 'Now Geoffrey,' he had said,
'one last matter. I know this will be next to impossible.
But what I would very much like to get for Castle
Wyvis — don't laugh, now — is an animal the like of
which has never been seen in Scotland before. A
crocodile, for example, or a salamander. I need it
for a certain ceremony that is to take place at midsummer. Here in this pouch are five marks — I'm
willing to pay so much for the kind of creature I've
been speaking of. I leave it entirely in your hands,
Geoffrey. You may chance to hear of a certain
Schvein in one or other of the Baltic ports — they
tell me he trades in such exotic creatures. But no —
on second thoughts forget it, Geoffrey, it's impossible.
Dangerous too. It's just the passing whim of an old
man — a piece of vanity, to astonish the great ones
of Scotland. Think no more of this Schvein. If only
the *Maria* was longer in the keel by forty feet, then
you and Wat might sail her as far as Africa or
Cathay. There are plenty of strange beasts in those
places.'

Sir Andrew de Ross had of late come to put great
trust in me. I in return had begun to reverence him,
and was anxious to forward his prosperity and happiness in every way possible. For seven months now I
had sailed in the *Maria*, and had quickly gotten to
know the trade-routes, and the various merchants
and the goods they offered, and rates of exchange
and how to draw up bills of lading; so that after the

first two voyages, to Holland and to the Orkneys,
Wat Glendinning the skipper left these matters entirely in my hands. I found, somewhat to my surprise,
that I was a good man of business, and could make
seven marks into ten on most voyages, and sometimes
into as many as twelve or twenty. Also I enjoyed the
ritual of bargaining, with merchants stubborn or
subtle, in the swarming ports of Western Europe.

The blight upon this fine new life of mine was
almost constant sea-sickness, from the time of setting
out till we dropped anchor again at Leith. Even what
Wat called a calm voyage prostrated me. On the
first voyage, to Holland, I lay so ill among the feet
of the sailors that I wished for nothing but death.
I convinced myself that Sir Andrew — who was cold
and silent to me still — had chosen this way to be
rid of me. At that time there was no particular
affection either between me and my shipmates.
When we lay at last at anchor in Amsterdam, I saw
one morning an English vessel lying there taking in
cargo. 'What is to stop me,' I thought, 'from telling
that skipper my woes, and throwing myself on his
mercy? He will bring me home. My father will give
him a good reward.' For the three days that we lay
at Amsterdam, I worked out in some detail this way
of escape. At the same time I began to be fascinated
by the life of the teeming port. I wandered, sometimes alone, sometimes with Wat Glendinning, among
the markets and the booths; and Wat, who is a good
man, answered all my questions patiently and pre-
cisely. Yes, that heap of white curves was walrus
tusks from Norway. No, those barrels held wine, not

beer — red rich Burgundian wine, that the Dutchmen would carry to England, Ireland, Iceland. Those men with the melancholy eyes and the long curled beards were Jewish bankers. That crate over there, in the booth beside the church, that the merchant was opening now, it contained most fragile merchandise, Venetian glass — look now how the merchant is shouting and shaking a fist down towards the sea-front — one of the delicate glass pieces has been cracked in transit. . . . I mentioned casually to Wat that there was an English ship in the roadstead. Oh indeed, he answered: these were bales of wool that she had put ashore. . . . So, on the third afternoon, the skipper and I wandered deeper and deeper into the market-place. There, at a certain counter, Wat quickly did his business, which was to sell in the name of Sir Andrew de Ross, of Castle Wyvis, Scotland, a hundred tons of Fife coal and five tons of barley in exchange for which a bond was written out and sealed. 'Pay attention, Geoffrey,' said Wat Glendinning. 'I fear I'm poor at this kind of work. The merchants take advantage of me wherever I go. You are to do the haggling in future — Sir Andrew says so. This is a poor day's work — I should have held out for twelve more guilders than they've given me. They say the market is glutted with coal and barley. Maybe they're right. How is an old sailor to know?' Indeed the huge warehouse behind the booth of this particular merchant, when we walked through it, had black mountains of Alsace coal along one wall and, further in, a fragrant hill of Irish barley.

When we got back to the seafront the English

ship was sailing out of the harbour.

All that winter and next spring the *Maria* sailed back and fore across the North Sea, trading, and always I was on board, with the ledger in my keeping now. And always I was green and miserable with sickness. We sailed to Scapa in the Orkneys, and Bergen, and Lubeck, and Calais. The cargoes we carried were not always Sir Andrew's; as often as not we carried the goods of Edinburgh merchants, or of rich teeming estates in the heart of Scotland. Once, hired on behalf of King Robert, the *Maria* landed forty foot-soldiers on the coast of Ulster. I trembled that day at the thought that I was doing a traitorous thing, for were not those soldiers sent there to fight against the English, who held by right the overlordship of Ireland? But I succeeded in purchasing in Antrim a dozen Irish horses very cheaply for Sir Andrew de Ross, and in the excitement of that dealing I quite forgot the question of my allegiance and the doubtful matter that had taken me into this rebellious province.

On the way home, between the north of Scotland and the Orkneys, in the Pentland Firth, I did not think there could be such violence in any waters. And yet on that voyage, for once, I was not sick. I sat against the mast and wrote and calculated in the ledger, while even Wat retched at the wheel, and the horses in the hold whinnied and reared and rolled their eyes with terror.

Now we were here, at the mouth of the Oder, with slack sails. 'I tell you, Geoffrey, it's impossible! I know all about this Schvein. He'll cut our throats!'

'Sir Andrew,' I said, 'is particularly anxious to buy one of those animals.'

'I don't believe in this menagerie of Schvein's,' said Wat. 'Has anybody seen it? There are plenty of beasts in that castle, but they're all in the shape of men.'

'I did not think,' I said, 'that a Scottish skipper would be afraid of a Latvian barbarian.'

'Me feared!' cried Wat. 'I'm feared of nothing, neither hog, dog, nor devil. Never say that again! But I saw the old moon last night bearing the young moon in her arms, and everybody kens what that means. It bodes bad weather. The sooner we're out of this Baltic the better pleased I'll be.'

'It will be necessary for me,' I said coldly, 'to inform Sir Andrew de Ross that we were not able to purchase the beast he so urgently requires on account of the fact that the skipper was perturbed at seeing a ring around the moon.'

'Due east!' shouted Wat Glendinning, red in the face. The helmsman John leaned on the rudder. Wat never spoke to me for the rest of that day, while the *Maria* surged gently through the Baltic, going east. It was the end of May, and the sea was bright and calm. Just before sunset we saw the huge darkening bulk of Schvein's castle, and cast anchor half a league from the shore.

I was a bit afraid myself now, I don't deny it. I woke once in the darkness and heard a weird cry across the water. I wondered if it could be a centaur or a griffon. The sailors snored uneasily all round me, all except Wat, who had decided to keep watch himself, a thing that had never happened before.

I woke again, at dawn, and found myself looking
into slanted eyes and a huge brown beard. I heaved
on to my elbow. The ship was full of strangers.
Wat Glendinning was arguing, in his Scottish tongue,
with a man who clearly did not understand a word
of what he said. This man kept shaking his head
and gesturing, sometimes towards the castle, and
sometimes over the side of the ship. The man with
the vast forest beard raised me not unkindly to my
feet. I went and looked over the side. There were
two open boats there, roped to the *Maria*, and rising
and falling gently on the swell. Clearly we were
being summoned, or invited, to the castle of Schvein.

I said to the skipper that we must go — there was
nothing else for it. Wat nodded, but he looked like a
man who expects rack and rope and fire.

The man from the castle indicated that there was
no need for the crew to come. Only Wat and I were
to go with them. They were treating us, thus far
at least, with consideration and an outlandish courtesy.
But half-a-dozen men, with bare swords, stayed behind on the *Maria*.

The coast that I saw from the *Maria*, in the light
of morning, was dominated by the castle. It was ten
times as big as the little keep of Sir Andrew de Ross
in Scotland. It was set massively into the side of a
hill above the sea. All behind it the countryside
surged with cultivated fields and blacker forest than
I had ever seen. The wheat lay heavy and green to the
sun.

Our hosts smiled. They excused themselves with

slow gestures for what they must do. Blindfolds were put over our eyes. We were handed down into the small boats. For a while I heard nothing but the regular splash of oars; then, after a time, the grinding of a keel among stones. A rower raised me by the elbow, my legs sank to the knees in cold sea. Then my feet were among loose clashing stones.

I could not help thinking then of the shudders of the German merchant Holl when he had described this place to me; and the great barbarian who laughed all the time, even when the victims were impaled screaming on the stakes in the courtyard.

'Well,' I thought to console myself, 'every man has his day appointed. I might have died in the battle near Stirling. I might have retched myself to a ghost in the North Sea. That strange sickness in Castle Wyvis might have carried me off'. . . . But it was cold consolation – these would have been deaths gentle or honourable.

I touched the crucifix under my shirt.

Feet, mine among many, moved from stones to greensward to cobbles. We were in the castle court-yard. What was the sound? Dark mournful rhythmic phrases issued, many male voices, muted, from the heart of a labyrinth of stone.

I was still urged forward by the elbows, but not brutally. The echo of my footsteps suggested to my ears a long corridor, then a high stone chamber. I was halted. Feet withdrew. I sensed a single authori-tative presence; also the presence of a hound flowing and lolloping.

There was a brief silence – I was being keenly

scrutinised. Then a voice spoke in the same savage musical tongue I had heard before. I did not understand a single syllable.

How would it be possible to communicate with the Letts? I had picked up a little Flemish, and Norse, and Irish in the past few months. But this place and people must be outside the bounds of Christendom. I had heard that Latin was understood in the furthest places of the world. It was worth a trial. I said, 'Scotus sum. Mercator sum ex Scotia. Pax vobiscum,' into the coldness, blindness, silence.

At once the response came, also in Latin, only with a different inflection to the Latin I had learned from Brother Stephen in the Priory school at home. 'A Scottish merchant. What are you seeking here?'

'We have heard of the lord Schvein,' I said, and the Latin began, after the first awkward phrases, to come more easily. 'I bring greetings to the lord Schvein from the lord Andrew de Ross in Scotland. The fame of the lord Schvein is known in all the seaports from Spain to Iceland. All men have heard of the wealth of the lord Schvein, and of his generosity, and of his prowess in battle both on sea and land.'

The same question was repeated, as if all that flattery and unction and lies were seen for what it was. 'But why have you come here?'

For some time the hound had been trotting softly back and fore behind me. I felt a lingering warmth and moisture about my knuckles. The hound had kissed my hand. I took it for a good omen, remembering the hound-tongue that had folded my bleeding wrist in the courtyard of Castle Wyvis, on the day of my capture — my only welcomer that dark time.

'My master in Scotland has heard of the beautiful and strange animals that roam through the lands of the lord Schvein. He wishes to purchase one, if the lord Schvein is willing to sell it for five marks.' (At least there was truth in the last statement.)

'The lord Schvein is not here. The lord Schvein is in the chapel. The lord Schvein has been in the chapel for six days past. He has neither eaten nor drunk. The head of the lord Schvein is bowed low with grief.'

I said, after a long respectful pause, 'What bitter chance has befallen the lord Schvein?'

The voice came again, 'The lord Schvein has many curious animals, that is true. He delights in their innocence and strangeness and beauty. What makes you think the lord Schvein would sell one of his creatures — the nasnas or the abtu or the unicorn — to a barbarian lord in the western sea? You have done wrong to come here, at such a time.'

'I am sorry,' I said. 'We will leave at once, if it is your will. We will hoist the sail and return to Scotland.'

'By no means,' he said. 'I have not satisfied myself that you are not spies. I intend to make certain enquiries. You are to stay in this castle meantime. If it turns out that you are a spy, from the Allemands or the Swedes, you must be a brave young man indeed, or an excessively stupid young man. Or perhaps one who longs to embrace the finer ecstacies of death.'

He issued an order in his native language.

The strange foreign breaths came all about me again, and the hound went circling back to his master.

Again the touch to the elbow, and I was turned away, and led along corridors and under arches and down stone steps — the rhythms and echoes of our feet altering according as the walls and ceilings broadened, narrowed, spiralled, sloped.

What lay at the end of it all — a fire? a block and an axe?

Everywhere, sometimes loud, sometimes so low it could have been the fall of dewdrops and cobwebs, the dark lament from the heart of the castle could be heard. Then a door was unlocked and I was let into a narrower cell than my cell in Castle Wyvis — it was hardly bigger, to my senses, than a sepulchre. They left me then. For a while I listened to the far-off elegy, a cold formal sorrow. Some master of music had reduced a shapeless meaningless mischance to its pure essence, by means of certain black markings on parchment. This the tongues, throats, lips of the choristers gave out, beyond any further change or chance. Sorrow, that seems so alien to the things that men strive for all their days, was made into a pattern acceptable and fitting, a necessary vesture for the soul. I pondered for a while the mystery of art. Then I drifted into the stone of sleep.

*   *   *

'I am satisfied now that you are not spies. I have made enquiries. That ship out there is indeed a Scottish merchant ship. There is therefore no question of punishing you in any way. On the other hand, you cannot speak with the lord Schvein. Perhaps, in ordinary circumstances, he would out of curiosity have wished to see you. But, as things are, his period of mourning has eleven days to run. He will be cloistered in the chapel, with the corpse, all that time.'

The man who spoke these words to me the next morning was thick-set and ruddy, and of middle years. He was dressed in dark cloth breeches and a coat of the same weave, belted in thick leather, that came down almost to his knees. His hair was greying, and he had a thick moustache that overhung his mouth like a thatch, but no beard. His eyes were gray and shrewd. He had told me previously that his name was Stanislaus, and that he was the chief steward in the castle. And always, as he uttered his rather pedantic Latin, the black hound flowed between us, kissing that hand, seeking comfort from this.

There was no doubt that he was now well disposed to me. I therefore asked, once again, in a low respectful voice, what sad bereavement the lord Schvein had suffered?

'His lover is dead,' said Stanislaus gravely. Before I could enquire as to the name of this mistress, or sweetheart, or wife, and the nature of the illness that had carried her off, the steward said that had been a terrible morning, the third day of the new moon, when Vladimir had been carried out of the forest with the red wound on him. A cornered boar had turned on the hunters, and though Vladimir's spear had grazed it, it had rushed screaming on that most beautiful and excellent young man and torn a gash in his belly with its tusks. This had been the sight that the lord Schvein had seen, coming down the

winding stair that led from his counting-house into
the courtyard: his beloved, all dabbled with blood,
carried in by six blanched hunters. The lord Schvein
had bent over Vladimir and kissed him, first on the
mouth and then on the wound in his white belly. He
had said to the hunters, "Carry your precious burden
into the chapel. Tell the priests and the master of the
music. Bring me the black robe out of the wardrobe."
These were the last words he had said. Since that
hour he had sat in the chapel, beside the corpse of
Vladimir, without food or drink. 'And this will go on
for eleven days yet, till the funeral.'

I murmured a few elegiac words.

'Ah,' said Stanislaus the steward, 'it is a sight to
break the heart, that in the chapel. I go, from time to
time, to see it, and also to listen for a while to the
death music. The chapel is starred night and day with
a hundred candles. The faces of the singers appear
here and there in the wavering light. Altogether
apart from them, under a single purplish flame, on a
catafalque, lies the body of Vladimir. Over it bends
the mourner, as still almost as the corpse. The death
song goes on, night and day. At regular intervals a
priest comes and spills smoke over the corpse from
his censer — that happens four times a day. The
voices go on, full of pain and reluctance and praise.'

There was a long silence. Then, in a lighter tone,
Stanislaus said, 'But the work of the castle must go
on. Fires must be lit and bread baked, even though
the beautiful hunter is dead. The wheat doesn't stop
growing — it must fulfil its circuit in the same way
that beasts and young men with spears fulfil theirs. So

the lord Schvein has left his old steward outside the circle of grief, to get on with the business of the estate.'

I thanked him, once more, for the delicious breakfast he had given me, at his own table; also for his assurance that the skipper Walter Glendinning was safe on the *Maria*, and was waiting for me to come aboard.

'Young man,' said Stanislaus, 'I like you. I knew, from the moment my hound Jervis kissed your fingers, that there was no evil or deceit in you. If you had been a spy or a thief, Jervis would have leapt at your throat. Now goodbye. It is not likely that we will meet again. When the lord Schvein puts off his sackcloth, I will tell him a thing he will scarcely believe, that a young Scotsman came to the castle wanting to buy a minotaur. How Schvein will laugh at that, once the time for laughter returns to his mouth! As for actually purchasing one of those rare animals, an elephant or a monkey or a leopard, that of course is out of the question. The lord Schvein could not endure to part with a single one of his precious beasts.'

Then Stanislaus embraced me and let me go. Two barbarians with huge brown beards escorted me from the castle to the shore. As I passed out of the courtyard I glimpsed, among the spikes that ringed the wall, dark clottings, as if pitch or mud had been thrown upon the sharp ends of six or seven; and then I realized with a shock of horror that those were the heads of certain enemies of the lord Schvein.

I was rowed courteously out to the *Maria*. As I

clambered on board, a thing happened that had never happened before, and almost certainly will never happen again — my old friend Wat threw his arms about me and put a wet cheek against mine.

After the anchor had been weighed I noticed a live sack on the deck. That is to say, it was an ordinary sack, but something struggled inside it. 'That,' said Wat, following my gaze, 'is a present to Sir Andrew de Ross from the castle.' He untied the neck of the sack. An outraged creature fluttered out — a crested bird with an immensely long tail, the like of which I had never seen before. As we gaped at it, the creature made, slowly, an immense fan of its tail — as splendidly dyed it was, too, as any church window. Then it screamed at us.

*   *   *

At the quay of Leith Angus stood. We greeted each other with smiles and handshakes. I left Wat Glendinning and the sailors to see to the landing of the cargo. I told Wat to be particularly careful with the bird. Then Angus and I turned out horses' heads northward. Angus was most anxious to hear news of the voyage. He listened amazed to my account of the Baltic barbarian and his castle. 'Well,' said he, 'thank God you're alive, Geoffrey. There'd have been a power of lamentation this day in Castle Wyvis if all that came home of you was a headless body!'

We left our horses at an inn, and refreshed ourselves there with ale and cheese until we got a ferry to take us to the north shore of the firth. I asked Angus how things were at Castle Wyvis. 'There's little news,' he said. 'Morag — do you remember Morag, from last year's harvest? Well, Morag was delivered of a boy at the weekend, and no father has come forward.'

My heart sank like a stone. 'What will become of her?' I said. 'She will be disgraced for this! She is a very good gentle girl. I must see Morag as soon as I get back.'

Angus was aware at once of my agitation, and, no doubt, of the cause of it, for he leaned towards me and clapped his great hand to my shoulder.

'Morag is in high honour,' he said. 'The bairn was delivered in the castle. The best midwife in Fife was summoned for the lying-in. Sir Andrew was delighted, man. A good husband will be found for Morag.'

We stepped ashore on the north coast of the firth soon afterwards. Two horses were waiting for us there, in charge of my old enemy Finn. I recognized the finest gelding in the stable of Castle Wyvis, called Independence, that only Sir Andrew was allowed to ride. He had rode it into the battle near Stirling the year before. The bridle was put in my hand. And Finn, that I had always known for a brash uncivil man, said to me in tones of the utmost respect, 'A good home-coming to your honour, with all prosperity.'

From that point on the day began to drape itself in artifice and illusion, like a mime. Whether it was that I had been too long at sea, I don't know, but the June grass and the corn in the fields through which we rode had an abundance and greenness that I had not known before, and the wild flowers in the ditches were fair and enamelled, and the sun shone out of the sky in aureate splendour, among quiet heraldries of cloud. We crossed the last ridge and saw Castle Wyvis below us. And it was brave and dream-like, with three pennants (blue and silver diagonal crosses on each side of a silver and scarlet cross) straining in the wind above the topmost battlement. 'There must be peace at last betwixt the two king-doms,' I thought with relief.

The horse Independence, at sight of home, snorted and pawed the air. Then Angus and I rode down into a deepening dream. (It was no dream for him — he chattered gaily all the way, but even thus early I was so far lost in the dream that I could not remember a syllable of what he said — or only one strange phrase, 'The ransom is to stand for the dowry.')

The courtyard was abrim with smells of cooking and brewing. There was much stirring about the stables, and every creature I saw had put off his workaday hodden and was dressed for fairs.

Young men whose names I did not know, though I recognized them from the harvest field, helped me to dismount. They clustered about me, smiling and winking. (At the oat-cutting they had been all hos-tility or coldness.) They led me up the stone spiral to my cell above the sea. The dream had invaded my cell too. It was as if a rose had burst from a stone. That bare place was utterly transfigured. A tapestry flowed in the draught all along one wall. There were fresh-varnished shutters at the window, to close against darkness and storm, but they were not required on a day like this, for the chamber (I must call it that now) was full of the warm light of June. Where was my bench and my stool? In their place was a wide white bed, surmounted by a bronze crucifix, and two elegant tapestried chairs stood one on each side of the fire. Yes, I said fire, for certain stones had been removed from the back wall to reveal an ancient hearth, upon which a fire of coal and turf burned briskly, with intertwinings of yellow and red flames. The stone floor was strewn with rushes. It was as pleasant a little room as I had ever beheld, and there hovered about it an air of expectancy — it seemed to be holding its breath against some happy and blessed event.

In the meantime the young men, with courtesy and despatch, had begun to take my clothes off. And truly these seamen's garments, smelling of salt and fogs and the verdigris of foreign marts, had no part in the strange dream that was fastening itself about me like a subtle web. When they had me naked, they washed me thoroughly; or rather, in dream-parlance, they put upon me lustre of water, and afterwards dried me, and then they brought white linen garments from the white bed — so spotless each whiteness that I had not noticed the one laid upon the other — and they put these immaculate dream garments on me.

By this time I had no will of my own. I had yielded myself utterly to the dream — let these bright creatures of fantasy do with me what they would. It seemed to me that any word or action of mine, or any assertion of my will, would shatter the good illusion beyond mending.

When at last the thin white woollen stockings were

on my legs and the white soft leather shoes thonged about my ankles, the young men conducted me to the door. They too — as I said — were dressed for holidays, but in blue and green and yellow.

Surrounded by the young men, I went slowly down the spiral to the courtyard. The smells and the sounds of revelry were much multiplied in the last hour. Long tables were being set on trestles here and there, and girls and serving-men ran and shouted between the kitchens and the courtyard. On a little platform that had been erected against one wall a group of music-makers was gathered, trying out their lutes and pipes. At the edge of the platform sat a jester, his conical belled cap hanging over a melancholy face.

All at once, it seemed, the bustling creatures in the courtyard spied me and my retinue. They all stood stock-still, and silent, as if I bore an enchanted mirror before me; but only for a second or two; they turned from me back to their tasks, laughing, and the musicians began again to try out random twangings and flutings. The jester cried in a falsetto, 'Here comes the unicorn to his jousting!'

So spell-like and compelling had the dream become now that it seemed I did not move from then on. But what was to be — and the people and places that defined the inevitable — moved about me and drew me into itself. My feet beat, and summoned all these things about me. A pointed arch passed over me. Candles and incense fumes beset me with holiness and brightness; I found myself embowered in a chapel. A cluster of faces familiar and strange came about me, summoned, all with the trance of ceremony on them. The face of Sir Andrew de Ross, weathered by many wars and harvests, was there. I saw without surprise my father's face, alert and smiling and sensual. (In a dream nothing surprises the dreamer; a goblin-eyed immortal, he drags out of a dull box gauds and masks and mirrors.) A long scarred face with a circlet of gold at the brow gave me a quizzical glance. (To the dreamer kings are as common, and welcome, as hop-pickers and herdsmen.) The great enemy of my king, the Bruce, had been summoned to make this royal masque. I remembered that face from the battle, and how I had urged it then on to my innocent axe. But now there was peace between us.

The dream was suddenly all whiteness and blessing.

I summoned, kneeling (but it was, I knew now, the realization of a sacred conspiracy that had been woven about me in my absence), mitre, crozier, music, book, ring.

Out of some impossible winter the bride had drifted to my side. The music stopped. The bishop spoke. He challenged me, the seed-keeper. And I answered, 'I will.' He challenged her who was to bear and nurture the seed. Who answered, 'I will.'

* * *

Before dawn, somewhere in the castle grounds, the strange bird shrieked three times.

SOLDIER FROM THE WARS RETURNING

The battle was over. I was well on my way home. How the battle ended I have no memory of. I did not hear the trumpeter sounding victory, nor did I see our standard planted on the ridge. The last thing I have a memory of is a knot of vivid faces, and yelling mouths and fierce frightened wide eyes. I was so deep in the battle then that I did not know whether these soldiers were mine or the enemy's. All faces, friend and foe alike, bore the same terrible mask. The only exception was our good marquis; he had sat since morning on his horse at the edge of the battle as if all that passed was falconry, or a game of tennis.

Presently out of that masque of terror and rage and cruelty a gun was produced and levelled at me, I thought; though the musketeer's hands shook so much that he may have had another adversary in view. I decided, to preserve life and limb, to do something heroic and decisive in the matter. I did not know the soldier with the gun, but he looked to me to be a usurper's man. I thrust my lance at his throat. I may have despatched him, but I think not. Hands pushed the lance away, a sword flashed somewhere to the right. There was a more vivid violent flash in my face, a thunderous noise, and white smoke.

About that time victory must have fallen to our good marquis. The battle ended. The hosts of Low-landers and mercenaries and bible-men broke suddenly. They turned and fled, in wild panic and disorder; and the men from the mountains after them, their naked legs splashed with blood and clay; they screamed out cries of Gaelic triumph; they cut the bleak air with their claymores. . . .

At least, this must have happened. And our marquis must have thanked those round the standard with his sweet mouth, and uttered also a few elegaic words concerning the dead — both our own and the usurper's, such a charitable heart he has. And we must have cried out our joy and thankfulness in each other's arms, and afterwards taken what we thought might be serviceable from the dead on the ground (who no longer needed brooch or cutlass). And very likely too some of the wolves in our army — even an army led by such a paragon as our general is likely to have a certain amount of the bestial and the depraved in it — some of these creatures, drunk with the victory, indulged I have no doubt in an orgy of looting, and took a special pleasure in despatching those who still stirred and moaned on the field.

I say this must have happened, for I have no clear memory of it. I seemed to emerge at last from a great and glorious banquet, and I found myself walking northwards, alone, along a lonely track. My lance lay aslant on my right shoulder, and there was an eager fire in the centre of my chest, such as a victorious soldier must carry afterwards to all the duties and affairs of ordinary life; for all the remainder of his days will have the blazon of victory on it.

I knew roughly where I was: the moor of Caithness. The mountains were behind me, where none of our Orkney volunteers had been at home; they had felt hemmed in and menaced by those huge presences. I

was walking towards the coast. Some fishing boat or
cattle boat would carry me across the Pentland Firth
to Orkney. At the thought of home a joyous trembl-
ling took hold of my spirit. In another day, at most,
I would see the farm again, and my mother and sisters; and after a decent period I would excuse myself
and take my cloak about me and make for the door.
And then my mother, for sure, would seem a bit put
out, and my sisters would laugh and touch their
fingers with their lips. All the household, even the
dog, knew that I was going to greet Marion in the
Mill, across a field and a burn. What I would say to
that sweet and precious girl I still did not know, but
even a spate of gibberish — even a rapt silence —
would show how glad and thankful I was to be back
with her once more. And then I would get a grip of
myself, and tell her, quietly and soberly, the story of
the victory; and explain to her how that victory had
put the true king on the throne of our land once more.
I quickened my steps.

It seemed to me rather strange that I was not walking in company with some of the other Orkneymen
who had followed the marquis. But then, I thought,
none of them is burning like me to get home. They
are all unattached young men. But I had a serious
business to do — to carry on my family estate, to
marry my sweetheart and to breed out of her a new
generation of hard-working loyal Thorbertsons.

I topped a low ridge and saw, a mile off, the bay,
the boats, the fishermen, and the molten pewter of
the Pentland Firth; and beyond that the dark sublime
shape of Hoy, the most southerly of the Orkneys.

I called to the fishermen through the clear air, but they kept their heads bowed over their lobster creels.

What churls they were, those Caithness fishermen! Not a man of them would speak to me, or even so much as look at me, though I asked over and over again if any of their boats would be crossing the Firth that day. 'I know how it is with you, my fine fellows', I said to myself. 'You have given your allegiance to the regicides and the traitors. And you will not speak to a man who has been loyal and true. Have it your way – the young king will know how to deal with creatures like you' . . . .

At the far end of the bay some flagons and boxes were being loaded on to a yawl, and I heard occasional words and phrases from the seamen: 'delivery to the Orkneys'. . . . 'Be back tomorrow, with eggs and feathers'. . . . 'Yes, sailing at once, a good tide'. . . .

I hurried over towards this boat, and had just scrambled on board when she was pushed off and the sail was raised. They were carrying passengers indeed. I saw two young women and an elderly man huddled against the sea-cold at one side of the boat. It was not a cheerful boat. The crew shifted about their tasks like men with a grudge against the world.

Once we were clear of the land, the skipper approached the trio of passengers – money was exchanged. I hurriedly searched in my breeches' pockets; there was not a bawbee; soldiers don't take coins into a battle with them. What excuse could I make? I decided to be bold and plain with him.

'Well, skipper', I called out, 'Have you come for my fare? I'm sorry to say, I haven't a penny. That's to say, I'm penniless as I stand, but the Thorbertsons aren't paupers exactly. There are one or two brass chests in the cellar at Coolin that have plenty of white and yellow discs in them. You'll be well paid, never fear, next time you're in Hamnavoe on a market day.'

The skipper paid no attention to me, nor did any other soul on board that vessel. Instead, he and the gray-beard passenger were muttering low and earnestly to one another. There were head-shakings. I saw that one of the young women was weeping; her sister put a hand on her shoulder to comfort her.

What kind of bleak spell was on this boat? I decided to break the spell, if I could, with good news.

I raised my voice, so that all the crew might hear, 'What's all this misery about? By rights you should be dancing on the deck. It seems you can't have heard the splendid news from the straths. The king has won a great victory. It's true. I saw it. I was there on the field of battle!'

My tidings made as much impression on their ears as the small surge from the prow. Not one so much as raised his head. The skipper and the father of the two girls were deep still in their dark conversation, and the girl who had quiet tears on her face now sobbed loud and openly.

The boat had indeed caught a favourable tide; she surged with hardly a quiver between the slumbrous whirlpools. Hoy shifted to the left. Other islands appeared. The boat drove fast towards the Orkneys. The sail creaked in the light wind.

By now fragments of their conversation came to my ears. 'Cut to pieces. . . . Every man of them killed, I hear. . . . A sad day for the women of Orkney. . . .'

What was the old man — a minister of the gospel? His voice rose, sonorous and ecclesiastical — 'I'm deeply sorry for those young ignorant men. What do ploughmen know about great affairs of state? They should have bidden at home. They should never have listened to that scented creature with the golden tongue. Well, he will soon have his deserts, the marquis. He's a prisoner in the Tolbooth of Edinburgh, I hear, and condemned. He's to be made a public spectacle. . . .'

I need not say how these words tore into me more cruelly than any sword or bullet. This, I knew, was the truth I was hearing, and the victory I had carried with me through mountain and moor had been a dream.

The second sister was weeping now.

So this is why they didn't speak to me — this is why they let on not to be aware of my presence. I am the survivor of a beaten host. It is, in their manner of looking at things, bad luck to have dealings with one whose fortune is a dark star. No, it is worse — it is treasonable. The wonder is that they allowed me on their boat at all.

The islands were all round us now. The boat dipped through a gray inland sea. I was nearing home.

The horror and pain and grief that the old man's voice had put on me was succeeded, after a time, by a pang of wonderment. How was it that I had not known defeat from victory? In the flushed heart of battle no soldier can know how the dice are falling. He is swayed by forces he has no control over — the numbers involved, the cunning and war-craft of his general, the slope of the ground, the morale of the enemy, even whether it has rained on the terrain the day before.

*   *   *

The village of Hamnavoe, with its tall merchants' houses and its fishing bothies, was before us now. Soon the boat was tied up at the pier. A few boys came down to meet us. I knew better now than to renew my offer of a fare to the skipper.

How glad I was to have my feet once more on solid ground! A walk of seven miles would take me home. I would get there just as they were lighting the lamps.

On the road home I met with a few more hurts and rebuffs, the worst one being that my friend and school-mate Charlie Scott passed me on his horse with a cold unseeing face. The horse's head drooped and snorted so close to me that I could have seized the bridle. Then rider and horse spurred on towards the village. He did not turn his head at my second disconsolate cry.

So Master Scott had turned his coat too, who had drunk all last winter to the king's return. I had seen his eager mouth on the hand of the marquis. To turn from a cause is bad. Is it not even worse to turn from the friend of a life-time? I stood for two desolate minutes in the middle of the road.

Here and there, further on, a farmer or a farmer's girl, who would have waved a greeting in fairer time, turned away from me, into barn or byre. Worst of all were the eyes, like Scott's, that looked right through me.

Timothy the hawker came up from the loch with a small trout in his hands. He would cook it over a fire in the quarry after dark. I had never had time to spare for such thieves and parasites, and I hurried on past him. 'Master Thorbertson!' he cried. The trout fell out of his hands. His face went white. 'God give you peace!' And he crossed himself, the way those vagrants still do though the papists have had no say here for a hundred years. Then he picked up his fish and turned and stumbled on towards the quarry.

It wasn't exactly a rapturous greeting. Why then was I so happy suddenly? A man had recognized me for the first time since that gunner had fixed me with frantic eyes on the battlefield. I walked on, filled with reassurance and a kind of wellbeing, into the sunset.

The dark smithy was seething with voices. Here I used to come and sit with the ploughmen and the shepherds many a winter evening, to tell stories and hear opinions. Sometimes, when the older men were absent, a bawdy verse or two would be sung. It was in the smithy that we had heard the first wonderful rumour that the marquis had arrived, secretly, in Kirkwall, with the king's commission.

It seemed to be all old men in the smithy this evening. They were talking of those who had been killed in the battle — a dark dreadful litany. 'Walter from Garth, he was seen on the field, though his face was half shot away'. . . . 'Yes, and Tom from Biggings — he was seen swinging from a branch — they hanged him'. . . . 'Willie Omand died in some bothy next day — Andrew Moar spoke to the man who kept the place'. . . . 'Andrew himself, he's wanting a leg. I doubt he won't live to see the harvest. He would be better dead. How can a farmer do his work with only one leg?'

All those young men I had known since childhood. We had marched singing from the sea to the mountains the day before the battle. Now I was home alone (except for Andrew Moar with his doomed remnant of limb).

'Ah', said an old voice, 'and what will they do now, the four women up at Coolin? Their strength and their hope cold clay. A sad bitter thing. They can't work a big farm like that alone. Never. I heard she was thinking of going to bide with her brother in Westray. She would be well advised indeed to sell the farm soon, for whatever sum she can get for it. For if she lingers there overlong, she might be made to answer for her son's treasonable doings.'

It took me some time to realize that the old man was speaking about me and my family and farm. Each man thinks that his own private world is the real one — others have no interest or entry there, they are shadows forbidden by the secret mark above the lintel. He resents an intrusion into his privacy.

I said in a low voice at the smithy half-door, 'No, I'm here. Look. I escaped from the battle. I got home.'

Did I speak so low that they couldn't hear me? Were they so afraid of the traitor in their midst that they resolutely shut me out of their talk?

'A bad business,' said Robbie Tuam the tailor.

'They were well told to bide at home. John Reid, too, he's another one. He was seen on the battlefield. Drew said it was as if a plough had passed over him.'

'That's the end of the Thorbertsons,' said the blacksmith. 'An old proud family.'

I stayed no longer in that ignorant doorway. I couldn't wait to get home, to prevent my mother from doing a thing not only unnecessary but desperate: to put an axe to the root of one of the old families — for it would be that, if she were to sell the estate, and their heir still alive and lustful and strong.

'They're sitting long in the dark tonight,' I said to myself when I stood on the ridge above the farm. But when I got closer the windows were shuttered and the door was padlocked. And the dog Trust, who had gone everywhere with me, he circled the yard, and he set up such a hellish hullabaloo of barking and howling that it set my teeth on edge. 'Come boy. Come, Trust,' I murmured to him. With a last frantic yelp the good creature turned tail and fled towards the hill.

By now the first stars were out.

Where else could I go now but to that dear person who must carry our seed on into the future, until in God's good time these evil things were done away with and the ancient kingdom was restored, even though that might take a century, and we were not likely to see it in our time.

A horse cropped the grass at the end of the Mill.

I knew how to get into the Mill without disturbing old Phil and his goodwife. I lifted the latch quietly and went in on tiptoe, and paused for a moment in the passage till my breath grew quiet again. Marion spent her evenings in her own sleeping-place at the far end of the house, where she had peace to sew her bridal linen, away from those tumultuous young nephews who kept the old miller and his wife in constant states of alarm and delight.

I felt my way to the door at the end of the long passage. I opened it. There was darkness and quiet breathing. I looked down on two faces asleep, it seemed, in the peace after love.

I had known for some time now — since the Caithness shore, I think — that indeed I had been killed in the battle, and was a homing ghost.

But death is never the end of any story.

Marion stirred in her sleep, and turned her face, faintly smiling still, towards the quiet beard on the pillow beside her.

I had not thought that pain like this was possible. In my body I had experienced nothing like it. Rage, and grief, and pride enwrapped me, a patched cloak of flames.

I will follow this harlot to the end of her days. She will have no peace.

And then, thank God, a passing wonderment touched me — I think it was a little of the ancient wisdom that we country folk absorb from the feel of the earth under our feet, and the taste of the broken oat in the barn. What is love, to a young country girl? (Men have put all kinds of sweetnesses, swoonings, raptures, sentimentalities into the word.) For a country girl like Marion love is simply the hunger in her womb for the seed. A hearth-stone of her own, a spinning-wheel, a lamp are waiting for her — but most of all a cradle in a corner. If one man cannot give her these things, she will find another who can and will. War, nor famine, nor earthquake will keep her from what is due to her.

She wants her man in his true place — ploughing his fields, harvesting, fathering children. It is the only glory that country folk will ever know.

I remembered Marion's bitter hurt face the day I took the old lance down from the rafters, and joined my comrades at the end of the road. Then, after the cheering, when I returned to kiss her goodbye, she wasn't there.

Out of loyalty to my king I had betrayed my fields and our unborn children. This is the way that women look on war and love.

What could a ghost expect: that a girl like Marion would spend the rest of her days weeping over a tombstone? The hunger in her body is more important than a fool of a lover who had marched away to a war he knew nothing about.

I opened my coat. There, where I thought the fire of victory had smouldered, was a terrible seeping wound. Andrew Moar had seen it on the field at Carbiesdale. He had brought the word home to Marion and to my mother and sisters. But where in the world was my place now, and my peace?

There came then a second infusion of sweetness. I had a sudden urge — it opened in me like a spring — that I should revisit the battlefield; find perhaps the musket that had killed me; kiss the barrel; forgive my enemy who had made the flash and the thunder and the smoke in my face.

I left the guardians of the seed to their sleeping.

I stood in the night outside. The horse that cropped the grass under the stars was Charlie Scott's — he who had had the wisdom to bide at home when the other young ploughmen had marched away. His farm at Althing would have a good mistress soon.

I turned away from the dark lovers in the Mill.

Then I set out on a journey without inns or tolls or milestones, for a tryst that I had experienced but had not understood.

PASTORAL

(1)

Honour'd Sir, I take leave to tell you there has lately been such a spate of sheep-thieving in this parish as I have never known. Howie Will of Brandon and Jeremiah Clett of Hammarvoe were at my door early in the week with their complaints. Five ewes gone in the one case, two in the other. 'We look to you, Master Blyth, as the factor, to see to it that the thieves are taken and punished.' That was the identical last words of each of them at my door. On the Wednesday it was Mr Tarff the minister. Two Glebe sheep were vanished from the hill. 'If Sir Thomas were at home,' says he, 'a thing like this would not have happened.' His reverence does not have a high regard for me.

I pray you give me leave to root out this lawlessness in my own fashion. I know well, in this parish some of them consider me over tolerant and complaisant. But more often than not in the end I make a sure finish of whatever business I embark upon.

As yet, Sir, I do not know who the thief or the thieves are. There are one or two gangrels and paupers on the roads who would not scruple to take a sheep, if they were starving and the night was dark. But such poor men would not raven to this extent.

I have written to the sheriff in Kirkwall.

Tomorrow, God willing, I will send Samuel up to the hill, in a casual way, to make as it were a rough count and assessment of the mingled herds.

But I think it is not one of our own people. I pray that it cannot be a tenant of yours. For if it were, and it were proven against him, I tremble to think of what must follow.

Norbister the shepherd tells me there is none of your sheep gone, so far. He made an exact count yesterday.

I will let you know, Sir, how things unfold with regard to this black business. (My pen has scurried over the page so fast and indignant that I have not said where my own suspicions fall. All I need say on that matter is that three Dutch boats were fishing off the Gray Head Saturday until Wednesday, and are now manipulating their nets off Hoy. Men who are long on the sea grow sick of herring at last — they have fair dreams of mutton broth.)

You ask kindly after Ella, my daughter and your god-daughter. Sir, with the years she loses nothing of the sweetness she had as a child. There is something more, a bloom on her since the ending of winter, a delight in everything that exists, that makes an ageing man like me both glad and rueful. It is as if the dear creature moved about the house to unheard music. She is a constant joy to me, in my loneliness and my troubles. What it is, I think the creature is, if not in love, at least in that condition that looks towards the seed-time of the body, and a fair harvest beyond. Thus, in spite of all this contentment that blesses my house nowadays, another worry has fallen. It's certain she can never marry with any crofter's son, to spend the rest of her days spreading dung and digging out peat. I think now seriously of sending Ella by the next boat to my sister Sophie in Edinburgh, her aunt. It is time that the girl learned some art and refinement and manners. If she were to spend a year in more polite society than she could possibly encounter in this bleak parish of ours, then it is possible she might meet a young man, a merchant or a lawyer, that will make her heart beat strangely, and she will recognise the true husbandman of her glebe.

In all other ways, Sir, the estate flourishes. The weather has been good for oats and barley and beasts, a sufficiency and balance of sun and rain and wind. The first green shoots are through, and all is full of promise, though there is yet a long time betwixt now and harvest.

The gangrels are still in the quarry, since winter. I know you would not wish me have them sent on into another parish or island, until they are rid in some measure of their winter thinness and coughings. Daily the woman Rachel gets a can of soup from Thomasina Skea at this door.

I hear of no betrothals, but I did observe in the kirk last Sabbath certain looks and blushings betwixt Robert of Sieves and Eliza the youngest daughter of Hillside, that had nothing to do with his reverence's discourse. And it has been whispered to me that little Willa Redd of Tensetter has had an autumn seeding, and is like to prove fruitful by the middle of summer. She will not mention a name, nor has the untimely sower declared himself.

I await your news and instructions, Sir, with more than usual expectation, and have the honour to remain, Sir,

Your most obedient servant,
Alexander Blyth.

2

. . . . The sheep-reft has died down, I am thankful
to say, but while it lasted it was worse than I thought,
for I have since heard belated reports of further
thieving in the course of these four nights. Hardly had
I sealed my last letter when I heard the voice of
William Erne of Burnlea at the door, demanding to
see me. Two of his lambs had vanished from the hill
on the Saturday night. 'And,' says he in that black
dangerous voice of his, 'let me get a whiff of the
thief, there will be no need to send for sheriff or
lawmen, I'll break him with my own hands.' Then he
leaves me, but not before he has put a look on me
sufficient to say, 'It is for you and for you alone,
factor, to seek out the criminal and have him punished.'
William Erne of Burnlea has little of honey in his
nature, yet he is a good tenant, and pays his rent
regularly, and I will satisfy him if I can.

The minister has been at my door again, ostensibly
to enquire what news there was of you, and whether
you had yet spoken in the Parliament on the question
of the new excise laws and the large amount of
smuggling that followed on account of their severity.
I answered that the debate was long over and done
with, and you had been too indisposed on that occasion to speak; matters with which he was perfectly
well acquainted. It was obvious to me that he had
come on other business. 'Does Sir Thomas know about
the sheep thieving? Have you written of the outrages
that occur nightly on the hill?' 'You know well (I
answered) that I have written to the laird in London,

for I told you so last time we spoke together.' Did I
know, he next enquired, that two unmarried girls in
the parish were with child? I said that the fruitful
bodies of the young women here are not my proper
concern, but indeed I had heard that Willa Redd would
give birth before harvest-time, and the child as yet
had no named father. 'Father!' cried Mr Tarff. 'Father,
indeed! I know who the father is! The whole parish,
except yourself, it seems, Master Blyth, knows well
who the father is. The father is none other than
James Tormiston. Yes, James Tormiston of Arbister.
That same James Tormiston has proved, in the past
winter or two, to be a worthless and a wicked young
man. The other girl too, Janet Kierfea, it's well said
(and I for one believe it) that James Tormiston has
intruded upon her virginity too. The girl has said
nothing as yet, not even to her mother, not even to
her father when he threatened her back with his stick.
But it will out, it will out!. . . .' So his reverence ranted on. This, it seemed, was why he had come to see
me, not out of concern for smuggling or sheep-reft,
but merely to put squarely before me the iniquities
of this young lad. I took Mr Tarff indoors, and decan-
ted a glass of brandy, in the hope that he might be
mellowed thereby. Rather, it inflamed his holy rage.
I declare his reddening face was a spectacle. He would
have the young scoundrel before the kirk session, if it
was the last thing he did; more, he would have him
standing in the sackcloth of shame before the entire
congregation.

'Mr Tarff,' I said, 'drink down your brandy. Tormiston and his lovers and bairns unborn are not my

concern. I am glad you have lost no more sheep. Good
day to you. I have much work to do in the laird's
ledgers and account book − you must excuse me − it
grows near to the term.'

I do not think a word of what I said sank in. He
nosed and lipped and grimaced over the brandy again
(and whether or no he knew it was a smuggled keg,
like the rest of our store, I do not know) and pro-
ceeded to make new variations on the theme of James
Tormiston. The blackguard was more than a fornica-
tor, it seemed. For one thing, he had not darkened
the kirk door since last harvest; but darken it again
he would, most certainly, if he had indeed put shame
on that poor lass Janet Kierfea, and that before the
month was out. But there was more still. Did I know
− this surely concerned me, as factor − that Jacob
Tormiston was working the croft of Arbister alone,
an old done man like that, without any help at all
from his wastrel of a son? It was true. And the croft
difficult to work, set as it was in what could only be
described as a moor. And what does the bold James
do while his father is digging and ditching and yoking?
He has built himself a yawl down at the shore, he
catches lobsters and haddocks. 'Ah ha,' cried his
reverence, fortifying himself yet again from the brandy
glass, 'you did not know that, did you, Mr Blyth?
And yet it is a part of your duty to know such
things, for a proportion of any fish that a tenant catches is due to the laird. I would see to it. I would stir
myself to make enquiries about that young man.'

I said, so coldly that even he must have felt my
displeasure, 'Young James is not a tenant. And

moreover Sir Thomas allows the fishermen to take what fish they want, without reckoning his own portion.'

He licked the last fiery drop out of his whiskers, and set down the glass, and clapped his bonnet to his head.

'Mr Blyth,' he said at the door, 'I have come here out of friendship and regard for you. You too have a daughter.'

'Good morning to you,' I said.

'You will let me know,' he said, 'if there are any developments with regard to the sheep stealing.'

Then with a scatter of hooves about the cobbles he was off.

I hope you will be in some measure entertained by the above over-lengthy account of the conversation I had with the parish minister. I must confess, I wielded the pen at such lengths not primarily to entertain you, Sir, but to rid my heart of a load that presses on it lately, I know not why or how. That outburst of Mr Tarff was pompous and ridiculous; yet I too sense something evil and dark and mysterious at work in the island lately. Perhaps it is only that I miss so greatly the sweet blithe presence of my daughter. More of her anon.

The 'mystery' I speak of manifested itself on the very day of his reverence's visit, in the afternoon. I was asleep in the great chair beside the fire – you must know, Sir, that this past year or two I have taken to falling asleep after the hearty dinner that Mistress Skea daily provides me with. Well, Sir, I woke up with a start to find someone standing over by the window.

You would do well to say impatiently, 'Someone. Who? Surely my factor knows all the hundred and eighty souls in the island.' I do indeed, or most of them; there are one or two very old people, or secret withdrawn people, that I am not so sure about – I have glimpsed them once or twice, and may even have passed words with them; a face abides in the mind, but obscured and forgotten about, so little need is there to summon up an image of it. Well, sir, such was the face that glimmered in the light from the tall window; one half-remembered and half-forgotten, yet unmistakeably of the island. I could not put a name to the woman, whoever she was. (One is never at one's brightest, awakening out of a day-time sleep.)

'Well,' I said, getting to my feet, 'you have given me a start! Has Mistress Skea let you in? Mistress Skea should have told you to come back later in the day.' (For I was displeased at the intrusion, and meant to let my visitor see my displeasure, though not too arrantly.)

'Now,' I said, 'what can I do for you?'

Her lips merely moved. She made a shape with her mouth. A low sound issued, hardly more than a breath.

So, she was one of those shy creatures who are stricken half-dumb in presence of authority.

'Come,' I said. 'You can be quite open with me. Tell me your trouble.'

Again the low brief half-articulate whisper.

'I remember you, of course,' I said. 'But for the moment I forget your name. Don't you come from one of the hill crofts? Which one?'

She shook her head impatiently — as if who she was and where she came from were of no consequence — and again, for the third time, made that mysterious utterance. This time I understood. It was a name she spoke. She said, 'James Tormiston.' There was no mistaking it.

'Well,' I thought to myself. 'This young man James Tormiston is fairly making a name for himself in the island. Here's another woman come to complain about the sullying of her daughter by James Tormiston. How many more will there be, before that young stallion stops his rampaging?'

'What about James Tormiston?' I said. 'You understand, his behaviour is no concern of mine, so long as he abides within the law.'

She gave me a last fierce look and made for the door.

'James Tormiston' — that was the simple burden of her message. A name merely, stark and unqualified.

I could make nothing of it. After a moment's perplexed lingering beside the table, I followed the woman through the door and along the corridor. I threw open the main door, meaning to call her back, and that sharply and peremptorily.

But there was no-one in the yard or on the road above. That emptiness did nothing to improve my humour.

'Mistress Skea, a word with you!' I said to my housekeeper in the kitchen. 'Why have you let me be interrupted? I have a sleep every day after my dinner. You know that. Who was the woman you let in?'

The good old soul is devoted, but deaf. Twice more I thundered out my displeasure, and demanded a name.

She shook her head dumbly. Her hand trembled. She was near to tears.

She knew nothing of what I was speaking about, she said.

At that, of course, I was sorry, and pressed her hand, and begged her not to distress herself — it was, I proclaimed into her deaf ear, a matter of no consequence. At that she smiled, and the kitchen was full of kindness and sunlight again.

It was a dream. I have convinced myself of that. The woman had no true existence. Her face was vivid but vague; I have thought about it; it was the kind of patchwork face that you glimpse in a dream, made out of many faces, it seems. And the name that she uttered so darkly — why, had I not heard the minister shouting it a score of times earlier in the day? No wonder it had strayed into the strange patterns and intonings of sleep.

As if the name of this unimportant lad were fated to dominate one entire day, I heard it spoken by a third mouth before sunset. I told you in my last letter, I think, that the gangrels were in the quarry, and have been since the start of winter. At this time of the year they generally move on into another parish, to see what hospitality lies in that airt; and then your tenants come down to take unhindered whatever stone they require for the repairing of kiln or byre. Thomasina Skea told me yesterday that they are still there, by reason that one of their infants is sick. And indeed just at sunset I glimpsed Ezra at the gate, through my window. Had I such a thing, he said in that sharp flashing voice all these tent-dwellers have, as a drop of brandy for a bairn that might be dead in the morning if it didn't get it? While Thomasina Skea was broaching the jar of brandy in the cupboard, I asked Ezra if he knew anything at all about the missing sheep. 'May God strike me dead,' he cried, 'it wasn't me! That's a hanging crime, mister. I get as many rabbits as I want for the stewpot. I never ate mutton in my life.' I assured Ezra that I entertained no suspicions against him. But the quarry was above the beach — had he seen the Hollanders come ashore any nights last week?

'I saw them with my own eyes,' said Ezra, 'four nights on the run, men blundering down to the shore with burdens. The few words they spoke I couldn't understand. There was a reek of blood as they went past.'

Mistress Skea returned with a phial of spirits. Ezra put all manner of blessing on me. Might I live to dandle my grandchildren's children, etcetera. And Mistress Skea, too, she was worthy of all temporal and heavenly blessings for the stew and broth and bread she gave to the poor wandering folk of the earth.

Ezra lingered awhile at the gate in the ebbing light. Then he said suddenly, 'That lad from Arbister — young Tormiston — he's a good lad that. He gives me a fish most days. God forbid I should ever have to rhyme a black ballad about him and sing it in the streets of Kirkwall!'

James Tormiston again! — the name was still wandering like a sinister echo through the day. What was it to me, if a fisherman gives a tinker a haddock, or gets a girl with child?

Ezra raised his bonnet. Then he turned and ran across the field, his feet splashed with dew and the splendours of sunset.

I know, Sir, what you must be saying, there at your table in London — 'What has gotten into Sander Blyth, that old factor of mine? He's written a letter as long as a sermon, that common-sensical man. And all about a dream, and the chatter of a tinker, and some randy fisherman or other. The islanders will get over the loss of a few sheep. It's high time I was getting back to Orkney, before my estate disintegrates in a whirl of words.'

Sir, the worst of the letter is past. I will hasten on to a conclusion.

Hear then some good news. The weather has favoured the crops of barley and oats this year more than I have ever known. The whole district within the dyke is a flush and tumult of green, and all the animals and their young on the hill are healthy. Earth and sea rejoice under a fruitful sun.

I know that you will want to know about Ella. Sir, she has been out of the island this past seven days. By now she will be in Edinburgh, at Sophie's house, and I trust with all my heart she is more composed and happy than the day she left. I never saw the dear child so upset. She pleaded with me to let her bide on at Garth. She would die, she said, if she had to live in the city. 'Now, Ella,' I said to her, 'now, my dear, all the preparations are made. Your aunt Sophie has been written to and expects you. Your chest is locked, the boat is waiting at Hamnavoe. There's no turning back now. All young women of your class must go to the city sooner or later, and taste society and manners. You're not a milk-maid.' 'I wish to God I was,' she said. Then, after a miserable silence, she actually turned on me with flashing eyes. 'You're wicked,' she cried. 'You're cruel! You'll suffer for this. Anyone that interferes with the heart, the way you're doing, deserves to suffer!' And then the poor creature, in sorrow for what she had said, flung her arms round my neck and wept long and bitterly and unashamedly. There stood Samuel at the gate, with her trunk on his shoulder, shuffling his feet and coughing with embarrassment. (In this island a man sees emotion like that once in a generation, perhaps.) At last she was quiet, and took her arms from about my neck, and put a small sad kiss on me. 'God bless you,' was all I could manage. And then she was off, a slow joyless reluctant adventurer, and Samuel jogging after her with that burden on his shoulder. They were round the corner of The Hall soon, and I saw her no more.

By this time, no doubt, my daughter will have had her first taste of the delights of city life, and this island will be a bleak fading dream to her. To enter society is her duty and her birthright. The day will come when she will bless me for having forced her out of this narrow life that we lead here.

Since Ella is gone, this house echoes like a tomb.

(3)

. . . . I keep my door open every Friday morning, and those with requests or petitions or complaints lay them before me at that time. Some Fridays I am sore taxed to satisfy them; on other Fridays I sit solitary at my desk till dinner-time.

Last Friday morning, as I was tying my cravat, I heard a shouting down at the shore. 'They're at it again, those fishermen,' I thought to myself, and went downstairs.

A petitioner was waiting for me, an old unquiet man. The face slowly emerged from the shadows — I recognized the tenant of Arbister.

He said, in that quiet fated voice so many of the old ones have, that he was feared for the safety of his son. Could I not do something to keep them from doing a mischief to Jamie? He had been wakened last night by a noise about the house — voices, a stone at the door, the dog frantic in the shed. He had gotten out of bed and unfastened the latch. Five men stood at the door. He knew the voices of some of them. It was a moonless night. Upon his asking what they wanted there at that ungodly hour, they said it was his son that they wanted to speak to. (But his son James had been at Kirkwall since the afternoon previous, with lobsters to sell — and this he had told them.) By this time, said the old man, his eyes had grown accustomed to the darkness, and he recognized all five — David Redd of Tensetter, George Kierfea of Scad, Howie Will of Brandon, Jeremiah Clett of Hammarvoe, William Erne of Burnlea. Their eyes, he said, seemed to smoulder in the darkness. One said they'd come at night because the night was Jamie's time for business. He had then asked David Redd if this visit was because his lass Willa was in trouble by Jamie; at which the man of Tensetter began to curse and

swear. They said it was a blacker business than that —
Jamie had gone trespassing on the hill in the night-
time. Then they had asked him if he had enjoyed
many pots of mutton broth lately. They said himself
and Jamie would surely have thick woollen coats next
winter. They spoke more about Jamie and his visits
to the hill by night, a thing the old man couldn't
understand. He had found nothing to say to them (he
told me) other than that Jamie was a good son to
him, and had never done harm to man or beast. They
answered that others would judge that. There was a
man in Kirkwall with a rope that would soon have
certain business with Master James. It would make a
good day's entertainment. And with that they had
gone away, and he had crept back, trembling with
cold and foreboding, under his blanket. He told me he
greatly feared they would do his boy some grievous
injury.

I assured the old man that they would harm Jamie
at their peril. I told him to find his way to the kitchen.
Mistress Skea would give him a bowl of ale and some
cheese; for it was plain to me (I said) that he had
hurried out into the cold morning without a bite to
eat. After that he must go home and wait quietly.
There was nothing to fear. I would see to it.

I had another reason for keeping old Tormiston
out of the way. The early-morning noise at the shore
had lately gotten louder. It was a kind of shapeless
song, flashing out and sinking away, composed of
several passionate voices; and it had been coming towards Garth for the past half-hour.

Presently it was in the yard outside: cries, irregular
footsteps, breathings, blows.

I knew who the 'dramatis personae' were to be. The door burst open. The full cast stood there — Redd, Kierfea, Will, Clett, Erne, and half a dozen others; and in the midst of them, his hands tied with rope, and badly marked about the face and right shoulder (for his sark had been half torn from him) James Tormiston of Arbister.

He has been, up to now, the kind of young man that I have given no particular consideration to. What is the son of a crofter to me, so he lives civilly and keeps the peace?

He is undeniably handsome, with the tall lissom carriage and the bright hair and the sea-cold eyes that (some say) bespeak a Scandinavian ancestry.

He looked heroic and beautiful among those shouting shuffling tillers of the soil.

I said nothing.

William Erne's voice rose above the babble. They all turned to him, nodding. William Erne of Burnlea would be their spokesman.

I said, 'Men generally have the courtesy to knock at my door. I am in two minds about hearing you.'

'You will hear us,' said Erne. 'You will hear us, or it will be the worse for you. There's a greater than you, Master Blyth, in this island (though, more's the pity, he's in London at this moment.) There's many greater than you in Orkney. If you won't hear us, they will.'

They growled and nodded approval all round William Erne. I had never heard such an insolent speech from any man in the parish.

'Such thunder, William,' I said. 'Such threatenings!

Why is this young man bound? It looks to me as if you haven't treated him kindly. Beware you don't suffer yourselves in the end, for taking the law into your own hands.'

'He struggled with us down at the shore,' said Erne. 'Look, I have a bruise on the forehead where he struck me. He bit David's ear.' (Indeed Redd had a blue swollen lobe.)

'And why,' I said, 'should there be such bruisings and blood in a peaceful law-abiding island?'

'Because we have found your sheep-thief,' shouted William Erne, turning from me to put his white staring face on James Tormiston.

'Here he is,' they all shouted; and Howie Will flung his hand resoundingly across the quiet face at the centre of the hullabaloo.

'Do that once more,' I said to the tenant of Brandon, 'and it is you who will be sent to the sheriff in Kirkwall.'

'What are you?' cried William Erne. 'Are you on the side of the law? Here we have your sheep-thief, without any stirring on your part, and all you do is rebuke us.'

'Sheep-thief?' I said. 'Who says this man is the sheep-thief? Have you any proof? Take care old Jacob of Arbister, the father, doesn't have you before the court for defamation, apart from the assault down at the shore. I have heard no evidence against this man.'

What was more strange than any other thing that dreadful day was the face of the young man in the midst of all this rage and rant. It seemed he had no part in the drama at all, and was in no way put out by

the horror of his situation. Indeed, there was a faint
smile on his pale bruised face, as if he was remembering some pleasant matter — a kiss or a pipe-tune — that
had drifted into his mind from an earlier summer.

'Untie his hands,' I said. They looked at each
other. Then Clett took out his knife and cut the rope.

'We have evidence,' cried Erne. 'We have plenty of
evidence.' He gestured to three farm boys who were
lingering in the doorway. The lads lifted a heavy
thing from the courtyard. The accusers made way
for them. A carcase of a sheep was dumped at my
feet. Its throat had been cut. The killing had been
done weeks before. The thing stank. The wound
heaved with maggots.

'We found this in his boat-shed,' said Erne. 'It has
Jeremiah's clip in the ear of it, look. The fisherman
would not say where he got it. There was no need.
We know where he got it.'

'Yes,' said Clett. 'That's my sign in the ear. It was
the ewe I called Peggy. She had two lambs in March.'

I said to James Tormiston, 'Is this true? Was this
carcase belonging to Jeremiah Clett found in your
boatshed? How came it there?'

He said nothing. There was hard dangerous breathing all about him. Then he said that he knew nothing
about it. It was his opinion that it was some matter
other than a dead sheep that made them so savage
against him. He said he could not tell how such a
loathsome thing had come to be in his shed that
morning. He had indeed noticed it in the ebb some
days before, rolled back and fore on the breakers, but
he had not touched it.

There is a kind of laughter more terrible than anger. It was shouted out all round him. I held up my hand for silence. Then I said I had strong reason to believe that the recent sheep-reft in the parish had been committed by certain foreign fishermen. There would be no more of it, for the Dutch were now fishing off Rockall; and if they did come back I would see to it that watch and ward was kept over the mixed flock on the hill, to prevent any further thieving. It seemed to me (I said) that in the case of this present carrion that was stinking out my entire house, the Dutch had been too greedy that night, and had overloaded their boat; and so one sheep had been left behind on the shore. James Tormiston had denied all knowledge of it. If it could be proved that someone, to incriminate James Tormiston, had lifted the carcase out of the ebb and placed it in the boatshed, it would go hard with that perverter of justice.

'Will you let him go?' cried George Kierfea. 'It seems to me Master Blyth is for letting him go.'

'He dare not,' said David Redd.

William Erne had been chewing the cud of new argument for a full minute. 'Dutch herring-boats,' he said. 'We know all about Dutch herring-boats. We know they had the benefit of our sheep. But it wasn't the Hollanders that stole them in the night. How could the Hollanders find their way round our hill in the darkness? How comes this, that the sheep taken were only from such-and-such crofts, but none from the laird's flock, and none either from Jacob Tormiston's flock? Did the Hollanders have wit to know one sheep-mark from another? The Hollanders ate the

sheep, I doubt not that. The Hollanders' wives will
see to the fleeces. But that lessens not a whit the
guilt of this creature. For he and none but he cut the
throats of the sheep and ferried them out to the Dutch
herring-men.' He turned then to James Tormiston.
'How much gin did they give you for those provisions?'
he shouted. 'I think old Jacob has been reeking clouds
of Dutch tobacco from his pipe lately. I saw rows of
herring curing in the chimney of Arbister.' He turned
his flaming face on me again. 'Let this man go,' he
said, 'and your days in this island will not be long.'
(Whether he meant that outraged justice would thrust
me out, as a protector of the guilty; or something
more sinister, such as that some dark night next winter the body of a certain factor would be found at the
foot of a cliff, or drowned in the bog, I do not know.)
I said, 'I want to be alone with this man. I have to
interrogate him. That's impossible in the midst of all
this insolence and threatenings.'

For a full minute I thought they would not go.
They huddled closer about James Tormiston; David
Redd even gripped him tightly by the arm. They
looked at each other. At last William Erne said, 'We'll
go, but we'll go no further than the yard gate.' He
nodded to the others. They made reluctantly for the
door. 'Take the carrion with you!' I cried. 'I won't
suffer the stench of it any more!' The three farm lads
came back and dragged the dead sheep out into the
air.

'Now, James Tormiston,' I said to the young fisherman, 'tell me, are you the sheep-thief? Tell me the
truth.'

He smiled. 'It doesn't matter what I say,' he said. 'It doesn't matter what the truth is. They're determined to hang me. There's not a thing you can do for me, Mr Blyth. My days are finished.'

'Young man,' I said, 'in this parish, in the absence of the laird, I am the representative of the king and the law. The law is stronger, believe me, than those ignorant perjured creatures. Their rage and their vindictiveness mean nothing in the end. I do not think that you did this thing.'

(I think I have never seen a gentler comelier young man than this, even with the spittle and the bruised blood on his face.)

'I am guilty,' he said.

'In that case,' I said, 'I can do nothing for you. I will have to send you to Kirkwall, to the law-men there and the sheriff. After they have done with you, God help you.'

'I was a prowler on the hills at night,' he said. 'I broke into their sheepfold. I stole their sweetest and best. They are right. Love is a dangerous thing.'

'James,' I said, 'listen to me. You are in great danger. This is no time for veiled words. I am not talking about love but the theft of sheep. Did you do that?'

He seemed to consider it seriously for a while; then he shook his head. 'There's no way out,' he said. 'I must be punished for it. It's sweet at the time, nothing sweeter. I had great sweetness and joy of it all last winter. But Willa and Janet, how will it be with them? They've had to put up with such rage and bitterness already, and there is a public shame being

prepared for them. I know I must suffer. I've tres-
passed deeper than into their sheepfolds.'

'I am not talking about girls,' I said. 'Love and lust
are outside my jurisdiction. If it torments you so
much, that fire in the blood, I will send for Mr Tarff
and have him sermonise you. All I require to know
is, did you steal and kill a dozen sheep in this island
at the end of May and sell them to the Dutch fishermen? Even if you deny it, I may have to send you to
Kirkwall to stand trial, but there's enough evidence
to acquit you. Of that I am sure. Tell me now, at
once.'

He smiled. 'Ezra Faa knows the truth', he said.
'But who would believe the evidence of a tinker?'

What was wrong with the man? Was it foolishness?
Was it vanity? Was it innocence? He seemed to have
no idea of the horror that gaped for him at the heart
of the labyrinth he was about to enter.

'Listen, Jamie,' I said. 'I have come this past hour —
because I did not know you properly before — to have
a regard and a liking for you. I am sorry that you
have been abused by those ignorant creatures this
morning. I would not have a hair of your head harmed
in time to come. What Erne said is true, I am eager
and anxious on your behalf. You're a young man,
not twenty years old, they tell me. You talk about
the sweetnesses of life. You've only had a sip or two,
boy — the whole deep chalice is waiting to be drunk.'

'Not by me,' he said.

'I spoke,' I said, 'to your father this morning, that
good old man. What will happen to him, do you
think? How pleasant, in his last few lonely years, to

think he had only one son, and that a hanged man buried in quicklime for a shameful deed. That is what will happen to you, if you make no move to defend yourself.'

He stood for another while in front of me, his head bowed. Then he smiled. He said in such a low voice that I could scarcely hear him, 'I wish Miss Blyth was here. Your daughter, sir, Ella. A sip or two — that cup was drunk to the last drop! There was never such a sweetness in my boatshed. The carcase they dumped on me — that rottenness! I can bear that now and all that must follow from it. Commend me to your ewe lamb, Mr Blyth.'

God forbid it was because of those words, Sir, that soon afterwards I opened the door into the yard, and bade Erne and Kierfea secure the prisoner again, and march him to the cellar of The Hall, until such time as the authorities in Kirkwall could be informed, and transport arranged.

Scarcely had these things been done when a letter was brought to me by Andrew Sutherland, skipper of the *Harmony* out of Leith. In it my sister Sophie informed me that Ella is with child. 'I think shame,' she writes, 'that you should have sent the girl out of your house in that state. Assure yourself, Sander, she was not put upon or debauched under my roof. The seed was sown in her before she left the islands. What am I to do with her? I am not wealthy enough to hide her away in some country place until such time as the shame is covered up. If she is to bear the child here, it will be an open disgrace to all our family. If I send her home — as she pleads eagerly and urgently to be allowed to do — it will make you a laughing-stock wherever you set foot in the islands. I am distracted between one course and the other. Write by return with your instructions in this matter, which concerns you a hundred times more than it concerns me. One thing I devoutly hope, that the lecher is made to pay to the uttermost. . . .'

As if that were not enough, the minister arrived at sunset. 'Well done, Blyth,' he cried. 'Well done, in-deed! When are you sending him on to Kirkwall? Well done, the sooner the better. A boil will be lanced in this island. I did not think, Blyth, that you had such smeddum and dispatch in you.'

Before lamp-lighting time, innocence turned the knife once more. 'Look!' cried Thomasina Skea in the kitchen. 'Look what Ezra has given me, a new pot and kettle. They've left the quarry. They must be in Kirkwall soon, he says, there's to be some great event there, a hanging or something'. . . .

Sir, I think there is no need for you to hasten home, as you might feel spurred to, on reading this letter. There is nothing now that either you or I can do in this affair; it is out of our hands. The law must take its course.

I intend to go down this evening to visit the tenant of Arbister.

I have never seen greener and heavier heads on the barley, nor such rich whispers among the oats, as if the sun were in love this summer with the bountiful earth. The beasts on the hill too move in brightness and peace and innocence.

THE SEVEN POETS

(In Memoriam S G S)

Finally, after very much suffering, the earth fled from cities and machines.

Yet the war had, in its dreadful way, fused mankind together. The peoples were one, in woe and horror and destitution.

A simpler species rose out of the ruins, no less intelligent, but with their faces set against science and the ruthless exploitation of the earth and its resources. "Progress" was a word they uttered like a curse.

On the fringes of the vast deserts of ruin left by the war, they lived in small villages of not more than 250 people. (It was forbidden to exceed that number: if a village was shaken with sudden fruitfulness one year, certain young people chosen by lot had to hive off and form a new community higher up the river, in the next valley, nearer the mountain snow.)

So the earth became an intricate delicate network of villages, each self-sufficient but aware of all the others. There was no possibility of war between neighbouring communities. The making of arms was forbidden; even a boy seen sharpening a stick was rebuked. The animals ranged unmolested in their separate kingdoms. Men kept their dominion over cattle, sheep, horses, swine, poultry, fish; because it was held that men had a very ancient relationship with these creatures, a sacred bond.

*   *   *

It can be said, with justice, that a great deal of excitement went out of the human story once this pastoral system was established. Men considered boredom to be a small price to pay for their new tranquillity. In fact there was little boredom. The simple village system had within itself endless variety.

There were however a few restless men here and there who could not endure the life of the villages. Allowances were made for them. They were called "the wandering ones". They had freedom to travel wherever they chose. If they wanted to stay in a village and help with a harvest, that was good. If they stopped till the last of the snow had gone from the mountain pass, that was good. If they passed through the village at night like a furtive shadow, and drank out of the well thanklessly, and were gone in the morning, that was good also. There was no need for them to thieve — they were welcomed and fed wherever they went. I know; I have been one of those wandering folk all my life.

*　　　*　　　*

I have never found the village system dull and repetitive, though I must have visited upwards of five thousand villages in my time. Always there was the cluster of houses, with the occupation carved or painted over each lintel — "Shepherd", "Blacksmith", "Baker", "Fisherman", "Vinter", "Weaver", "The House of the Old Men", "Shoemaker", "Priest", "The House of the Women and Children", "Poet", and the three "Houses of Lovers".

A village in China is very different from a village in Greenland or Africa. The legends over the doors are in a variety of scripts; so are the offered foods, and the dances in the village square, and the faces of the people in the sun.

It happened that, wherever I went after the age of forty (being then too old for the delectable House of Lovers), I chose to stay in the house of the poet. You may say "a strange choice", and so it was. In almost any other house I would have been better fed and more comfortable; in the "House of the Old Men" I would have heard more entertaining lies; in the "House of the Vinter" my head would, night after night, have been transformed to a happy bee-hive. But it was the poet in every village that fascinated me; they were so various, so unlike, so unpredictable.

The main duty of the poet was to write a masque, or chorus, or group of poems, for the villagers to perform in midwinter. Those entertainments were in the main naive, and crudely performed; but the villagers entered into them with deep enjoyment, and so the poets were honoured people in the communities, and never lacked for flowers and wine.

Most of them were honest workaday craftsmen. But here and there I stayed overnight, or maybe for a full week, with an extraordinary poet. In Spain, in a village high on a mountainside, the poet read me his new work. Rehearsals were about to start on it as soon as the grape harvest was in. It was an uninspired piece, and the man knew it. He poured some of the tar-smelling wine of the hills into two cups. We drank in silence. He was one of those that wine makes morose. At last near midnight he said, 'I think often of the boundless power of words. A Word made everything in the beginning. The uttering of that Word took six days. What is this poetry that I busy myself with? A futile yearning towards a realization of that marvellous Word. What is all poetry but a quest for the meaning and beauty and majesty of the original Word? (In most languages the poet is "the maker".) Poets all over the world since time began have been busy at the task of re-creation, each with his own little pen and parchment. We do not know the great poetry of the past — the libraries are dust. But I think that Shakespeare in his lifetime made perhaps the millionth part of a single letter of the Word. Will the complete Word ever be spoken for the second time? When it is, stranger, then the world will be perfect again, and time will have an end'. . . . He looked at his manuscript. 'This is my contribution to the Word — such a sound as a speck of dust might make falling on grass — no more.' He sighed among the harsh wine fumes. He did not speak again. When the flagon was empty he went to his bed. I was glad to leave the house of that gloomy man before dawn next morning, breakfastless. From the vineyards the harvesters greeted me in the first light.

They would enjoy the masque two weeks later, whatever the only begetter thought of it.

In a Mexican village the poet had done nothing for twenty years. 'The bird inside me has stopped singing,' he said. He was quite cheerful about it. The villagers bore him no grudge. The bird had stopped singing, there was nothing more to be said. The poet in the next village had to compose two entertainments each year, one for the songless village. 'I say to them,' said the once-poet, ' "I gave you many fine poems before the bird stopped singing. They still remember these poems in The House of the Old Men. Why not perform them again, with the dances and tunes to go with them?".... But no, they refuse to do that. There must be a new entertainment each year. It is a sign of death, they say, to repeat a masque. These end-less repetitions, they say, the worship of the husks of dead art – that was one symptom of the sickness of pre-Village Man.'

I left him with the wish that the bird inside him might soon start singing again. He laughed, delighted at the possibility; but then shook his head.

In a Swedish village the poet was a great heretic. His poems and plays were all about machines: tanks, tractors, motor-cars, aeroplanes, the internal com-bustion engine. . . . 'These great times will come again', said the young blond visionary. 'Next time we will know how to use them without danger to ourselves. There must come an end to this cutting of corn with scythes, and sailing out into the teeth of the fishing wind with only a patched sail! That is bar-barism!'. . . . A hundred years ago he could not have said such a thing; he would have been ritually strangled if he had whispered a tenth part of it. Even in some villages today they would see to it that his mouth was stopped. But in all the villages in that part of Sweden the people have arrived at such a mildness of the spirit that they are tolerant of their poet. They take part in his midwinter drama, in which the heroes are made of metal and have oil for their blood, but they manage to do it in such subtle ways that the drama, far from being a noble vision of the future, is reduced to burlesque, and becomes by implication a celebration of the pastoral simplicity they have attained. 'The truth is,' said this poet to me, 'they have not sufficient talent to perform my work properly.'

Once I came to a village in an African jungle. The poet, a little old withered man, made many poems every day, sometimes as many as ten. They were all about the praying mantis, its wisdom and beauty and power. He clicked with his teeth, made deep clonking noises with his tongue against his palate. 'Praying mantis, my delight, my brother, you wise one. . . .' He had never composed a poem on any other subject. I could imagine, in the darkness of that jungle, the village performers declaring all one night the joy that the universe felt for that stick of an insect.

Somewhere in Siberia, one spring, I stayed several nights in the house of the poet. This man did not compose in any language. He repeated a few poems to me — not one word was familiar; there was a syllable now and then that seemed to come out of the speech of the people. (You will have to believe me when I say that I have a fair knowledge of many languages, having been on the roads since I was a boy.) I listened to his theories late into the night. I only partially understood what he was trying to do. There was some kind of kinship, it seemed, between the speech of a people and their natural surroundings. Birds, winds, waterfalls, the coil of a river, the shape of a hill, even

the hush of falling snow, moulded speech. 'That is
why the speech of this village is subtly different from
the way they talk in that village twelve miles back,
where you stayed last night. It is a matter of the utmost fascination. Human speech cannot be left to
itself — it will wither — its roots are deep in the
elements, our tongues take nourishment from the
splash of a salmon in the river, the black howl of
blizzards, the thunders and glories of the Siberian
spring. So, in my poems I am steeping speech in
elemental sound. This is a powerful, mysterious, and
dangerous art. It will be the death of me before
long'. . . . He was so absorbed in theories about his
art that I was poorly fed and sheltered, day after
day. As I was leaving the village, having thanked him
at his door for the veiled but stimulating vistas he had
opened for me, I met The Blacksmith at the end of the
street. 'Tell me,' I said, 'how is it possible for his
masques to be performed? People can neither speak
them nor understand them.' 'That is true,' said The
Blacksmith. 'I used to take part in the mid-winter
masque when I was young — now I stand among
the audience. Always we feel that we are one with the
earth. We understand the silence of stones. We re-
affirm our kinship with fish and stars' . . . .

*   *   *

Once, when I was younger, I nearly died among
ice. Why I wandered so far north I can't remember —
a young man must always be tempting providence.

I had no food in that white wilderness for three

days, or maybe four. I remember biting my right hand like a wolf and sucking the warm blood. ("Better you than the wolves," I said to myself.) I expected such a grey savage death.

Instead it was a small befurred man with a face genial as the sun who found me. In a very short time I was sitting in his ice-house, among a cluster of ice-houses. There were no legends over these doors, for the villagers could not read or write.

They spoke a language I did not understand, too.

My rescuer gave me to know that I should spend the night in his house. Obstinate as ever, I shook my head. I made signs to him — striking an imaginary harp, kissing an imaginary pipe and making my fingers dance. At last he understood. His smile was broader than ever. I would rather pass the night in The House of the Poet than with him. He was not in the least put out.

A boy took me by the hand and led me through a squat white labyrinth of a village to a house exactly the same as all the others. Inside the smells of blubber and fish-oil were dreadful. I discovered, to my deep surprise, that the poet could speak several languages. He had been "a wandering one" in his youth. He had gone through Scandinavia and Central Europe; he had lingered among the isles of Greece for a while; then he had walked eastwards, through Persia and India, intending to get as far as Japan. But while he was being entertained by a village in the Himalayan foot-hills, word had come to him that he was wanted back home. The poet in his village on the shore of Baffin Bay had died; it was for him now to make the songs of his people. I interrupted him — how had this news come to him? The poet in the Indian village had told him, he said. All true poets all over the world have this gift of divination — an exquisite network of sensibility binds them together. (I had not known this before.)

Meantime the igloo grew more and more uncomfortable. People were crowding into it — men, women, children, even infants. The air got steadily hotter and ranker. There was no room to sit — we crowded shoulder to shoulder. Others stood in the freezing night outside. All waited patiently for the poet to begin.

The word flowered out of a long deep silence.

I did not understand it, of course. The mouth cried, whispered, sang, whistled, shouted. There were seven poems in the recital. At the end of each one the villagers showed their delight with silence and sunlooks. Nowhere had I seen happier faces.

At last the recital was over; it must have been an integrated group of lyrics. They went away as mildly as they had come, leaving only that intolerable fish-stench behind, and a silence enriched.

I said to the poet when we were alone again, 'These are happy poems, surely.' 'All poetry is gay,' he answered. 'Are they love poems?' I asked. 'One is,' he said.

> The young man says, "Come into my hut."
> The girl answers, "I have a bird for a lover."
> The man, "I will hunt that bird. There will be
>   red drops in the snow."
> The girl answers, "No.
> For the bird is to take me under his wing into

the north. His nest is on a black cliff. You
will never find us."
'There is the hunting poem then.

The boy says, "Tomorrow I will hunt for the
first time.

Beware, walrus. Beware, reindeer.

I am coming to play at arrows with you."

At the end of the snow

The great bear stood, who does not like the
game of arrows.
'Then there is the poem of the whale.

The whale grew tired of eating little cold
fishes.

It swallowed the sun.

Then fell the black time, winter.

The people said, "Must we always stumble
about in blackness?

The stars are too feeble.

We want our children to play among the
beautiful snow crystals."

They hunted down that whale.

They filled a hundred lamps from his belly.

Just when the last lamp was empty

The sun peeped at us over a low rim of ice.

Dead whale, drowned hunters, devoured sun.

Inside this circle all dances are made.
'There follows the aurora poem.

"Come, children, into my house of crystal.

Come, the feast is set.

Here kings sit and eat, and heroes, and the
bravest hunters."

We are bidden, night after night,
To feast in that house of marvellous shining.
But we linger here sick,
Growing old, filled with regrets, in hovels of
    snow.
'My own favourite is the poem of the women.
        "Go away, man.
        I will not open my door to you.
        Quench your fires in the snow.
        I will never leave the dancing children."
        The witch moon kissed me as I slept.
        I am her blood-servant now.
        She has put a sign on my doorpost.
        Now many hunters come. All are welcome.
'Did you not see how the old men smiled at the poem
of childhood?
        "I am a salmon."
        "I am a bear-cub."
        "I am a reindeer."
        "I am the moon."
        "I am the hole in the ice where ivory is."
        Stop your games.
        Three hunters are coming to teach you the
            trade —
        Winter, Age, Death.
'You understand, stranger, these translations I am
making for you are poor things, withered leaves
plucked from the tree of our language. (I remember
groves, woods, forest.) The sequence ends with the
winter poem.
        I don't mind winter.
        I listen to stories.

I make love.
I don't mind winter now, in my youth.
My eyes, some morning,
Will be caught like two fish in the sun's net.
Tell me, poet
The cruellest things that can happen.'

'Sombre songs,' I said. 'Yet the people tonight drank them like wine, cup after cup.'

'Wine,' said the poet, and smiled. 'I remember the raptures and rages in the house of the Vinter when I was one of the wanderers. Here in the far north is neither grape nor barley. We have only poetry. The word whispers, like a ferment, in what seems to be the futility, pain, idiocy of life. It is my duty to attend to the pure essences. And I am potter here as well as Vinter. I make cups that remain beautiful in their withering hands.'

In that latitude there is a night six months long. The arctic poet tried to give me some idea of the masque that takes place in the ultimate darkness. I could only guess at the glory of it. Since — as in the lyric — this people, though eternally invited, can never enter the house of the Aurora Borealis, the imagination of the poet builds about them a palace of unimagined beauty, their primitive words and gestures are clothed in ceremony, and there they kept a tranced revelry for one night in the year.

*   *   *

Now, thirty years later, I find myself for the first time among the mountains of Scotland.

FIFE EDUCATIONAL
RESOURCES CENTRE